A wake-up call . . .

Leigh moved toward the hammock, her uneasiness wrestling with her annoyance. The scene was just too bizarre. Who would leave a life-size dummy in someone else's backyard at three in the morning? Especially one dressed like an idiot?

She peered down closely at the moth-eaten hat. It was of a greenish fabric, with half a red feather stuck in a dusty brown band. Wondering if this dummy had a face as demonic as the one from *Magic*, she lifted the brim.

Later, she would say she hadn't screamed. Nevertheless, the sound that echoed through the backyard and into the house was shrill enough to make waves in her cousin's decaf.

Leigh attempted a dignified retreat, but her legs didn't seem to be working right. She tripped and fell on her face, eye level with Cara's approaching feet. Struggling up, Leigh grabbed her cousin's arm and propelled them both back into the kitchen.

Leaning against the back door and taking deep breaths, Leigh slowly regained her poise. "I need to call Maura. Now."

Before Cara had time to respond, Leigh grabbed the phone and dialed. She soon heard a woman's voice, deep and pleasant.

"Avalon Police, Maura Polanski. What can I do for you?"

"Get over here now, Maura," Leigh said intently. "I want you to look at a corpse."

NEVER
BURIED

A Leigh Koslow Mystery

Edie Claire

A SIGNET BOOK

SIGNET
Published by the Penguin Group
Penguin Putnam Inc., 375 Hudson Street,
New York, New York 10014, U.S.A.
Penguin Books Ltd, 27 Wrights Lane,
London W8 5TZ, England
Penguin Books Australia Ltd, Ringwood,
Victoria, Australia
Penguin Books Canada Ltd, 10 Alcorn Avenue,
Toronto, Ontario, Canada M4V 3B2
Penguin Books (N.Z.) Ltd, 182–190 Wairau Road,
Auckland 10, New Zealand

Penguin Books Ltd, Registered Offices:
Harmondsworth, Middlesex, England

First published by Signet, an imprint of Dutton NAL,
a member of Penguin Putnam Inc.

First Printing, April, 1999
10 9 8 7 6 5 4 3 2 1

 REGISTERED TRADEMARK—MARCA REGISTRADA

Printed in the United States of America

PUBLISHER'S NOTE
This is a work of fiction. Names, characters, places, and incidents either
are the product of the author's imagination or are used fictitiously,
and any resemblance to actual persons, living or dead, events, or locales
is entirely coincidental.

BOOKS ARE AVAILABLE AT QUANTITY DISCOUNTS WHEN USED TO PROMOTE
PRODUCTS OR SERVICES. FOR INFORMATION PLEASE WRITE TO PREMIUM
MARKETING DIVISION, PENGUIN PUTNAM INC., 375 HUDSON STREET, NEW
YORK, NEW YORK 10014.

For my friends at
Ingomar United Methodist Church

ACKNOWLEDGMENTS

This book would never have existed if not for the willingness of several individuals to provide the patience and/or persistence I lack. For graciously reading assorted chapters in paper-clipped stacks and unformatted text files, then hassling me mercilessly until I finished the book, I thank my first guinea pigs, Kim Gibson and Teresa Stewart. For their benevolent nit-picking and endless emotional support, I thank my fellow writing workshoppers, Hairy and the Maidens. And for their constant encouragement and occasional virtual kicks in the rear, I thank all my Compuserve Sisters in Crime, especially Paula Matter and Sharon Zukowski.

For technical assistance, I am indebted to Joe Szabat, Gregg Otto, Teresa Stewart (yeah, you get mentioned twice!), Laurie Lehew Rees (copywriter extraordinaire), and the *real* Avalon Chief of Police, Robert Howie. Any slight manipulations of the truth—or more likely, blatant errors—are entirely my fault and not theirs.

Last but not least I thank my family, especially my husband, Mark, for not insisting I get a real job.

Chapter 1

The sounds filtered through Leigh's sleeping brain, nagging her into consciousness. She knew them all too well. First the series of short, wet, hiccoughs—then the muffled splat. Her cat, Mao Tse, was throwing up. Again.

Leigh groaned and pried up an eyelid just long enough to read her clock.

3:37 A.M. *Wonderful.*

She was almost asleep again when she remembered she wasn't at home. The image of Tom Cruise in silk boxers faded out to a picture of her cousin's favorite throw pillow laced with cat vomit.

Get up, you ingrate. You have no choice.

The bed was warm, the mattress comfortable. Leigh's eyes remained closed as she rationalized. The mess was probably in the kitchen on the linoleum. It wouldn't matter if she waited till morning. It wouldn't matter at all.

She lay quietly a little longer, trying to believe herself. Then she settled into her pillow and tried hard to reconjure Tom, preferably toting a blueberry muffin and some orange juice.

It didn't work. She sighed and opened her eyes. "Who am I kidding? Stupid cat heads for upholstery at the first sign of nausea."

She swung her legs over the side of the bed, letting

the momentum pull her upright, then slipped on her
house shoes (a lesson well learned) and hoisted herself
up. The corridor outside her room was pitch dark.
Yawning, she slumped over against the wall and fumbled for a light switch, using a brass sconce for a head-
rest. Her fingers soon found a switch. Unfortunately,
it was the switch for the sconce.

By the time the dancing dots had faded, Leigh was
alert. She remembered her mission and looked down.
The hardwood floor seemed an unlikely place—it
would be too easy to clean. The other upstairs doors
were closed. She padded down the front staircase and
flipped on the light in the entry hall.

*Not on the Persian rug. Anywhere but the Persian
rug.*

Experience led her to the room with the densest
concentration of fine fabrics—the parlor. The cat was
there, of course, resting comfortably on one of the
antique wingbacks. Leigh resisted the urge to throttle
her. "All right, girl. Give me a hint. I'm really not in
the mood for this."

Mao Tse, a large black Persian with an imperial
attitude, turned up what little nose she had and
stared blankly.

Leigh's eyes scoured the rug, the furniture, the pillows. *Nothing. Good girl.* She moved into the dining
room and turned on the chandelier. The floor was
clear. Perhaps the cat had settled for linoleum after
all? The hope faded as her eyes traveled upward.

Fabulous.

Right in the middle of the handmade tablecloth.

Spouting curses, Leigh shuffled off to clean up. Two
swinging doors led her to the large kitchen, dimly visible by moonlight. She sighed. She hadn't a clue where
her cousin kept anything. With Cara's sense of organi-
zation, the paper towels would probably be next to

the dill weed. Once again her fingers fumbled for a light switch. Nothing.

After a few more moments of grumbling, she found a set of switches by the back door and flipped one. The outdoors turned bright as day. Squinting through the back window, she counted no fewer than six stadium-sized spots trained on the patio. Her brow wrinkled. Sure, the patio had a nice view of the Ohio River, but weren't six lights a bit excessive? Perhaps she shouldn't be surprised—most everything about her cousin was excessive.

Leigh was about to turn away when she noticed movement. It happened quickly, but she could just see the back of a head and shoulders—a person standing on the bluff below the level of the patio. One second the figure was there, the next it was gone. She shook her head and blinked her eyes. There was nothing more to see.

Her heart beat fast. She wasn't into bravery, but she did try to avoid panic. Panic could be terribly embarrassing. She took a deep breath and tried to think of legitimate, unthreatening reasons why someone would be wandering around her cousin's backyard in the middle of the night. It took a while, but eventually her creativity won out. Someone had been walking down the boulevard and cut through Cara's yard to see the river. *No problem.* She smiled. Sure, Pittsburgh's borough of Avalon had its share of wacky residents, but most of them were harmless. The doors were locked and the security system was on. Hysterics were not called for. Neither was waking up Cara in the middle of the night.

Promising herself she would get butch and check out the backyard in the daylight, Leigh found the paper towels (next to the Bisquick) and headed back to the dining room. She tore off a few sheets and began sopping up the mess.

Damnable cat.

Mao Tse appeared in the doorway to the parlor, stretched her front paws gingerly, and let loose with a dignified yawn. Leigh wanted to throw the roll of paper towels, but her conscience forbade it. She couldn't be too hard on the beast. After all, she had missed the embroidered trim.

Leigh walked into the breakfast nook the next morning feeling less than vital. The ecstatic chirping of her finches, who were enjoying the morning sunshine from their cage in the bay window, only vexed her. Cara sat at the table looking bright-eyed and energetic, savoring a pastry with the morning paper. Leigh groaned. "I'm glad somebody got a good night's sleep. Hey, aren't pregnant women supposed to eat healthy? You keep this kind of food in the house, and I'll gain more weight than you will."

Cara, seven months along and still leaner than Leigh would ever be, smiled cheerfully and held out the bakery box. "Consider it a special occasion—your first breakfast in the March house. Eat. I got cake donuts."

"Maggie Mae's Bakery?"

Cara nodded.

"You know me too well," Leigh sighed. "I can't fight you and Maggie Mae both." She pulled out a chocolate-frosted and sat down. Moving in with Cara temporarily had seemed like a good idea. With Gil March off globetrotting and the baby's due date fast approaching, Leigh's normally independent cousin had had a sudden yearning for companionship. Leigh, after spotting a family of roaches under her apartment sink, had had a sudden yearning to move out before her lease expired. Unfortunately, the night's events made her wonder how long her menagerie could coexist with antique furniture and parquet floors. "Um . . . Cara, about the tablecloth . . ."

Cara dismissed the subject with a wave of her hand. "No problem. I've already got it soaking in Woolite."

Her generosity only made Leigh feel worse. "You shouldn't have done that. She's my cat and we're your guests. I'll clean up after her." On cue, the cat strolled into the breakfast nook, contentedly licking her lips. Leigh knew what that meant. "You shouldn't have to feed her either, Cara, even if you are up first."

"I didn't have much choice." Cara laughed, reaching for another pastry. "She was driving me nuts meowing and pawing up my legs. I haven't had my shins attacked like that since Tiger Lily."

Leigh smiled at the reference to their shared childhood pet. She and Cara had grown up like sisters, but since high school graduation they'd seen very little of one another.

Cara stretched out a toe and stroked Mao Tse's shaggy back. "You didn't sleep well?"

Leigh started slightly, her eyes drawn over Cara's shoulder to the window. "The bed was heavenly," she answered, "but Mao Tse kept me up. You didn't— hear anything, did you?"

"I heard you moving around, but don't worry, it didn't bother me."

Leigh got up and walked over to the big bay window.

Cara's house, perched on top of the high northern bluff of the Ohio, stood a few miles downstream from the river's birth at the junction of the Allegheny and Monongahela rivers—known to Pittsburghers as "The Point." The Victorian had once stood in good company along the old brick River Road, but time and progress had been its enemy. When River Road was replaced by the busy Ohio River Boulevard, the bluff houses were cut off from the rest of Avalon and re-zoned commercial. Most either fell into disrepair or just plain fell, but this one had been stubborn. It had also been lucky—Cara had wanted to fix it up and live in it ever since she was a child. And what Cara wanted, Cara generally got.

Leigh looked out the window to the east, where she could just see a sliver of brown water flowing lazily from the point. Carefully placed trees obscured the view across the river to Neville Island, whose looming smokestacks were a dead ringer for those in Dr. Seuss's *The Lorax*. She walked into the kitchen and opened the back door, sniffing tentatively.

Although the Pittsburgh air was practically sterile compared to the glory days of the steel industry, the blue-collar borough of Avalon could not escape an occasional foul blast from Neville Island. This morning, thankfully, the breeze was from the east. It was, in fact, a perfect warm June morning. Leigh allowed herself a deep breath. Had she really seen someone outside, so close to the house? A gray pigeon flapped down from above and landed on a patio chair. Nothing appeared amiss. Nevertheless, last night's trespassing nagged at her.

"That pigeon is aiming right for your love seat," she called to Cara. "I'll go out and manhandle him." She walked out the back door and closed it quietly behind her.

Cara, used to such inane comments, returned to the morning paper.

Leigh stepped out onto the concrete patio, looking down at the intricate swirling pattern on its shiny new surface. The old Victorian seemed more of a plaything than a home. Gil's high-profile consulting work had provided plenty of cash to fix it up but little time to enjoy it. And because nothing short of advanced pregnancy could keep Cara from tagging along with her husband, the house had, up until the last month, been little more than a weekend hideaway.

Walking purposefully around the expensive patio furniture, Leigh tried to remember if everything was in the same place it had been the night before. She came within two feet of the pigeon, which didn't seem to notice her.

Take a number, beakface.

If the furniture had been moved, she couldn't tell. Remembering where she had seen the figure, she crossed to the patio's edge. Had he been standing on the steps to the terrace?

Beyond the patio, the yard dropped off suddenly in its descent to the railroad tracks and river below. Trees and thick undergrowth blanketed the lower portion of the slope, but the upper part had been cleared to make the river visible. Jutting out from the hillside below the patio was a narrow terrace, just wide enough for a hammock with a treetop view. Leigh leaned over the short stone wall that bordered the upper yard and glanced down. She would say she didn't jump. But she did.

Lying there, in Cara's hammock, was a small man in a pinstripe suit. An old-fashioned top hat shielded his face; his hands were clasped serenely over his chest. He wore black dress shoes, dull and scuffed with dirt.

Leigh frowned. Whatever she had feared in a nighttime visitor, this wasn't it. This bizarre little person had cost her a good night's sleep, and she didn't appreciate it. She started down the steps to confront him. She was almost to the bottom when she stopped cold.

Something was wrong. This man wasn't lying in the hammock. He was levitating in it. His head and feet touched the nylon mesh, but his midsection hung above it. His body was straight as a board.

After several seconds she exhaled. "It's a dummy," she decided finally. "Somebody's stupid old mannequin."

She moved toward the hammock, her uneasiness wrestling with her annoyance. The scene was just too bizarre. Who would leave a life-size dummy in someone else's backyard at three in the morning? Especially one dressed like an idiot?

She peered down closely at the moth-eaten hat. It was of a greenish fabric, with half a red feather stuck in a dusty brown band. Wondering if this dummy had a face as demonic as the one from *Magic,* she lifted the brim.

Later, she would say she hadn't screamed. Nevertheless, the sound that echoed through the backyard and into the house was shrill enough to make waves in Cara's decaf.

Leigh attempted a dignified retreat, but her legs didn't seem to be working right. She tripped up the last of the steps and fell on her face, eye level with Cara's approaching feet. Struggling up, Leigh grabbed her cousin's arm and propelled them both back into the kitchen.

"What on earth is wrong with you?" Cara demanded. "Why did you scream like that?"

Leaning against the back door and taking deep breaths, Leigh slowly regained her poise. "I didn't scream. But I need to call Maura. Now."

Before Cara had time to respond, Leigh grabbed the phone and dialed. She asked the dispatcher for Officer Polanski, and soon heard a woman's voice, deep and pleasant.

"Avalon Police, Maura Polanski. What can I do you for?"

"Get over here now, Maura," Leigh said intently, wasting no time. "I want you to look at a corpse."

The husky voice on the other end of the line chuckled.

"Yeah right, Koslow. Don't tell me—some plumber called you ma'am and you smashed his head with a pipe wrench. Am I right?"

Leigh breathed deep. "Will you just get your carcass off that chair and get down here, please!"

She heard the squeak of Maura's ancient swivel stool. "Chill out, Leigh! Just tell me what the problem is."

"I already told you what the problem is. There's a corpse in my cousin's backyard. Now, are you coming over or do I have to track down Mellman?"

The only answer was a loud click, then silence.

Leigh hung up the phone. When she turned to speak to Cara, the kitchen was empty.

Breaking into a run, she caught up with her cousin about six paces from the edge of the patio. "Don't, Cara. *Don't*. It's not a pretty sight. Stress is bad for the baby, remember?"

Cara's mouth opened as if to protest that Leigh was being ridiculous. Then awareness flickered in her eyes, and she closed her mouth in a petulant scowl. Leigh felt a sweet sense of triumph. Trying to stop Cara from doing something was like trying to hold back the tide, but the baby was proving an excellent trump card. Leigh had promised Gil, her aunt, her mother, and half of the Greenstone United Methodist Women's Association that she would do her best to make Cara follow doctor's orders, and she wasn't going to let them down.

Cara sulked as Leigh pulled her back into the kitchen and steered her to a chair. "I'm not an invalid, you know," she said with a pout. Then she smiled slyly—a fresh gleam in her blue-green eyes. "I'm supposed to avoid stress, not intellectual challenge. You know I'm good at detective work!" She leaned toward Leigh expectantly. "So spill it. You said there was a body?"

"Well . . . yes," Leigh answered, uncertain what to say. Finding a bright side to the discovery of a body in one's backyard was vintage Cara, but hearing morbid details surely qualified as stressful. Perhaps the less Cara knew, the better.

"I can't tell you much more than that," Leigh said unconvincingly.

Cara shook her head sadly. "You're a wonderful actress, dear, but a pathetic liar. Now, *talk*."

Leigh searched for an unalarming way to describe the dark, cracking lips, the thin lids parting over shrunken eyeballs—it just wasn't possible. She squirmed in her seat and waited for inspiration. What she got was an interruption.

Leigh and Cara both jumped as the front door opened and slammed hard. Heavy footsteps crossed through the parlor into the dining room. Even though the six-thousand-person borough of Avalon covered only five-eighths of a square mile, it was physically impossible for Maura to have arrived from headquarters so soon. But then, Maura always seemed to do things that were physically impossible.

The doors between the dining room and kitchen swung open to admit six feet two inches and two hundred ten pounds of Avalon's finest. Maura Polanski was a big woman, period. Ordinarily she was rendered less imposing by a cherubic baby face, but no dimples could obscure her current displeasure.

"Leigh Koslow!" she boomed, hands on hips. "You had *damn* well not be jerking me around." Beads of sweat stood out on Maura's broad forehead, and dark brown hair clung limply to the sides of her face. Mao Tse uttered a trademark hiss and took cover under the kitchen stepladder.

"Would I do that to you?" Leigh's sarcasm held respect. Four years as Maura's college roommate had taught her just how to diffuse her friend's wrath. The skill was necessary, as she was also expert at invoking it. She pulled open the back door and swept her arm across the opening. "After you!"

Maura nodded to Cara, scowled at Leigh on principle, and ducked out the door.

Leigh turned to Cara. "Stay here," she said firmly. "Have some more decaf." She started out the door but ducked back in. "Just think about that baby!"

Leigh pointed Maura down the steps and followed close behind her. She couldn't suppress a sadistic sense of glee. Maura was always telling Leigh she over-reacted to things, always accusing her of being melodramatic. . . .

Not this time.

Maura's ability to remain cool in a crisis irritated Leigh to no end. Never mind that the policewoman came from law enforcement stock (her late father had been the police chief and patron saint of Avalon), Leigh just didn't find it normal. She could make her friend blow a fuse on a moment's notice, but had never managed to spook her.

Maura's department-issue shoes clomped heavily down the concrete steps. When she reached the bottom, she let out a sigh and walked casually over to the hammock. Leigh stayed at the base of the steps and held her breath.

Maura looked carefully at the folded hands, the position of the body, and the odd clothes. She pulled a notebook out of her breast pocket and began to write.

Leigh exhaled with a groan. "For God's sake, Maura—aren't you at least going to flinch?"

Maura kept scribbling and replied without looking up. "You would prefer hysterics?"

"Well yes, actually," Leigh snapped, coming closer. "How many bodies have you seen before, anyway?"

"More than you care to know about. Did you touch this hat?"

"Of course I touched the hat! I thought it was a dummy. I only knew it was real when I saw the head."

Maura lifted the brim of the hat with her pen and slid it off the face.

It was a man's face, no doubt about that. An old man. Wrinkled skin hung loosely off his facial bones, and his head was bald except for a few short wisps of gray hair. He might have looked like any other old dead man, but he didn't. His skin was unnaturally dark and shriveled, the folds above his collar looking dry enough to crumble off his neck.

Leigh stepped back again and waited. Maura said nothing, but began a rhythmic tapping of her pen against her notepad. Leigh waited some more.

"Well?" she finally asked. "Is there a dead man in Cara's hammock or isn't there?"

The tapping ceased.

"Oh, yes," Maura answered in her police voice, sliding the notebook back into her pocket. "That's a dead man, all right."

"So," Leigh continued, "what do we do about it?"

Maura clucked her tongue. "*We* don't do anything. *I* make some calls." She left the body and started up the stairs. Leigh followed, trying to catch up.

"Don't you need to dust for fingerprints or collect hair samples or something?"

Maura snickered. "That's not my job, Koslow."

"Well, it's somebody's job, isn't it?" Leigh stifled

her irritation. Maura had an annoying habit of not saying what she knew Leigh wanted to know. "This *is* a possible homicide, right? The man is dead. I'm no coroner, but I don't think he just keeled over while taking a snooze. He looks to me like he's been dead longer than he's been in that hammock."

"Oooh . . ." Maura answered, pursing her lips. "You're right about that one. Mr. Vaudeville there didn't die last night."

They reached the patio, and Leigh stepped around to face her friend. "Well then, how long do you think he's been dead?"

"Hard to say," Maura answered. "They decay a lot slower after they've been embalmed."

Chapter 2

Cara greeted them by the kitchen door, anxiously twirling a lock of strawberry blond hair between her fingers. Her face was pale, her pupils wide. She was doing an excellent imitation of a damsel in distress, but Leigh knew better. What Cara wanted was information. Pronto.

"Is it true?" Cara asked in a stage whisper. "Is there a body in my backyard?"

Maura assumed a calm, professional demeanor Leigh hadn't seen before. "Yes, there is a body. I know that's alarming, but from what I can tell at this point, the individual appears to have died some time ago. Quite possibly of natural causes."

Cara took a deep breath and nodded, her normal complexion returning. Whether she was relieved or disappointed, Leigh couldn't tell.

"So what happens now?" Leigh asked, looking at Maura with new respect. Police procedure, outside of detective shows and mystery novels, had never interested her. She presumed Maura spent most of her time writing traffic tickets and bouncing drunks. A cop's life suddenly seemed more intriguing.

Local Woman Stops Grave-Robbing Ring: Police Grateful.

"Koslow? Did you hear what I said?" Maura's stern gaze implied she knew what Leigh was thinking, and wasn't amused. "This is what happens. First, nobody goes near the body again. Second, I make the necessary contacts. Third, you two relax and get ready to answer some questions."

Cara nodded cooperatively. Leigh did the same, but Maura eyed her skeptically. "Could I use your phone, please?" she asked Cara.

Leigh frowned. She had been looking forward to hearing both sides of the conversation. She tapped a finger on the two-way radio clipped to Maura's belt. "Why can't you use this thing?"

Maura's eyes narrowed. "This 'thing,' as you so eloquently put it, is for communication between on-duty officers. Chief Mellman is not on duty this morning. In fact, I have a pretty good idea he's sitting on his fanny in the Chuckwagon Café, stuffing down pancakes and sausage with Vestal Fields. But he gets beeped for all unusual deaths, and this qualifies. The phone?"

Cara threw Leigh an admonishing glance and led Maura inside to the kitchen. Leigh followed eagerly, but her attempts at eavesdropping were unproductive. Maura called several different people, but she talked to all of them in numbers. Her radio conversation with the dispatcher was no help either—all Leigh heard was static. When the squeal of brakes finally sounded, Leigh trailed Maura outside. Perhaps now someone would speak English.

A dilapidated sedan sat parked in the drive, its chassis springing up a foot as two hefty occupants scooted out.

Donald Mellman, recently named chief of police after a lifetime of playing second fiddle to Maura's father, stood up with an automatic tug at the waistband of his uniform pants. He was a large man, over six feet tall with a roundish midsection and slightly oversized head. His nose, large even for his head, was distinctly crooked. Leigh watched him run a pudgy hand through his graying hair and stifle a belch with a fist.

Sausage. No doubt.

Vestal Fields, owner of the Fields Funeral Home, rose quickly to his feet and adjusted his tie. Vestal missed Mellman's six feet by a fair margin, but in weight they were about even. He scrambled immediately to Maura, rubbing his hands anxiously. "You've got a body you think's already been embalmed, eh?"

Maura let out a barely perceptible sigh. Vestal was trying hard to act somber, but his glee about being a "police consultant" was poorly contained. "The body's in the hammock in the backyard," she replied. "You can take a look at it yourself and see if it's anyone you recognize. But don't touch anything!"

Vestal nodded soberly while his baby blue eyes danced. He turned on one heel and started around the corner of the house.

Chief Mellman ambled slowly up to Maura. He looked at Leigh as though he thought he should recognize her, but didn't. She wasn't surprised. Almost a decade had passed since her days at the Koslow Animal Clinic. Then she had seen him frequently. Whenever a dog was hit by a car or a crazed raccoon wandered into somebody's yard, Officer Mellman—the animal lover—got the call.

"County's on the way, Chief."

The stiffness in Maura's voice was hard to miss. Leigh sympathized. It couldn't be easy to have a man you'd grown up calling Uncle Don suddenly become your boss. Especially if you'd always considered him kind of a nincompoop.

Mellman nodded once. He smiled politely at Leigh and lumbered off after Vestal.

* * *

Leigh drummed her fingers impatiently on the patio table to which Maura had threatened to chain her.

A secured scene, indeed. I found the damn thing, didn't I?

Cara, incapable of idleness, made coffee. Finally, the privileged trio of Maura, Mellman, and Vestal climbed up from the terrace and were persuaded to sit down for some java. Cara buzzed hopefully about with her pot until Leigh, still worried about her cousin's stress level, made baby-rocking motions with her arms. Cara scowled but went inside.

After Maura's stoic reaction, Leigh hadn't expected either of the men to be upset by the corpse. Mellman had been a cop ever since he graduated from high school, when he and Maura's dad had joined the force together. Vestal, who had inherited the family business, had been pickling friends and relatives even longer. It seemed odd, therefore, that he should now be pale as a ghost.

Maura and Mellman both looked at Vestal with concern. "Take it easy there, old buddy," Mellman said nervously, giving a hearty slap to his friend's back.

"Is there a problem, Vestal?" Maura asked, studying him carefully. "If the body isn't familiar, is there something else about it that concerns you?"

Vestal waved off her concern and swiped the beads of sweat forming on his upper lip. "No, no. Delores's white gravy didn't agree with me, that's all." He reached out a shaky hand and grabbed the coffee cup in front of him. Some of the brown liquid sloshed out over the rim. He turned to Leigh. "Straight?"

"Decaf," she replied.

He brought the cup to his lips and drained it without putting it down, then looked better. He wrenched a handkerchief out of a tight pocket and cleared his throat. "I can tell you a few things," he said in a steadier tone, mopping his brow. "The body's been embalmed, no doubt about that. But it's desiccated. It's been around awhile."

Leigh's eyebrows rose. "Awhile? How long is awhile?"

Vestal turned to look at Leigh, and a dash of color returned to his cheeks. The spotlight must have suited him, because the more he talked, the more animated he became.

"I'd say that body was embalmed, oh, at least five years ago. Hell, it could have been twenty years ago! You can't tell without knowing how it's been stored, you see."

Vestal went on to describe the effects of humidity on decaying tissue, but Leigh's mind drifted. She tried to imagine where a body might lie for twenty years without being noticed. Other than a grave, nothing sprang to mind. Why would anyone rob a grave? She didn't think scientists bought off the street anymore, but didn't medical schools keep embalmed bodies in stock? She ran through a mental list of twisted acquaintances who had wanted to be doctors. There were several. "Some medical student's idea of a joke, perhaps?" she interrupted.

"Now, let's not get carried away," Mellman said in his usual even drawl. "We won't know anything for sure until the coroner's had a look."

Vestal, now thoroughly full of himself, glared at Mellman indignantly. "You don't think I can tell when a man's been embalmed?"

Leigh sensed an argument coming on, but Maura broke in. "The county detectives will notify the coroner. If it's a homicide, it'll be out of our hands anyway. If it's not . . . Well, we'll see what they report."

Mellman stood up. "Let me give you a lift back to the Chuckwagon," he said to his friend. "Once the detectives get here, I'll be tied up for a while." Vestal nodded impassively and rose. He smiled at Leigh and handed her a business card. "Anytime I can be of service, my dear."

Leigh took the card, colorfully embossed with the slogan GRATEFUL TO SERVE YOU.

Charming.

Mellman nodded to Maura. "I'll be back in a few." He and Vestal walked around the side of the house, their departure confirmed by a series of squeaks and groans from the sedan. Maura leaned forward and took a swig of coffee. Leigh watched her.

"What are you staring at?" Maura asked.

"I'm just enjoying seeing you in action." Leigh smiled. "All those criminal justice classes. Now you're the real thing. And here, on my first day in your jurisdiction, I bring you a body. Am I good, or what?"

Reluctantly, Maura smiled back. "You'll get yours, Koslow. Be prepared for a grilling when the detectives get here."

Leigh's brow wrinkled. "They won't have to question Cara, will they?"

"Of course they'll question her. Why shouldn't they?"

Leigh's fingers tapped nervously on her coffee cup. "She's having these abnormal contractions. Her OB said she's supposed to restrict her activity and avoid stress, or she could go into premature labor."

"Oh." Maura was out of her element. "I'll ask them to go easy."

The sounds of arriving vehicles echoed around the side of the house, and Maura rose. "That'll be the county. Why don't you go back into the house and stick with Cara for a while? I'll let you know when we need you."

Leigh chafed at the dismissal, but collected the coffee cups and headed back inside. The door swung open for her. "Just put them in the sink," Cara said, a little too pleasantly.

"Sit down and have another donut. We need to talk."

Leigh winced but complied. A donut sounded good, bribery or not.

"I've been good so far," Cara began, lowering herself into a chair on the other side of the table. She was using her debating tone, which was bad news. Leigh was good in an argument; Cara was better. "I haven't looked at the body, and I've let you handle the gory details with the police. My obstetrician would be proud. But you can't expect me to forget all this. A body is in my backyard. I need to know why, because not knowing is more stressful than hearing the truth. Did he drown and wash up on the bank? Did he trip and roll down the cliff? Did he OD sucking gas out of my grill? *What?*"

Leigh propped her elbows up on the table and sank her chin into her hands. What could she say? It wasn't just the pregnancy. Protecting Cara had been a childhood mission; now it was habit. Cara was everything Leigh wasn't—naive, tenderhearted, optimistic, and drop-dead gorgeous—in other words, a disaster waiting to happen. Leigh was amazed her cousin had survived this long. Yet survived Cara had—through a degree from the Rhode Island School of Design and the building of an illustrious career in graphic design. Not to mention marriage to a handsome husband and the conception of a much wanted baby.

Lucky breaks.

Leigh sighed. Cara had a point. Being too secretive might make things worse; the quest for information could become a game in itself. But the mystery aspect had to be played down—one shred of encouragement and Cara would be crawling around the terrace with a magnifying glass.

Leigh looked away, reached for a strawberry-frosted, and tried to think. "All right. I'll give you the short version. A man died, probably of natural causes. He was embalmed. His body took a wrong turn on the way to its coffin and ended up in your hammock. The police will find out who it is and give him a proper burial. End of story."

Cara's eyes grew wide. "You've got to be kidding. Somebody stole a body?"

Leigh stuffed the rest of the donut in her mouth and chewed as slowly as she could. Cara waited politely for a moment, then stretched a foot under the table and kicked Leigh's chair. "*Where* was it before? *Who* took it? *Why* did they leave it here?"

After recovering from a melodramatic choke, Leigh shrugged her shoulders.

"Don't be ridiculous. You know more than that! And I'm going to find out everything soon anyway." She looked out the window over Leigh's shoulder. "The detectives will want to speak with me. Those men wandering around out there *are* detectives, aren't they? As in homicide?"

Leigh swallowed and cleared her throat. "Calling detectives is standard procedure for any discovery of a body, homicide or not," she said authoritatively. She had no idea what she was talking about, but it sounded good. "They'll remove the body, identify it, bury it. It's not a big deal to them. And if Maura's methods are any indication, they'll ask a heck of a lot more questions than they'll answer."

Cara studied her cousin, then tried another tactic. She leaned closer, eyes beaming, voice conspiratorial. "Come on, Agent L. It's debriefing time. You do remember The Agency, don't you? Mrs. Peterson's missing cat? The bicycle speedometer?"

Sentimentality—Leigh's Achilles' heel! She felt herself beginning to weaken and stood up. "We were just kids then," she answered, pushing images of bowler hats and spy rings out of her mind. "Now we're adults, in case you haven't noticed, and we know better. You're a twenty-eight-year-old artist on the mommy track, not a private eye. Just stay out of it and concentrate on the baby. I'll work with Maura and take care of anything that needs to be done."

Cara swept some table crumbs into a napkin. "Last time I checked," she said smoothly, "you weren't a private eye either. What exactly makes an ad copywriter more qualified at assisting the police than a graphic designer? And even a thirty-year—"

"Don't say it!" Leigh interrupted. "I'm not there yet and you know it."

Cara smiled smugly.

Someone knocked softly on the back door.

It would be a long morning.

Chapter 3

Leigh's nocturnal activities had never been considered so fascinating by so many people. Nor had Mao Tse's digestive problems. The questioning was almost fun—for about fifteen minutes. Then the monotony began. By mid-morning Leigh had described the figure on the bluff so many times she was tempted to embellish the story just to amuse herself. Cara had hung on every word, disappointed at not having a story of her own to tell and annoyed at not having heard Leigh's earlier. Then, much to Leigh's chagrin, Cara had insisted they play brunch hostesses to the army of public servants and journalists streaming in and out of the yard. By the time the body was removed and the crowd gone it was almost twelve-thirty, and even Cara was drained enough to lie down for a nap. It was around this time that Leigh remembered she had a job.

Deciding against a phone-in apology, she grabbed some low-fat breakfast bars from the pantry and took off in her Cavalier. The more disheveled she looked for this explanation, the better.

She practiced. "I'm terribly sorry, Mr. Lacey, but there was this corpse, you see, on the hammock, and what with the police and everything I just clean forgot about the deadline on the DecoDripless account. . . ."

Oh, sure. That'll go over in a big way.

Leigh pulled into her usual spot in the stadium lot

and walked across the Sixth Street bridge to down-town. It wasn't a bad day for a walk—warm but not too humid. Perhaps the fresh air would help her think.

It didn't. When she reached the lobby of the USX building she was tired but no more inspired. She boarded the elevator to the fifth floor, where for the past four years she had worked more or less happily at the offices of Peres and Lacey Advertising, Inc. She loved her work, but the advertising climate in Pitts-burgh was fiercely competitive, with certain undesir-able consequences for a young copywriter. She had lost two jobs already—one to a merger, one to bank-ruptcy. And although Peres and Lacey was a relatively stable mid-sized firm, the last six months had not gone well.

Although everyone on Leigh's team agreed that she had done an excellent job of making the patented Twist-it Rim sound exciting, they had lost the ac-count—by far their most lucrative—anyway. Appar-ently the Carttran Milk Caps CEO had a relative who was starting up her own agency, and what else could he do? Leigh considered herself fairly powerless against nepotism; her boss hadn't agreed. She'd been busting her butt to make up for the loss, but this morning's no-show would create problems. Big ones.

She stepped off the elevator just as Jeff Hulsey, her team's manic but capable account representative, stepped on. She greeted him optimistically, with her usual humor. "Going the wrong way, aren't you?" Her smile faded as Jeff looked through her with hostile eyes, cracking his knuckles in tandem. He leaned to one side and pounded the control panel with a fist. The elevator doors closed.

OK. Let's not panic.

Leigh turned around to face Esther Reed, the office receptionist. "What was his problem?"

The perpetually work-weary Esther studied her wrinkled hands with discomfort. "Good morning, Leigh. Mr. Lacey said he wanted to see you as soon as you got in."

Now let's panic.

Esther turned away and pushed a button on the office intercom. Leigh felt the artificial smile she'd been wearing slosh down into her shoes. What was the point?

She plodded down the hall to the door that bore Mr. Lacey's brass name plate. She and Lacey hadn't had a heart-to-heart in his office since the last big catastrophe. From all indications this meeting would prove comparable. Leigh took a deep breath. It was her own fault; she could have called this morning. But then, she had been involved in official police business. She shouldn't be too apologetic, should she? She knocked.

Almost instantly she heard the booming response. "Come on in, Leigh."

She slipped around the heavy door, her level of wariness increasing. The voice was loud but not angry. In fact, it was almost kind.

Mr. Lacey was slouching in his high-backed recliner. He was a giant man, about six feet four inches, and bald as a cue ball. The Daddy Warbucks image was ill-suited, however. Despite his apparent efforts to be a good ole boy, his demeanor was decidedly sharklike. He motioned for Leigh to sit, then tapped his fingers together lightly beneath his chin.

Conversation with Lacey never came easily. He had the creative instincts of a Xerox machine, and tended to avoid any discussion that couldn't be summarized with a spreadsheet. After about fifteen seconds of silence, Leigh felt obligated to jump in. "I'm sorry I'm so late getting in, Mr. Lacey, but the fact is, I encountered a rather strange situation this morning. You see . . ."

He wasn't looking at her. He stared at his desk, shook his head slowly, and waved her explanation away. She stopped talking. He let her suffer in silence for a few more seconds, then stood up and walked around to the front of his desk.

It was not looking good.

As he opened his mouth to say something, then stopped, deciding against it, Leigh fought the urge to grip her armrests tighter. He exhaled, leaned back, and perched himself on the edge of his desk. If he was trying to be casual, it wasn't working.

After about six hours, he spoke. "I told the rest of your team this morning."

NOT a good intro.

"I'm sorry, but the DecoDripless account is gone. Wainwright called me yesterday."

Leigh's heart seemed to stop. DecoDripless was the only major account her team had held since the milk cap fiasco. They couldn't survive the loss of two big accounts in six months.

"We just can't carry your team through this one. . . ." Lacey continued. "We've already shifted as much work as we can."

It was Leigh's turn to gaze at the floor. She was being laid off. Again.

"So I'm afraid your team is being laid off, effective immediately. You'll receive a severance package, of course. . . ."

"Of course," Leigh echoed.

"And a top-notch recommendation." Mr. Lacey was doing his best to sound warm. Leigh tried to appreciate it. "You've done a good job for us, Leigh. I don't think you'll have any trouble finding another position. I wish we could keep you on, but we can't."

She stood up and faced him. "Why did Wainwright pull the account?"

"Nothing to do with our performance, at least, that's what he said. He claims they're restructuring and pulling more work in-house."

Mr. Lacey didn't say anything else, and Leigh gathered she was being dismissed. She started to leave, but he spoke again just as she was opening the door.

"Mrs. Reed will give you the details about your severance package . . . and the office situation."

You mean, how soon I have to be out of here.

Leigh turned around. "Good-bye, Mr. Lacey. Thank you."

She went out the door and shut it behind her.

Thanks a lot.

Had Leigh been an actress in a movie, she would have headed straight for Point State Park. She would have watched the pigeons fighting over bread crumbs, then let the spray of the Point fountain settle on her hair while she reflected on the meaning of life. As it was, she walked straight to her car, drove to the nearest Co-Gos, purchased a Tootsie Roll, a Snickers bar, and a Diet Coke, and consumed them in the parking lot. Her only reflection was that she had neglected to buy a lottery ticket. When the Snickers wrapper was licked clean, she started the car. An ancient instinct took control of the wheel and steered her to the Koslow Animal Clinic.

Her father's pride, joy, and lifetime obsession was only slightly larger than the other brick row houses that flanked it; a tiny lot in the back passed for a parking area. Leigh squeezed the Cavalier into a slot behind the Dumpster, throwing in the candy wrappers as she headed toward the clinic's back door. She opened it and stepped into the kennel room, wincing when a canine chorus announced her arrival. A harried-looking veterinary assistant paused in the midst of dumping cat litter and raised her eyebrows at Leigh. "Sorry, Denise," Leigh said sheepishly, closing the door. "Just need a word with The Man." The younger woman tossed her head in the direction of the exam rooms and went back to work.

Leigh found Randall Koslow, DVM, sitting on the wheeled stool in exam room 1, snipping away at the feathers of a displeased blue and gold macaw. The uncertain-looking teenage employee holding the bird was sweating bullets; the patient seemed to have an unhealthy fascination with her hot pink Press-On nails. Leigh's father was, as always, oblivious to such signs of distress. "Tighter around the neck, don't squeeze the chest," he said mechanically. "Now, let's do the claws."

Leigh nodded at the bird's owner, a thin, fiftyish-looking woman wearing a Grateful Dead T-shirt. The woman responded with a plastic smile, her hands fidgeting over a pack of cigarettes protruding from her denim handbag. When the trim job was finished, Leigh's father replaced the bird in its cage. The bird's owner nodded hastily in all the appropriate places during the avian husbandry lecture, then swept out in search of a more carcinogen-friendly environment.

Dr. Koslow turned to his only daughter with his usual no-nonsense manner. "It's the middle of the day, Leigh. What's happened?"

She waited for the teenager to finish running cold water over her fingers and leave. Randall Koslow sat patiently, adjusting dark-rimmed glasses over his thin nose. He bore an amazing resemblance to Dennis the Menace's father, a burden that might have annoyed a man of lesser self-esteem.

"I got laid off again," Leigh said simply.

Dr. Koslow's wince was almost imperceptible. He removed his glasses and blew on them, then wiped an imaginary smudge with his smock. "Hard times for the company?"

"That, and I got caught dancing naked on the boss's desk."

Dr. Koslow's answer was matter-of-fact. "Then you'll get another job in no time. You have a good record, you're a talented writer. I assume you can dance half decently." He replaced his glasses. "This sort of thing is happening to everybody now. Don't beat yourself up over it, just go get another job."

A shrill bark from the crowded waiting room echoed through the door. Dr. Koslow rose. "Anything else?"

Leigh smiled. Her dad wasn't the gushy type, but he could always make her feel better. "Um, actually there is," she answered. "Mao Tse's throwing up again. I need some Laxatone."

"Take whatever you need," he answered, reaching for the door. Then he turned. "I assume you don't want me to mention this to your mother."

Leigh shivered. "God, no! She wouldn't eat for a week. I'll tell her after I've found another job."

Dr. Koslow nodded. "Good plan." He opened the connecting door to the waiting room and poked his head out. "Sugar Fedorchak?"

Leigh slipped out of the exam room, grabbed a tube of Laxatone from the pharmacy shelves, and left through the back door. The kennel dogs had no comment.

It was late afternoon before Leigh returned to Cara's house. Balancing several Office Max bags with one arm, she let herself in the front door. The phone was ringing as she stepped inside.

"Cara?" she called around the bags. "You here?"

There was no response. Leigh looked for a place to put her packages, but seeing only a spindly antique table, she dropped them in a heap instead. She ran to the security box, punched in the code, and dove for the phone in the study. The lady of the house didn't believe in answering machines; she rarely even answered in person. Apparently, letting someone think you weren't home was more polite than ignoring a message.

"Hello? March residence."

A cranky, shrill voice spat into the other end of the line. "Is this the maid?"

Leigh controlled her annoyance. "No, it isn't. Whom were you calling?"

Throaty laughter echoed out the earpiece, and Leigh's face reddened. "Maura Polanski! What the hell is your problem? I about gave myself a hernia running for this phone!"

The laugher funneled down into a dramatic exhale. "Just couldn't resist, Koslow. You sounded so formal."

Leigh was in no mood to be the brunt of somebody else's joke. "So what do you want, anyway? I've got work to do."

"What do I want?" Maura asked after a short pause. "Have you forgotten you're living at the site of an official police investigation?"

She had. "Of course not. But I thought you finished with all that. What is it now?"

This pause was longer, and the voice that followed was more serious. "I don't have the best news for you. In fact, it's rather worrisome."

Leigh was unmoved. Worries? She had her own to deal with.

Maura continued. "I just got a call from the medical

examiner's office. They haven't finished the autopsy report yet, but they did find something when they removed the clothing."

Leigh tapped her foot on the new Berber carpet and thought about whether or not she had bought the right printer cartridge. Perhaps she should invest in a laser printer anyway. Résumés had to look good in her line of work. . . .

"There was a note pinned to the shirt. Handprinted on plain notebook paper—new, fresh paper."

"Yeah, all right," Leigh said impatiently, debating whether she could afford any computer supplies now that she was unemployed. "So what did it say?"

Maura cleared her throat. "It said: GET OUT OF MY HOUSE."

Leigh's brain shifted back to the present. *Get out of my house.* Whose house? Her brow wrinkled. "What is that supposed to mean, Maura? Was the note intended for Cara and me?"

"I got no way of knowing that yet, Koslow. The medical examiner still hasn't officially stated that the body was embalmed or how long the man's been dead, much less cause of death. Then there's the matter of identity. . . ."

Leigh clenched her teeth. Perhaps, on a better day, she might be more patient. Probably not. "So, why did you even call me?" she barked. "I don't know if the note was meant for us, I don't know who he is, what house he's talking about. . . . Oh, for God's sake. The man's dead! He didn't write the damn note anyway!"

A long pause followed. When Maura spoke again, it was in her best calm-the-hysterical-citizen voice. "I realize this embalmed-body thing has been unsettling. But you're sounding a bit over the edge. Is something else going on?"

Leigh remembered why she liked Maura so much. She was one perceptive human—a trait that undoubtedly served her well as a policewoman. Leigh's temper cooled. "Yeah," she said more quietly. "I lost my job."

"Geez, Leigh," Maura sympathized. "I'm sorry. Did you see it coming?"

"I should have." The offer of an empathizing ear proved too tempting to pass up, and before Leigh knew it, she had vented a few years' worth of job frustrations. She could hear several other phones ringing at the station, and her cheeks reddened. "Thanks for listening, but I don't want to hold you up."

"No problem," Maura answered with ill-disguised relief. "I'll let you know if I hear any more about the case, but I doubt I will. The detectives will contact you themselves. My butt is back on traffic duty."

Leigh thanked Maura and hung up. To hell with disoriented corpses. She had résumés to write.

Chapter 4

Leigh unrolled the Thursday morning *Pittsburgh Post* with great expectations, her little-used optimistic side in full swing. First, she was going to be a celebrity. Second, she was going to find a new job.

The mood didn't last long. "Body Found in Avalon" held not a hint of sensationalism; in fact, it was downright dry. Leigh cursed the lackluster reporter who had interviewed her the day before. A journalistic purist—what were the odds? To add insult to injury, he had spelled her name "Lee," which was unforgivable.

The classifieds were no better. Not only were no advertising agencies dying for copywriters, but the only reference to a journalism degree came next to the words SALARIES TO 14K.

She tossed down the paper and tore the wrapper off her fourth low-fat granola bar. *Coffee. I need coffee.* She was about to search for some when Cara joined her in the breakfast nook.

"Morning," Leigh said, sounding more cheerful than she felt. Cara looked awful. Her normally perfect hair hung limply over her shoulders, several renegade strands sticking out in odd directions. Her eyes were red-tinged and her lids puffy.

"Yeah, I guess," she groaned, shuffling over to open

the refrigerator. "Did you and Maura eat all those donuts?"

Leigh sniffed. "You, Maura, I, and half the coroner's office finished them by noon, yes." She rose. "You can have some breakfast bars if you want," she said, holding out the box. "They're sweet."

Cara looked at the box skeptically, but pulled out a bar and sat down. Leigh poured two glasses of orange juice and joined her. "Bad night?"

Cara glanced up in surprise. "Why do you say that?"

Leigh smiled slyly. "Um, gee, I'm just psychic, I guess."

Cara looked at her hair out of the corner of her eyes and tried to smooth it down.

"Your were out at your mom's house pretty late last night," Leigh continued. "Did she make that great lasagna?"

Cara nibbled the breakfast bar with distaste. "If she'd been making lasagna, I would have invited you. Actually, she served chicken salad—it was a Ballasta basket party. I thought the guests would never leave."

Leigh gave thanks for being spared the invite. Her aunt's chicken salad was second to none, but not even lasagna could make her spend an evening with thirty Martha Stewart fanatics cooing over Ballasta baskets.

"But even after I got back," Cara continued, "I didn't go straight to bed. Something Mrs. Rhodis said made me want to look around the bookshelves in the study."

This statement begged several questions, but Leigh decided to take first things first. "Mrs. Rhodis?" she asked. "That's the older woman who lives next door, right? I didn't know she knew your mom."

"She didn't," Cara answered. "I invited her. She was fussing over my Ballasta laundry basket the other day, and she's a neat lady. She hangs her clothes out on the line too. She has a dryer, but we both think there's nothing like that fresh smell—"

Leigh's efforts at polite conversation did have limits. "You were saying something about searching the house?"

"Yes." Cara backtracked, becoming more animated. "It's all very interesting. You know about how I found the money?"

Leigh nodded. A few days before, Cara, who was used to thinking in geometric terms, had noticed a discrepancy in the woodwork around the master bedroom fireplace. She thought there must be a potential space not accessible through the existing cabinets, and a more thorough examination revealed she was right. A camouflaged door opened to a small compartment, which contained a blank book and a metal tackle box with $300 in cash and some old coins. From Cara's reaction you'd have thought she won the lottery.

"You still have it, right?" Leigh asked.

"For now," Cara answered. "But I think I'll give it to charity. It must have belonged to the man we bought the house from, but he's dead, and apparently he had no family."

The image of a small piece of paper flickered through Leigh's mind. *Get out of my house.*

Cara continued. "Anyway, this man, his name was Paul Fischer, lived in this house practically his whole life. Mrs. Rhodis lived next door to him for over forty years, but never got to know him very well. Do you believe it? She says he kept to himself, went to work and came back, and didn't have much of a social life. She only saw him when he was outside working on the house. He kept it in great condition, as you can see, so he clearly was a decent handyman and carpenter. Which led me to believe that he designed and

built the compartment himself." She bit off a larger
bite of breakfast bar.

"A miserly type who didn't trust banks?"

"That's what the police suggested when I found the
money. Apparently he had no bank account, at least
not when he died. So building a safe seemed a reasonable enough thing for him to do. But then I talked to
Mrs. Rhodis."

A tiny bell went off in Leigh's mind. Hadn't she
known a Mrs. Rhodis in her days at the Koslow Animal Clinic? She closed her eyes and tried to get a
picture. "Yep," she said proudly, opening her eyes.
"Got her. Short, round, wild hair. Polyester. Dynasty
of clairvoyant white poodles."

"That's her"—Cara grinned—"but I think the current poodle is apricot. Or maybe it's what you'd call
champagne?" Realizing she was getting sidetracked,
Cara shook her head and moved on. "The point is,
she told me that before Paul Fischer died, he hinted
that he had some important papers at his house."

Leigh's stomach twitched unpleasantly. "You mean,
like a will?"

"No will was ever found. Nor were any other papers. The closest thing he had was an address book,
and no living relatives could be located."

Leigh remembered the legal hassles Cara and Gil
had gone through to buy the house. The sale had
taken years. Just thinking about it made her head start
to pound. Or was the pounding from another source?
Her eyes panned the kitchen anxiously. If she didn't
get some caffeine in her veins soon, civil conversation
would become impossible. Maybe on the very top
shelf? "So, Mrs. Rhodis has got you believing that this
Paul Fischer guy hid something in the study? A treasure map perhaps?" Leigh fetched the stepladder and
started to climb.

Cara watched with amusement. "If you can control your cynicism for a minute, I'll tell you exactly what she said. But as I told you yesterday, you won't find any regular. I went cold turkey when I found out I was pregnant."

Leigh stepped down reluctantly.

"I'm not expecting gold doubloons," Cara continued. "More along the lines of an answer to an old mystery."

Leigh couldn't help rolling her eyes. Once again, the promise of a mystery had Cara drooling. *Thanks a lot, Mrs. Rhodis.*

Cara caught Leigh's expression and set her jaw in irritation. "And what's so wrong with trying to solve a little puzzle here and there? What else am I supposed to do for the next seven weeks? Sit around and file my nails?"

Leigh could think of several better suggestions but stopped herself. Cara clearly enjoyed such things. So much so that she had stayed up till all hours of the night rattling around measuring bookshelves. Harmless fun, right?

The image of a dusty hat and pinstripe suit formed unbidden in Leigh's mind. She rounded up her breakfast bar wrappers and threw them in the trash. A real mission was hers this morning—one that didn't involve catchy slogans for industrial soap dispensers. She needed to make sure Cara wasn't getting herself into trouble, and she needed to do it without Cara knowing about it.

But first she needed caffeine.

It was twenty minutes later when an angel of mercy finally leaned down from heaven to hand Leigh the cup of life. "Thank you for choosing McDonald's," the pimple-faced teenager said flatly, slamming the glass window.

Leigh placed the brew delicately between her knees and steered into a parking spot, a technique she had perfected long before scalding your crotch had become a national cash cow. After half a large cup her mind began to clear, and she tried to connect Cara's rantings with the appearance of the corpse. The note on the body had been written in first person: get out of my house. Unless the deceased had the presence of mind to write it himself before he kicked off, it seemed reasonable that the note was planted by whoever left the body in the hammock. Since writing a note to a dead man would be pointless, the note must have been intended for whoever found his corpse. And with the body placed at the old Fischer house, it seemed reasonable to assume that the deceased was Paul Fischer himself.

Leigh took another long drink. When had Paul Fischer died? Years before Cara and Gil bought the house, she knew that. And they had owned it a few more years before they fixed it up and moved in. No need for a nice house when you spend ninety percent of the time living out of a suitcase bopping around the world.

And what could have happened to his body? She was fairly certain that most residents of Avalon ended up at Fields Funeral Home, intestate or not. But then again, Vestal hadn't recognized the body. Where had Fischer died? And where had his body been between then and yesterday night?

The more Leigh considered that the body might be Paul Fischer, the more certain she became. Surely Maura already suspected him—he was an obvious choice for anyone who knew about the note, which Cara, Leigh remembered, did not. That was just as well.

Finishing off the last of her coffee, she drove to the

parking lot pay phone and placed a call to the station. After a considerable delay, Maura's voice came through in a harried bark.

"Polanski here!"

"Hi, it's Leigh. What's up?"

The officer sighed. "What's not? Look, I'm really swamped right now. Has something happened?"

Until yesterday Leigh would have assumed "swamped" meant a stack of reports to fill out. Now she wondered if any other bodies had turned up. She was smart enough not to ask, however. "No, Maura, I called because I wanted to know if Paul Fischer is being investigated as a possible ID for the body."

"I'm out of that loop now, like I said. But that was my first thought too. I do know that Paul Fischer died in 1989, and that his body went to Fields Funeral Home."

"How do you know that?" Leigh asked.

"Real heavy-duty investigative police work, Koslow."

"Your mother told you?"

"Yeah."

Leigh smiled. Maura's father might have been a legend in Avalon law enforcement, but her mother was a legend, period. Mary Polanski had a memory for names, faces, and minutia that boggled the mind. She knew who had twins in 1958, and she knew who got audited in 1974. Better yet, she wouldn't tell unless you had a good reason to ask.

Maura's chair was squeaking again. "Look, Leigh, if you want more information, you'll have to call the detectives. The coroner's report should be in sometime today. I've really got to go."

"OK," Leigh said idly, her mind working. "Take it easy."

"Always do," Maura replied, and hung up.

Leigh returned to her car, crumpled her coffee cup

and tossed it over her shoulder into the backseat. So
far her instincts were on the mark. And with fresh
caffeine surging happily in her veins, she was ready
to roll.

Chapter 5

Fields Funeral Home was located on California Avenue, Avalon's main drag. It was a spacious stone building spread out on a large, treed lot, and it could have passed for a house if not for the telltale awning over the side porch. The parking lot was filled.

Who has a funeral at nine o'clock in the morning? Leigh grumbled as she circled the lot looking for a space. She found one near the back door, which was just as well. It wouldn't do to walk in the front and interrupt.

She opened the unlocked door and surprised an older man in a red Fields-issue suit as he collected a Coke from the vending machine. This was an informal lounge, most likely for employees only. *Oh, well.*

"Can I help you?" the man said politely. If he was annoyed at her, he did a good job of hiding it.

"I hope so," Leigh said with a smile, stepping forward to shake his hand. "My name is Leigh Koslow; I'm a writer." She felt a slight pang of guilt for the misrepresentation, but dismissed it. She *was* a writer—sort of. "I was hoping to talk to Mr. Fields, but I can see he's a bit tied up right now."

The man smiled and nodded apologetically.

"You may be able to help me. I'm doing some genealogical research on Avalon families. I'm particularly interested in a man named Paul Fischer who died in

1989. I was hoping you could tell me if he had his funeral at Fields, and where he was buried."

The man smiled broadly. "Well, certainly." He then looked up at the ceiling thoughtfully, scratching his stubbled chin with a fat, liver-spotted finger. "Paul Fischer . . . he lived in one of those big houses on the river, didn't he?"

Leigh nodded enthusiastically.

"Didn't know the man personally," he went on, "but I suppose Mr. Fields might have. Our burial records are open to the public unless the family requests otherwise. Have a seat and I'll check for you. Do you know how his last name is spelled?"

Leigh answered the question, and her benefactor obligingly shuffled off. She plopped down on the red vinyl couch, feeling smug. If investigating was this easy, perhaps she was in the wrong line of work. After fifteen minutes she began to get worried, but her red-suited servant did return, pink "while you were out" note in hand.

"Sorry it took me so long," he apologized good-naturedly. "We put everything on computer in 1992, and the old records are a little disheveled. But I think I found what you need."

He handed Leigh the paper, which bore some illegible pencil scribbles. "Paul Byron Fischer was entered into the books on June 5, 1989. He was buried over at Peaceful Acres on the Eighth. Was he a relative of yours?"

"Not a blood relative," Leigh answered honestly.

"The records say that Fields Funeral Home picked up the cost of the burial plot, so evidently Mr. Fields did know him. Would you like to wait and speak with him?"

Leigh's brow wrinkled. "Fields paid for the funeral? Is that typical?"

"No, no," the man responded. "The funeral arrangements were made in advance, but apparently Mr. Fischer had not yet purchased a plot at the time of his death. It happens sometimes. Fischer being a lifetime resident of Avalon, and having already paid for the funeral, I suppose Mr. Fields was willing to help out. He's a good man."

Leigh took the pink note and thanked the man profusely. She slipped out the way she had come in and returned to her car. The funeral, thankfully, was still in session. With luck, the procession wouldn't be following her to Peaceful Acres.

The old cemetery was in West View, another of the many Pittsburgh boroughs which, although a stone's throw from the metropolis, had a distinctive small-town feel. It was in this larger borough to the north where Cara and Leigh had grown up in red brick row houses, side by side. That situation had occurred partly because their mothers, who were identical twins, were inseparable, and partly because Cara's father had abandoned the family before his daughter was born. Leigh drove through West View in a circuitous fashion, careful to avoid her parents' neighborhood. God forbid her mother should see her driving about on a Thursday morning.

She pulled up to the small wood-frame structure that served as the cemetery office, and was relieved to see the door propped open. Someone was home. She parked the car, walked up to the door, and looked in. A small sitting room was empty. Leigh knocked on the door's inner surface. "Hello? Is anyone here?"

A thin interior door opened slightly, then stopped. A woman's voice swore. With a grunt from the other side, the door broke loose from the buckled floorboards beneath. It burst open, followed closely by the shoulders of a stout woman of medium height and middle age. She slammed the door behind her and turned to look at Leigh with eyes eclipsed by black eyeliner and glittery blue mascara. She sighed heavily. "Damn door. I told Pete last spring to fix the thing." She gave Leigh a saccharine smile with lips that were a little too pink. "But then, men never do what you tell them, do they?"

Leigh returned a smile. She wasn't sure she wanted to male-bash with this particular individual, but she did need help. "My name is Leigh Koslow. I'm doing some genealogical research, and I'm trying to find the gravesite of a Paul Fischer, who was buried here in June 1989."

The woman's mouth twitched slightly in disappointment, as if she had been hoping Leigh was selling Avon rather than visiting a grave. She sighed. "Sure, honey. Just let me take a look at the book." She pulled the door open again with a heave and a few strong words, not bothering to close it. Leigh couldn't see into the inner office, but she could hear heavy books being moved about, pages turning, and even more choice words. When the woman reemerged, her dyed-black hair looked a bit moister around the roots, and her expression was less friendly. "Paul Fischer's in section C, lot fourteen." She pointed out the area on a faded wall map encased in yellow-tinged plastic, and Leigh was dismissed.

Leigh hiked out to the far hill, careful not to step directly on any graves. It was an inefficient route, but eventually she reached the area of flat stones where the woman had directed her. They lay close together in rows, a bit more orderly than the hodge-podge of graves with upright headstones. She walked up the fence line and read the stones as far as she could see. When she reached the fifth row from the top and read the third stone over, she stopped. "Paul Byron Fischer; Born February 13, 1925, Died June 5, 1989."

So, Mr. Fischer, here you are. Or—here you were.

There was nothing special about the marker, which looked just like those around it. The grounds were well tended, and no weeds covered the stone's edges. Remembering the purpose of her mission, she stepped back to look at the ground. It was covered with healthy grass that blended perfectly with that around it. Not a blade out of place. No telltale clods of dirt, no obvious swell of the landscape. No one had dug into this ground in months, maybe not even years.

Leigh sighed softly, then felt a little foolish. And she had thought she was doing so well as a sleuth. Had she really expected to come out here and find a gaping coffin-sized hole that no else had noticed? She exhaled in disgust and started back toward the car. She was better off doing résumés. The body, whosoever it was, probably had nothing to do with Paul Fischer or Cara's house. She should let the police handle it. At least they were getting paid.

Seeing the maroon Taurus parked in Cara's driveway did nothing to improve Leigh's spirits. She parked behind it and walked into the house, shoulders drooping. A prim, heavily accessorized woman sat in the parlor with Cara, teacup in hand. When she saw Leigh, she hastily put down the cup and rose, her face a perfect blend of concern and irritation. "Well, there you are! Are you feeling all right? I've been worried about you, you know. Why didn't you call me yesterday?"

Leigh took a deep breath, wheels turning in her mind. She had to tread carefully. "I'm fine, Mom. Why do you ask?"

Frances Koslow's orange-tinted lips formed an exaggerated O. "Why do I ask? *Why* do I ask? I read in the morning paper that my daughter is a witness in a murder investigation, and I know nothing about it. And you ask me why I'm concerned?"

Leigh exhaled. If her mother only knew half the story, she was in good shape. "It wasn't a murder investigation," she answered calmly. "I just found a body, that's all."

"That's all?! And poor Cara here alone and unprotected?"

Cara bristled a little but said nothing.

"Mom," Leigh tried again, "there's nothing to be upset about. Maura thinks the man probably died of natural causes. We're fine. I didn't mention it because I didn't want to worry you."

"You didn't think I would read the paper?"

Leigh had no response to that.

"And if you're so fine—"

Here it comes.

"—why aren't you at work? Your receptionist told me you weren't coming in today, and Cara didn't know where you were either."

Today? Leigh sighed in relief. *Thanks, Esther. I owe you one.*

Cara rose and looked at Leigh around Frances's shoulder, a question in her eyes. Leigh shot her a warning look.

"Well?" Frances insisted. "What's wrong with you? You know you just can't go taking off from work all the time. You'll lose your job for sure."

Leigh bit her lip, and inspiration came. "I have plenty of time off coming, Mom. In fact, I just talked with Mr. Lacey yesterday, and he encouraged me to go ahead and take it."

Frances's brow wrinkled slightly, but she seemed

satisfied. "Well, good. I'm sure Cara can use some help around the house. No point wasting money on maids and nurses when family can pitch in." She scooped up her oversized embroidered purse and fumbled for her keys. "Thank you for the tea, Cara dear, it was lovely. I have to run. Music club is at noon."

She motioned for Leigh to walk her to the door. "I want you to let me know what's going on with this investigation, do you understand?" she said in a hushed tone. "Cara shouldn't be exposed to this. You know what her doctors said."

Leigh rolled her eyes but nodded. She opened the door wide.

"Oh, and I almost forgot." Frances continued, gesturing with her keys. "I want you both to come over for dinner on Saturday. It's been too long since we had a nice family meal. I want you to invite your friend Maura too. I haven't seen her in years."

Leigh wondered what was motivating the latter invitation. "Maura may have to stay with her mother," she reminded. In a cruel twist of irony, the woman with the near-perfect memory was now in the early stages of Alzheimer's disease.

"Oh, of course," Frances responded thoughtfully. "Then invite her too. The more the merrier."

"OK, Mom. Good-bye."

Leigh shut the door, but soon heard a gentle rapping. She opened it to face a look of stern disapproval. "I can't go anywhere, dear. You have my car blocked in. Oh, and by the way—"

Leigh steeled herself for the honey-coated insult she knew was coming.

"—your car is looking a little neglected. You can come over and use our hose if Cara's won't reach the driveway. No sense paying for a car wash. You should vacuum it out too—I'm sure it's long overdue . . ."

Leigh slipped into zombie mode and followed her mother out to the cars. Saturday would be a blast.

With Cara off at an afternoon doctor's appointment, Leigh had settled herself in front of the computer with good intentions of updating her resúmé. But when the phone rang a half hour and one rewritten sentence later, the interruption was welcome.

"Hello again, Leigh," Maura said, sounding tired. "I have some news for you."

Leigh wondered whether she should tell Maura of her own investigations. Probably not.

"This doesn't usually happen," Maura continued. "In fact, I don't know if it's ever happened, but the county has kicked your case back to us. Seems this whole business boils down to an abuse of corpse, and the detectives are up to their eyeballs in real homicides."

Leigh was lost. "Abuse of corpse?"

"The coroner's report came out earlier today. The man whose body you found died at the approximate age of sixty, and was embalmed about ten years ago. The most probable cause of death was advanced pancreatic cancer—i.e., natural causes. There was no homicide. The body isn't where it should be, but messing around with a corpse is only a second-degree misdemeanor. Long story short—the county no longer cares. You're stuck with the locals."

Leigh smiled. Maura was back in the loop. The detectives had been a disappointment anyway. She hadn't expected raincoats and cigars, but an unattached, thirtyish one with a sardonic smile and a cute posterior would have been nice.

"I'm not sure who Mellman's going to put on it, but I've already made a few phone calls. Paul Fischer's records from his first and last admission into Suburban General Hospital match up with the coroner's findings."

Leigh's stomach tightened.

"He died at Suburban General on June 5, 1989, at the age of sixty-four, of complications of pancreatic cancer."

Leigh tried to reconcile Maura's words with the smooth, flat lawn below Fischer's headstone. "But that's not possible," she said without meaning to.

"Come again?"

"I just came back from looking at Paul Fischer's grave, up at Peaceful Acres," Leigh answered hesitantly. "There wasn't a blade out of place."

Maura was quiet for a moment. "Perhaps the body hasn't been there for a while. Landscaping can change in a decade."

A long silence followed. Finally, Maura broke it. "Look, Koslow, I know this is creepy. But we're going to get to the bottom of it, I promise. I'm going to grill the hell out of Vestal as soon as I can, but first I've got to check on a domestic situation, and that may take awhile. What I'm wondering is—" Maura broke off, as if she were about to give away more than intended. "Sit tight, Leigh. You guys have a good security system over there, right?"

"Yes."

"Well, use it. Just in case this prankster isn't the friendly type."

"Comprende," Leigh answered mechanically. They hung up.

She sat for a long time, staring into space. Something was nagging at her. If the body was Paul Fischer, then she'd been looking at an empty grave. But empty for how long? She closed her eyes and pictured the site: the carefully tended green grass, the rows of long flat stones, laid out so precisely.

Her eyes opened. She knew what was wrong. And she knew that not only was Paul Fischer's body not in that grave—it never had been.

Chapter 6

When Leigh's Cavalier pulled into the driveway of Fields Funeral Home for the second time that day, the parking lot was nearly deserted. She parked near the main entrance and walked up to the heavy wooden double doors. She started to pull one open, with no small amount of effort, and quickly found herself aided by another red-coated man. This one was considerably younger than the last she had encountered, and not nearly as polite.

He looked condescendingly at her T-shirt and jeans. "Can I help you . . . ma'am?"

She bristled. "Yes," she said firmly, and more than a little high-handedly. "I'd like to speak with Vestal, privately."

"He's busy in his office right now," the youth replied. "Is there something I can help you with?" His eyes twinkled evilly. "Perhaps you'd like to have a look at one of our advance planning programs?"

Leigh stared at him hard, wondering how their relationship had gotten off to such a fabulous start. "I've already made plans with a taxidermist"—she smiled sweetly—"but thank you." She pushed past him and started walking in what she believed to be the general direction of the main office.

She found Vestal's office without difficulty, at the end of the hall across from the lounge she'd entered before. The door was ajar, and she could see the funeral director sitting behind a cluttered mahogany desk, phone in hand. She waited patiently in the hall and tried to put the obnoxious doorman out of her mind. Her tough nineties woman act wouldn't cut it with Vestal. If she wanted information from him, she'd need her smelling salts. When he hung up the phone, she knocked.

"Come on in." He beckoned cheerfully. Leigh walked on bright red carpet in between dark red walls and sat on a chair covered with maroon-colored vinyl. She made a mental note to send over an interior decorator when her ship came in. "Hello again," she said demurely. "I'm Leigh Koslow. I'm not sure we were formally introduced yesterday at my cousin's house, but we've met several times over the years."

"Of course," Vestal said with enthusiasm. His eyes, however, betrayed a hint of nervousness. He leaned forward over the desk and pumped her hand hard with damp, chubby fingers. "Oh, yes, you're Randall's daughter. Good man, Randall. He always took great care of my Pete, God rest his soul."

The words "God rest his soul" slipped off Vestal's lips like butter as he settled back in his chair. Leigh wondered if he used the phrase in ordinary conversation. "Well, it certainly is nice weather we're having, God rest his soul!"

"I'm here because my cousin and I are concerned about the body that was left in her hammock," she said with downcast eyes. "It's just the two of us there, you know, and Cara's expecting." Vestal responded with a look of fatherly concern.

"There's something that's been troubling me," she continued. "The police know now that the body we found is that of a man named Paul Fischer. . . ." She stole a look at Vestal out of the corner of her eye, and was pleased to see the color draining from his face. She thought again of the headstones that were lined up in rows, close together. Too close together. "But according to Peaceful Acres, Paul Fischer's body was cremated here at your funeral home. So I'm wondering, how could his ashes be buried there when his body is at the coroner's office?"

Leigh looked up, and for a moment she thought she had actually killed the man. His face was a whitish gray, his eyes glassy, his chest unmoving. She sat up quickly. "Mr. Fields? Are you all right?"

He blinked, shook his head, and quickly rose. Then he crossed to the door, closed it tightly, and returned to his seat. He grabbed the glass of water set on his desk and took an interminable swig. Finally he pulled out a handkerchief and wiped his brow. Leigh said nothing.

"Miss Koslow . . ." he began in a hoarse whisper.

"Leigh, please," she said warmly, feeling more than a little guilty.

His pasty white lips tried to smile. "Leigh. I see that an explanation is in order here. But for reasons that will become obvious, I would appreciate your discretion."

Leigh's heart skipped a beat, and she leaned forward. Such speeches were generally followed by something worth hearing. If she played her cards right, Vestal might just wrap this case up for her. She was proving to be pretty good at this detective stuff, after all.

"I'm happy to help you and your cousin in any way that I can," Vestal continued stiffly, "but I really don't know how Paul Fischer's body got into your yard, or who could have put it there." He took a deep breath and ran a fat finger beneath his nose. "You see, I haven't seen the body since the day it was brought here ten years ago."

Leigh let that thought sink in, then asked another question. "Did you embalm it?"

He nodded.

"And you knew him, right? So why didn't you recognize the body?" Leigh asked. She knew the answer, but the innocent act had served her well so far.

"I did, of course." Vestal admitted with a touch of defensiveness. "But it spooked me. I knew that eventually the whole mess would come out. I was just trying to delay the inevitable so I'd have a chance to think."

Vestal rose from his desk again and walked to one of the floor-length windows whose thick red velvet curtains blocked out any light. He parted the curtains slightly and gazed out, eyes unseeing.

"I've been wanting to get all this off my chest for ten years. Now I have no choice. Maybe it's just as well."

Leigh held her breath. Vestal needed a confessor? That suited her perfectly.

"What happened to Paul Fischer's body?" she asked softly.

Vestal took another long breath, then drooped his shoulders, resigned. "It disappeared," he said simply.

Leigh squirmed in her seat. "Disappeared?" she echoed.

"I had never been so angry in my life!" Vestal's apple cheeks quickly turned to balls of red in a sea of white. "I embalmed the body soon after it came in from the hospital. That's standard procedure. I had finally sold Paul on an advance package about a year before: bottom-of-the-line, no frills. The cheapskate. I remember he hadn't bought a plot like he was supposed to, which was going to be a pain. With no family coming forward, the loose ends would be left to us. I was wondering what I was going to do with him. But the next day he wasn't there."

Vestal pulled out his handkerchief again, this time blowing into it loudly. "I had hired this kid as a night janitor. He was a pathetic sort, but I was trying to give him a break. He was the only one in the building that night, as far as I know. When I confronted him, he made up some cock-and-bull story about hearing funny noises, and said he didn't know anything. I grilled him and another teenager I had doing some odd jobs for me, and what did I find out? The second guy told me that the first one was—"

He broke off suddenly, remembering his audience. Leigh kept her face impassive. "Well, the other kid told me that he had seen the night janitor acting, how shall I say it, 'inappropriately' with some of the cadavers. God, what a nightmare. Do you have any idea how a scandal like that could affect my business?"

Leigh could imagine.

"I made a decision. Maybe it was a bad one, but it seemed like the best thing to do at the time. Fischer had no relatives, nobody. People in Avalon who had known him his whole life didn't give two hoots about him. He was that kind of man. No one was going to ask questions about him, much less visit his plot."

Leigh couldn't help breaking in. "So you never reported the body as stolen?"

"No," he said, perhaps with regret, "I didn't." The confession seemed to be helping him; his color had improved to a pale pink. He went on.

"Maybe the kid had the body, maybe he didn't. Maybe he sold it. I just hoped that whoever had it would keep it. I changed the advance order from embalming to cremation and let the world think Fischer was buried right on schedule. And I made sure those two kids would let the world go on thinking that. The janitor promised to leave town, and I'm sure he did. He could have gone just about anywhere with the wad of cash I gave him. Nobody else ever knew."

He returned to the chair behind his desk and sank into it. "So that's it. That's all I know. The body disappeared. I've spent the last ten years hoping it would stay missing. Until yesterday I thought it was going to."

Leigh had to ask him one more question.

"I don't understand why you weren't more worried about the body turning up somewhere and being identified by the police."

Vestal looked slightly embarrassed. "That was always a risk, and in the end, I suppose it happened. But you see, I knew Paul Fischer. The man didn't trust anybody. Bankers, lawyers, especially not doctors. That's why he died so young, you know. Refused to believe he was sick. Didn't see a doctor till he collapsed in his driveway and a Samaritan called an ambulance. I wasn't too worried about dental X rays being on file somewhere. And he didn't look much like himself when he died. He was emaciated, you know, from the cancer."

"Surely some of his neighbors would recognize him?" Leigh asked tentatively.

"If they had a chance to look at the body, maybe." Vestal replied with a calculating tone. He had clearly been over these thoughts before. "But with Paul Fischer supposedly cremated and buried, no one would have any reason to be looking for him." He paused a moment. "Maura Polanski didn't recognize him. Hell, even Mellman didn't recognize him! But then, Donald's never been too good with faces. Now Chief Polanski, he would have known in a minute, God rest his soul."

Vestal's voice trailed off in thought, but soon he remembered who he was talking to. He cleared his throat and sat up, fatherly once again. "You realize that whoever had the body must have known whose it was," he said carefully. "They did leave it at Paul Fischer's old house. Frankly, that makes me a little nervous for you and your cousin. There are a lot of crazy people out there."

Leigh couldn't disagree with that. She nodded appreciatively, then rose to leave.

"Thank you for trying to help," she said sweetly.

Vestal beamed. "Anything else I can do, you just let me know. You girls be careful, now."

"We will be."

Vestal opened the heavy oak door and Leigh started to scoot outside, but he gently grabbed her elbow. "By the way," he said quietly, "how *did* they identify the body?"

Leigh stiffened as she heard a familiar voice echoing down the hall. Maura hadn't seen her yet—which was good. Something told her the policewoman might not be thrilled with her and Vestal's little chat.

"I'm sorry, Mr. Fields," she said quickly, "but I just remembered I left a roast in the oven. I've got to go!" She dashed across the hall and into the lounge. "My car's out here," she lied. "I'll just go on out. Thank you again!"

With a smile and wave befitting Melanie Wilkes, she was gone. She started the Cavalier and smirked with pride. Perhaps she should become an actress. She'd never put a roast in an oven in her life.

When Leigh returned to the house, she found Cara in the kitchen creating a marvelous-smelling pot of spaghetti sauce. "What's the occasion?" Leigh asked with a smile.

"A craving, naturally." Cara stirred the wonderful concoction gingerly as she tapped in an extra dash of oregano.

"Smells great. I could eat the whole pot myself."

"Oh?" Cara's eyebrows lifted. "You're not having cravings now too, are you?"

"If I am," Leigh said with a snort, "it'll be the start of a whole new religion."

Cara laughed. "Would you mind climbing up to that top shelf and handing me the minced garlic? It's by the candles."

Leigh knew better than to ask why. She found the bottle and handed it down, then sank into a chair.

Cara put a lid on the pot and sat down across from her. "Are you going to tell me what you and Maura found out today," she asked pleasantly, "or am I going to withhold your dinner?"

Where to begin?

Cara tried to help. "The body is Paul Fischer's, isn't it?"

Leigh stared. Cara didn't even know about the note, much less the coroner's report. "What makes you think that?"

Cara's response was matter-of-fact. "As I tried to tell you this morning when you went into caffeine withdrawal—by the way, I bought regular—I'm convinced that Mrs. Rhodis is right and that something is hidden in this house. Something somebody else wants. The gender and age of the body seemed right for Paul Fischer. I think serving up the body of the house's last resident was a scare tactic to make us move out."

Leigh was in awe. "Well, you're right. The body is Paul Fischer's."

Cara smiled with pride, though the implications seemed nothing to be happy about.

"We need to take this seriously, Cara. Whoever

wants us out of this house is perverted enough to steal a body. Who knows what else they might do? Maybe you should think about staying at your mother's for a while."

Cara's eyes blazed. "I'll do no such thing! I will not be frightened out of my own home by some nutball. I've wanted this house forever, and if there's something here to find, I'm going to find it first. I own the contents of this house, and I intend to keep them!"

Leigh had known her cousin long enough to know when to back off. As mild-mannered as Cara was, when her buttons were pushed, a tigress emerged. "It's just something to think about," Leigh said softly. "We need to be careful about remembering to turn on the security system."

Cara's face returned to its normal color. "I've been very careful about the security system ever since the body was found," she responded calmly. "I'm not an idiot."

They were interrupted by the sound of a slamming car door, followed closely by heavy knocks on the front door. If Leigh hadn't known who it was, she might have been concerned. Knowing who it was was even worse.

The cousins looked at each other. "I'll get it," Leigh said bravely.

She opened the door and braced herself.

"What in the hell were you thinking, Koslow?! Don't you know when you're interfering in an official police investigation? You could have given away vital information—tipped off a suspect, for God's sake!"

"I didn't *tell* Vestal anything," Leigh placated, wiping flecks of spit off her forehead. "I just got him to tell me things. And I was good at it!" she protested. "He spilled his guts without so much as a whimper."

Maura took a deep breath, but her voice was still

strained. "You just don't get it, do you? *It's not your job!* You are merely a bystander, do you understand? You leave the investigating to me from now on, or I swear—"

Maura broke off as Cara slipped quietly into the hall. Leigh knew her cousin had been listening to the whole exchange, undoubtedly with some glee, but at least she had the decency to intercede before the real violence started.

"Oh, hello, Maura," Cara said graciously. "You have wonderful timing. We were just about to have some rather excellent homemade spaghetti marinara. Please join us."

Maura looked from Leigh, the picture of innocence, to Cara, the picture of sincerity, and gave up. "Hi, Cara," she answered calmly. "That sounds great. Thanks."

The spaghetti marinara had not been falsely advertised. When it was gone, Cara passed around a bowl of fruit salad. "Well, now," she said in a well-polished hostess's voice, "you ladies have been rather quiet. I was hoping we might have a nice, animated conversation over dessert. Shall we?"

Leigh shot a warning look at Cara, and Maura shot one at Leigh. Both were ignored. "All right, fine," Cara continued. "I'll pick the topic. Today's topic is corpses, specifically those that reappear at a previous place of residence. Oddly enough, I happen to have been party to just such an occurrence. I was told that— for the sake of the baby, of course—I should not trouble myself over the corpse's motives. So naturally I haven't. However, it would appear that *someone*—again, not me—has been possessed by the spirit of Miss Marple and has been doing some investigating herself. Am I right? Would anyone else like to comment?"

Leigh sat with her arms folded. Maura's eyes darted from cousin to cousin.

"All right," Leigh said, resigned. "Yes. I have been doing a little sleuthing. But I shouldn't have, as you clearly overheard earlier. And I'm done now, so there's no point in belaboring the issue. The Avalon police can handle things just fine without either of us getting any more involved."

Maura laughed sarcastically. "A lovely speech, Koslow. I'll believe it after I get a tracking device embedded in your neck."

"No, really," Leigh insisted. "The body has been identified, but there's no real reason to think that anyone is—" She broke off, realizing she was at cross purposes with herself. She wanted to protect Cara from the more unpleasant details, yes. That seemed logical since the doctor had told her to take it easy. But if they really were in any physical danger, Cara had to know the facts for her own protection.

"All right," Leigh sighed. "It's like this, Cara. I was worried that the body wasn't left here as a random prank, so I decided to speed things up a little. You know, help Maura out." Maura started to open her mouth, but Leigh gestured for her to be patient. "I wanted to know if we really should be alarmed. The note did concern me."

Cara perked up instantly. "What note?"

Maura looked at Leigh with surprise. "You didn't tell her about the note?"

"Well, no," Leigh said, feeling distinctly uncomfortable, "not right away."

Cara's eyes blazed. *"What note?!"*

By the time Leigh had completed her confession and Maura had filled in the details she left out, all three women were on their second cup of coffee.

"Well," Cara was insisting, "it seems to me that the next step ought to be taking a good look at Paul Fischer's life. We need to know what might be in this house that someone else could want badly enough to steal a corpse."

"Not just any corpse," Maura pointed out. "This person got hold of Paul Fisher's corpse. Now, that either happened totally by coincidence—he ran into some necrophile and offered to buy it off him—or else we've got to assume he stole it ten years ago with some particular purpose in mind."

"If that's true," Cara reasoned, "this is the first time in that ten years that the house has been regularly occupied. Maybe that's what he was waiting for. Or she."

"But what would be the point?" Leigh wondered out loud. "If there was something in the house this person wanted, why couldn't they have taken it out while no one was here? Why wait for someone to move in first? Unless they want the house vacant for some other reason . . ."

Maura rose and stretched. "You two keep brainstorming all you want. But your main goals should be to keep your security system running and take the extra precautions we discussed. Leave the investigating to the police, OK? Nobody needs to get hurt trying to do our job." She looked purposefully at Leigh as she stressed "our."

"Leigh will behave herself," Cara said with a devious smile. "I'll watch her."

Maura headed for the door. "That was a fabulous dinner, Cara. Thank you again."

"Hey!" Leigh interjected. "I got down the garlic."

"Don't make me laugh, Koslow," Maura snorted, opening the door for herself. "I'll never forget that time you tried to make chili in a hot pot—" She broke off the sentence and turned around. "And by the way . . . how *did* that 'roast in the oven' turn out?"

Cara looked questioningly at Leigh, who shrugged and held up her hands. "You can't believe everything you hear, you know."

Chapter 7

At first the sounds echoing into Leigh's bedroom brought on pleasant dreams of seagulls and sand. But as the screeching caws intensified, reality took over. Puzzled, she woke reluctantly. No one was watching a Hitchcock movie. Why the racket? She swung her feet onto the plush carpet and crossed over to one of the two windows that faced the Ohio.

In the dawn light she could see smoke from Neville Island curling above the trees while the river flowed peacefully below. Considerably less peaceful was the collection of birds clustered around the patio. At least a dozen black crows squawked and fought as they picked at some unidentifiable mess on the concrete. She turned and shoved her feet into a pair of slippers. It wouldn't be the first time she had picked up scattered garbage.

She moved into the hall, and as she passed her cousin's bedroom door, it opened. A groggy-looking Cara slipped out. Even half awake and seven months pregnant, she managed to look elegant in a pale silk gown. "Are those crows?" she asked, stifling a yawn.

"Yeah," Leigh answered with equal enthusiasm. "In the garbage. You go back to bed, I'll take care of it."

Leigh started down the stairs, and Cara, ignoring the offer, followed. When they reached the back door, Leigh banged on it with her hand to scatter the crows while Cara turned off the security system. The birds grudgingly flew away from the patio, only to resume squawking from the nearby trees.

Leigh unbolted the back door and swung it open. She was right, the crows were picking at garbage. She just wasn't sure whose garbage it was.

"Cara," Leigh asked with a yawn as her cousin joined her outside, "when did you throw out fish?"

Cara stepped over to investigate the assortment of fish and fish portions scattered over her patio. "I didn't," she said matter-of-factly. "I hate fish, especially lately."

Leigh raised her eyebrows. Cats were prone to dragging in their kills, but even if Mao Tse was allowed outside, which she wasn't, the odds of her catching a half dozen fish in the Ohio River were not worth contemplating. Furthermore, no other pet she knew made fishing a regular pastime. Perhaps a dog dragged someone else's garbage over?

Cara stooped and poked a nearly whole fish with her toe. Her eyes narrowed. "Leigh," she said intently, "look at this."

Leigh walked to her side and squatted down for a closer look. The fish was missing one eye and a good bit of brain tissue, but its scaly side was intact, marked with red paint. She squinted at the red streaks. "It looks like a U," she announced.

Cara grabbed a stick from the grass and picked the edge of another fish to flip it over. "And here," she said, "this one is marked too. It looks like somebody tried to make a six, or a G." Leigh and Cara exchanged a brief glance, then began gathering the fish and turning them paint side up.

There were five fish in all, but thanks to the crows, several were no longer in one piece. Leigh undertook the anatomic reconstructions while Cara puzzled over the red markings. When fish number five had most of its body reoriented, the women stood back.

"We have two T's, a G, a U, and an E," Cara announced. "Lovely. Any ideas?"

"Well," Leigh said intelligently, trying to pretend she was looking at a puzzle book rather than a bunch of mutilated fish, "how about GUTTE? Maybe that means 'gut me' in French?"

Cara laughed. "I'm afraid not. Try again."

"TUTEG?" Leigh hypothesized. "UGTET?"

"Maybe it's two words," Cara said thoughtfully. "Like EAT GUT without the A." She raised her head, and her eyes met Leigh's as a new possibility struck them. Wordlessly, they began searching again. After a few moments Leigh found the majority of a sixth fish under a shrub.

"Well," she announced, pushing it next to the others with a stick. "It's not an A, it's an O."

Suddenly her blood ran cold.

GET OUT.

Get out of my house.

Leigh said nothing as she tried to decide whether to share her thoughts. But Cara soon sighed in disgust and dropped into one of the patio chairs. "You know," she said in a tired voice, "this is really getting on my nerves."

Leigh looked at her questioningly.

"Oh, please!" Cara said with a wave of her hand. "Don't pretend you don't know what it means! You're the word-game master, not me."

Oddly, Leigh couldn't think of anything to say. How exactly should one respond to a threat spelled out in fish?

"Of all the idiotic wastes of time," Cara continued, glancing at the newly risen sun. "I could have slept in this morning."

Leigh's eyes widened. "You don't sound as though you're taking this too seriously."

Cara laughed and spread out her hands. "You call this serious? Painting letters on fish? I call it . . . well . . ." She faltered, searching for the right word. "I call it just plain stupid!" She put her hands by her sides for leverage and rose from the chair. "I'm going back to bed."

Leigh blinked. She wondered for a moment if she was the only sane person she knew. "Cara," she said maternally, "you can't tell me you don't find two threats in three days a little disturbing."

Cara stopped momentarily in her progress toward the back door. "Disturbing, yes. Convincing, no. Although I must admit the tactics are original."

Leigh dropped her shoulders in disbelief. Was she the only person in the world who knew when to be scared? "Cara, you can't just forget that, for whatever reason, someone wants you out of this house."

Cara stopped with a sigh. She really did look tired. "So. Someone wants me out of this house," she began calmly. "Well, tough. I happen to want me in this house. I've spent a lot of time dreaming about it, not to mention a lot of money and energy buying it, decorating it, and furnishing it. If some wacko thinks it's worth his time to steal corpses and paint fish to get me out, fine. I'll play. I'm going to find out who this person is and what it is he wants. Then I'm going to keep it."

Speech finished, Cara shuffled to the back door and went inside. Leigh watched her retreating form. She knew from a lifetime of experience that Cara was not an easy person to intimidate. Bravado was all well and good, but somebody had to be reasonable.

She collected the fish in a empty shoe box and set the mess down by the back door. Mao Tse made a break for it as soon as the door opened, but Leigh swept her up with a well-practiced gesture and carried her back inside. "Sorry, girl. Chain of evidence and all that."

The cat was not appeased. "OK, OK. How about some of the gourmet stuff as a compromise? Ocean perch in aspic, perhaps? I'm sure I brought some from the apartment. . . ." After a half hour of rattling around Cara's kitchen feeding the cat, the finches, and her caffeine habit, Leigh had developed a plan. As soon as a more respectable hour of the morning approached, she would take the fish down to the police station. Maura could lift fingerprints off the scales—or whatever. Then she would find out what the heck Mrs. Rhodis had been babbling to Cara about.

An answer to an old mystery? Maybe. Leigh was skeptical. Crimes of passion were plentiful in the movies, but reality was usually more mundane. Avarice was the root of all evil. They had evil. The money must not be far behind.

Chapter 8

Leigh was dressed and ready to head for the police station when the phone rang. She eyed it suspiciously. It had brought her only bad news so far. She crossed to the kitchen counter and picked it up.

"Hello?"

"Hello!" rang a cheerful tenor voice, muted somewhat by static. "Leigh, is that you?"

Leigh allowed herself a smile. It was Cara's husband, and it had been awhile since she'd heard his voice. "Yeah, it's me. How are you, Gil? And where are you now, Istanbul?"

Her cousin-in-law laughed merrily. "Don't start with that. You know I'm still in Tokyo. But not for much longer. I'm counting the days!"

Leigh felt the slight knotting in her stomach that she always felt when reminded of Gil's happiness with Cara. Not that she was jealous. How could she be when she had had the first shot? Leigh had met Gil through work, and was astonished when he asked her out. Gil was the type of man one normally sees only with the aid of photography. His admirable physique, square jawline, and impeccable taste in clothes were not to be sniffed at. Furthermore, he had the kind of twinkling eyes and carefree grin that most estrogen-dominant individuals would kill for. Unfortunately, he hadn't really understood Leigh's sense of humor. So what would have been the point? Instead of acting interested, she had referred him to Cara for a specialized design project. The rest was history.

"So how's my little family doing?" he continued happily. Leigh could picture him lounging on a bamboo mat in an Armani suit, his hazel eyes beaming with pride. Her stomach twitched again, and guilt surged.

"Cara's fine. And she says the baby is kicking up a storm."

"That's great!" he enthused. "Is she up yet?"

Leigh's guilt was suddenly replaced by recall of her cousin's predicament. Had Cara told Gil about the body? Leigh's brow furrowed in thought. She probably wouldn't have—she wouldn't want him to worry. But he certainly deserved to know. Besides, she had promised to report anything that might get Cara upset. She cleared her throat. "Listen, Gil, do you have a minute?"

Leigh shrieked as long fingernails scratched her hands. Cara, materializing from nowhere, snatched the receiver with a fierce look of disapproval. She covered the mouthpiece with her palm. "Don't you *dare* tell him anything!" she whispered. "One word and he'll be on the next flight back to Pittsburgh, and all his hard work will be for nothing! He's got to finish up this project now, so that after the baby's born he can stay put for a while. I'm not going to let this mess spoil all our plans!"

Sufficiently chastened, Leigh retreated. Cara smoothed her hair and spoke cheerfully to her husband. "Hi, honey. Sorry about that. Leigh wanted to talk to you some more, but I couldn't wait any longer, so I wrestled the phone away from her." She paused. "Oh, I'm wonderful, and so is little Pippi or Bobo. Except that we both miss you."

Having no desire to hang around and eavesdrop, Leigh decided it was time to visit the Avalon Police Department. She arrived five minutes later, shoe box in hand. Finding a place to drop it on Maura's cluttered desk was difficult, but she managed. It landed with flare—just enough to displace several sheets of paper and send a stray pen rolling to the floor.

Maura, who had been too buried in paperwork to notice her approach, glared. "Koslow," she acknowledged, her voice not without a hint of chagrin. "Nice entrance." She examined the box as Leigh stooped for the pen. "You bought me air soles? How sweet."

"Um," Leigh hedged, glad that Maura was being sarcastic, "not exactly. Are you a seafood person?"

"Turf and surf in cardboard? I'll pass."

Leigh sighed and sat down. "It's fish. They were scattered over Cara's patio this morning."

Maura's eyes flickered. She sat up and opened the box lid. Then, with a grimace and a wrinkle of her nose, she dropped it closed.

Leigh couldn't help laughing. "I can't believe that got more reaction out of you than a ten-year-old corpse."

"I've never liked fish," Maura said simply, settling back in her chair. "So what's the deal? I don't get it."

Leigh took a breath. "The deal is, those fish have letters painted on their sides. And the letters spell 'GET OUT.'"

Maura's eyebrows rose. "You're sure?"

Leigh nodded.

Maura rose from behind her desk and leaned over the cubicle wall. "Hey, Chief! Got a minute? Fish question." She sat back down and turned to Leigh. "Lucky for you, we have an award-winning angler on staff."

Donald Mellman's bulky form soon loomed over

them both. As Leigh explained the morning's events, his pudgy fingers stirred the collection of fish pieces.

"Bluegill," he said with pride. "And this one's a crappie."

Leigh wondered what possible difference it made what kind of fish they were. She started to ask, but Maura interrupted.

"Are these the kind of fish you could buy in a grocery store?"

"Not hardly," Mellman answered, poking his finger into one of the fish's mouths to show the hook scar. "These fellas are a pretty common catch around here. If you just went out and starting fishing, this is what you'd end up with. Pan fish. Most people throw 'em back."

If they'd been store-bought, Leigh thought, a clerk might have remembered the purchase. *Rats.*

"Koslow," Maura began with a heavy tone, "one threat could be a fluke. Two threats, and you need to take it personally. This could be a dangerous situation."

"You don't have to convince me," Leigh said sincerely, "but Cara refuses to leave. She thinks the whole fish thing is just an amateurish stunt to keep us from finding something that's hidden in the house."

The chief shook his head. "She's taking for granted that the perp's got all his marbles. What if he doesn't?" His voice assumed a paternal tone. "The safest thing would be for you and your cousin to find another place to stay—at least until this blows over."

Leigh sighed. "I'm all for that. I'll keep working on her."

With a trademark nod Mellman retreated to his office.

Maura pulled a large Ziploc bag out of a cabinet and dumped in the contents of the cardboard box.

"You know, Koslow," she said in her police voice, "you should have just called us over. It would have been better if we could have seen the way everything was laid out."

Leigh sighed. "I told you, the fish weren't laid out. I suppose they were once, but our slightly dense lunatic didn't count on a bunch of crows picking them to smithereens before we woke up."

Maura offered the empty box, but Leigh declined it with a grimace.

"So what's next?" Leigh asked. "Is Vestal being charged with anything?"

Maura's eyes narrowed slightly as she relived her annoyance with Leigh. "Vestal's legal problems are not your concern. Your safety is. We don't know what this perp is capable of. Perhaps you and Cara could move in with your parents for a week or so?"

A chill ran down Leigh's spine. Back home? Horrors. And the lease on her old apartment had just expired. How had she gotten herself into this situation? *Hi, Mom! I'm unemployed again! Just as you predicted. What's for dinner?*

She shivered.

Maura looked at her, eyebrows raised. Leigh decided that a truthful explanation would be a bad idea. Her friend had barely had time to mourn her father's fatal heart attack before her mother had started showing signs of dementia. After Mary wandered out of her house and into a neighbor's house a block away, interrupting a friend's husband during a bath and demanding to know where Chief Polanski was, Maura made a decision. She left her cozy apartment in town and moved back into the family duplex with her mother and two elderly aunts—waylaying her plans to make detective by taking the first available spot on the

Avalon squad. Leigh could hardly expect sympathy for her own petty phobias.

"I don't think our moving out is necessary," she said carefully. "The house has a top-notch security system." Maura opened her mouth to speak, but Leigh went on. "And besides, our best chance of getting out from under this threat is to figure out who's delivering it, and why. We have a much better chance of doing that in the house than out of it. If this guy is as big a moron as we think, he's going to get himself caught pretty soon."

"What makes you so sure it's a he?"

"I told you already," Leigh said impatiently. "I saw a man on the bluff the night the body appeared."

Maura's expression turned serious. "What if I told you it was me you saw that night?"

Leigh's eyes widened. Nonsense. Why wouldn't Maura have said something? "The figure was a man," she insisted. "It had broad shoulders, and—"

"Yes?"

Well, perhaps it could have been Maura, after all. But why?

Leigh's thoughts were cut short by a sly smile from the policewoman. "That's OK, Koslow, don't torture yourself. It wasn't me. But you've just proven that it could have been a woman."

Leigh's face reddened.

"You also said he or she was a moron," Maura continued. "What makes you think that?"

Leigh sniffed. "What intelligent person that you know writes messages on dead fish and dresses corpses up in stupid-looking hats?"

"A criminally insane one," Maura said heavily, "and there may be a method to his madness. Using the fish, for instance."

Leigh looked at her blankly.

"Fish? Paul Fischer?" Maura said slowly. "Get it?"

Leigh hadn't. "Well, sure," she said quickly. "That much is obvious. But it doesn't prove this guy is really dangerous."

"Of course not," Maura said, "it doesn't prove anything. That's my point. We don't know what this person is capable of."

Leigh exhaled in defeat. "I understand what you're saying. But I'm telling you, Cara won't leave. And with the security system going and the police driving by now and then, I'm sure we'll be fine." She got up to leave. "But we have some detective work to do—"

The glare aimed at Leigh could have kindled a fire.

"I mean," she backtracked, "we have some genealogical research to do. If Cara and I make a mission of finding out all about Paul Fischer's life and the history of the house, we're bound to stumble across something suspicious."

Maura's eyes appraised Leigh carefully. "All right, Koslow. But let me tell you this. My official advice is for you both to get the hell out of that house. Sadly, I have no legal right to make you. That said, as far as doing *library-type* research on Paul Fischer and the house, that's fine. You and Cara working together can make faster progress than the overworked Avalon PD. But if you find anything"—she pointed a finger—"and I mean anything, you tell me about it right away. Understand?"

Leigh raised her hand in a salute. *"Capiche!"* she said with a smile, then rose to leave. Her eyes rested momentarily on Maura's gun holster. "Hey, Maura, do you think—"

"Go, Koslow!"

Leigh decided to comply. Fun was fun, but she had work to do.

Chapter 9

Leigh offered Cara her arm for balance as the two walked up the crumbling concrete steps of the Rhodis home. There were only six, but when Cara reached the top she stopped to massage her bulging abdomen.

"What's wrong?"

"Oh, nothing," Cara replied unconvincingly. "It's just another Braxton Hicks."

Leigh felt a flicker of panic in the back of her mind. She was supposed to be a companion, not a midwife. And where the hell was Gil when you needed him, anyway?

Cara looked at Leigh's expression and laughed. "Oh, knock it off! I'm fine. You're getting as bad as your mother!"

Leigh scowled. That was hitting below the belt.

Cara laughed again and put her hand on Leigh's arm, a form of apology. "Really. It's no big deal. As long as I don't have more than four an hour, there's nothing to worry about. I'm just supposed to be taking it easy, which I am. I'm the quintessential lady of leisure, in case you hadn't noticed."

Leigh was only partially reassured. "Are you sure you're up to this?" she persisted. "You could just tell me all this stuff yourself, like I asked."

Cara shook her head. "I think you should hear this firsthand. Besides, what's so stressful about having a chat with my next-door neighbor in the middle of a Friday morning?"

Giving up, Leigh rang the yellowed plastic doorbell. Adith Rhodis appeared in a matter of seconds. She opened the flimsy screen that separated them and flashed a wide smile. "Well, hello, Cara dear! Come in, come in! And you must be her cousin Leigh. So nice to see you again!" The older woman grasped Leigh's hand and held it tightly. "I can't believe how you've grown up into such a lovely young woman. Last time I saw you, you were just a little thing holding cotton balls for your daddy!"

Leigh smiled painfully. That was at least one poodle ago. "It has been a long time, hasn't it?"

Mrs. Rhodis turned back to Cara. "So, how are you, dear? I can't believe you walked up those rickety old stairs to get here. It's a wonder you didn't fall to your death. I've been on Bud for years to get them steps fixed, and he always says the same darn thing: 'I'll do it in the spring, Adie!' " She leaned toward Leigh conspiratorially. "Old buzzard ain't got much spring left in him!"

Leigh grinned back at the older woman. Adith Rhodis appeared to be somewhere in her seventies. She had wavy white-gray hair that stood up in all directions, an image fitting well with her flowered polyester house dress and knee-high stockings. Her eyes, on the other hand, were those of a disobedient thirteen-year-old with a wild imagination.

An ear-piercing yapping suddenly erupted from within the house. "Oh, that Pansy!" Mrs. Rhodis continued with a smile. "She can't hear the doorbell anymore, but *somehow she knows*!" She tapped her forehead with a spindly finger. "Some animals know a whole lot more than we do, you know."

Cara nodded pleasantly, and Leigh, who had heard

it all before, tried to. Mrs. Rhodis led them through a dark, slightly musty-smelling but well-furnished living room into the back kitchen. They could see Mr. Rhodis sitting peacefully in a lawn chair on the attached screened porch, while a frantic poodle wildly clawed the screen door that led inside.

When Mrs. Rhodis opened the door, the obese little dog scampered in and sniffed the visitors' feet. Pansy was what the staff at the Koslow Animal Clinic affectionately referred to as a "coffee table dog." Her chunky, rectangular body was smoothed with ample pads of fat, each corner precariously suspended by a spindly limb. "Easy, Pansy, don't scare them to death!" Mrs. Rhodis laughed. She turned to Leigh. "She's a bit overweight, you know. Your daddy's always on me about that. But I only give her this much food a day!" she said defensively, holding her fingers to outline a volume of food that wouldn't keep a cat alive. "You know what it is," she said, leaning close to Leigh's ear and pointing a thumb toward the porch. "It's Bud. He's always giving her them Pupperonies."

Cara's face was beginning to break out in a sweat at the stagnant heat of the kitchen. Mrs. Rhodis noticed and quickly clamped her hand to her mouth. "Where are my manners! You poor thing. Let's go outside on the porch and sit. It's nice out there. I'll bring you girls some lemonade."

She opened the screen door again and pushed Cara gently toward it. "Go on, go on," she insisted, "have a seat on the rocker. I'll be right back. Why, I remember when I was pregnant with Jimmy . . ." Mrs. Rhodis's voice trailed off as she wandered back into the kitchen.

Leigh and Cara settled themselves on a suspended love seat and started up a gentle rock. It was pleasant on the breezy porch. They could see snatches of the

Ohio through the trees, but a tall hedge lent privacy to Cara's small backyard. Mr. Rhodis sat quietly smoking a wooden pipe, whose bowl was carved into a bust of Sir Walter Raleigh. Mr. Rhodis was long and lanky, with weathered skin and a thick crop of snow white hair. He nodded at them pleasantly but didn't say a word. Cara leaned down to scratch Pansy's broad back, and the little dog panted and squirmed in contentment.

In a few moments Mrs. Rhodis returned with three tall tumblers of lemonade. Cara and Leigh took them thankfully. "Please sit down, Mrs. Rhodis," Cara insisted. "We didn't mean to make more work for you. It's just that, with what's been happening lately, Leigh and I are trying to find out everything we can about Paul Fischer and my house, and I knew you could help."

"Well, you've come to the right place!" Mrs. Rhodis began merrily, but then her face turned grave. "I can't believe what you said about his body. That's the most scandalous thing. . . . I don't believe it really *was* his body. How could anyone know for sure, anyway? When it's that old—" She broke off in a grimace of disgust that was purely theatrical. She leaned toward Leigh, eyes sparkling. "What exactly *did* it look like, anyway?"

Cara grinned expectantly. Leigh searched her mind for a way to avoid the question, then turned from Mrs. Rhodis and swallowed hard. "If you don't mind, Mrs. Rhodis," she said softly, looking down into her lap, "I really don't think I can talk about it."

Cara rolled her eyes. Mrs. Rhodis, however, was suitably taken aback. "Oh, my! I'm sorry, my dear. Me and my big mouth! I didn't mean to make you uncomfortable." She leaned forward to pat Leigh's knee. "We won't talk about it *anymore*." She sat back in her chair and adjusted her polyester skirt, clearly disappointed.

Leigh felt ever so slightly guilty. "That's all right, Mrs. Rhodis," she said, quickly recovering, "we did come here to talk, after all. But what Cara and I wanted to know more about was Paul Fischer's life. You know, what he was like, what kinds of things he kept in his house. We're trying to figure out who might want something that he left behind."

Mrs. Rhodis's eyes gleamed. Mr. Rhodis continued to puff on his pipe. Thankfully, the breeze carried the smoke well away from the love seat. "I can tell you anything you want to know," Mrs. Rhodis said proudly, taking a swig of her glass of lemonade and settling back in her chair. "As they say on TV, shoot."

Leigh and Cara looked at each other. Cara gave Leigh a nod. "Well, for starters, how long have you lived next door to him?"

"How long? Oh, let's see . . ." Several moments elapsed while she proceeded to describe in excruciating detail the various residences of her childhood. Leigh politely bit her lip while waiting anxiously for information from the relevant decade. Eventually it came. "Bud and I moved in here in 1940, right after we got married," Mrs. Rhodis continued. "His parents lived here too for a while. Anita was still married to Harlan back then, and she had little Robbie."

Leigh restrained herself from asking who the hell Anita, Harlan, and Robbie were. "And how long did you say Paul Fischer had lived next door?" she interrupted. Cara flashed her a look of annoyance.

So, I'm not a saint. OK?

Mrs. Rhodis didn't seem to mind the redirection. "Oh, Paul moved in with his father after Norman— that's his father—married Anita. Paul was already a grown man, but he wasn't very mature for his age. I always thought it was a little odd that a man should expect his new wife to house his grown son, but Anita, she put up with a lot. Why, I remember one time when that knife salesman's car broke down out on the boulevard . . ."

Leigh was starting to sweat. She buried her face in her lemonade cup to suppress a scream.

"Excuse me, Mrs. Rhodis," Cara said politely. "Let me backtrack a moment for Leigh's sake." She gave her cousin a sly glance. "This house was built by the Stewart family, of which Anita was the last remaining member by the 1930s. She lived here first with her husband Harlan and her son Robbie. In the forties, after her husband died, she married Norman Fischer. Paul was Norman's son by a previous marriage."

Leigh nodded appreciatively and turned to Mrs. Rhodis. "So if you and Paul Fischer were neighbors that long, you must have known him pretty well."

Mr. Rhodis scoffed. Leigh and Cara quickly turned to look at him, but he sat, impassive as ever, puffing away.

Mrs. Rhodis, ignoring the interruption, answered. "I suppose I knew him as well as anyone, but that wasn't very well. He spent all his time at work or inside; I only talked to him when he was hanging out laundry or making repairs on the house. He never seemed to have much to say. I always figured he was kind of simple until he showed me how he could write."

Leigh sat up expectantly. "Paul Fischer was a writer?"

Mrs. Rhodis smiled. "I guess you could say that. I had cause to . . . well . . . look in his windows a time or two, and the house looked clean as you please, but there were papers and books stacked everywhere. Nobody can be too simple if they spend their whole life reading and writing, that's what I say." She turned up her nose with authority.

"Did you ever read anything he wrote?" Leigh asked.

Mrs. Rhodis cracked a wide grin and glanced at her husband. "Just once, a few years before he died. He showed me a poem he wrote about Bud. 'Man on the porch, smoke's a blowing . . .'" She cackled. "You remember that, don't you, Bud?"

Mr. Rhodis rolled his eyes.

"Bud wasn't too impressed," she continued, "but I thought it was good. Paul said he wrote other things, but I don't know what." Mrs. Rhodis suddenly turned to Leigh, a distinct gleam in her eye. "Well, I do know one other thing he wrote. He wrote a will."

Leigh leaned forward. "But no will was found, right?"

Mrs. Rhodis looked smug. "Just because nobody ever found it doesn't mean he never wrote it."

Leigh's heartbeat quickened. "What makes you think he wrote a will?"

"He told me so!" Mrs. Rhodis answered proudly. "About a year or so before he died, he said he'd made up a will, but he hadn't paid any lawyers or anything. He just wanted me to sign it and maybe keep a copy of it at my house."

"You didn't think that was strange?" Leigh asked.

Mrs. Rhodis scoffed slightly. "Honey, everything about Paul Fischer was strange. But no, I wasn't surprised about him not spending an arm and a leg on lawyers just to write a will. He was only around sixty, anyway. Bud and I are half dead already, and we still haven't gotten around to making one up!"

"So what happened to Paul Fischer's will?" Leigh asked hopefully.

Mrs. Rhodis sighed. "I haven't a clue. He never brought it up again."

Leigh's hopes faded. "You mean, he asked you about signing it and keeping a copy but never went through with it?" she asked.

"That's about the size of it," Mrs. Rhodis answered. "That sort of thing wasn't unusual either. He also promised to build flower boxes for the bedroom windows."

Mr. Rhodis coughed. Mrs. Rhodis shot him a look but didn't say anything.

"What did bother me," she continued, "was not finding his writings later. After he died, I offered to help out—you know, box his things up for the next of kin. But there was nothing there. Not a scribble. I couldn't even find the poetry notebook he'd showed me before."

Cara jumped in with sudden energy. "What I was trying to tell you the other day, Leigh, is that Paul Fischer may have hidden some of his writings in the house. He told Mrs. Rhodis that he wanted her to keep a copy of the will because it contained important information that people needed to know after he died."

Cara's eyes shone with the same fiendish excitement they had when she was making mud pies as a six-year-old.

"Important information," Leigh repeated. "And do you have any idea what that might be?" she asked Mrs. Rhodis.

The older woman smiled as if she had been waiting for years to answer that question. She took a long swig of lemonade for dramatic effect, then spoke. "I always thought that boy knew a whole lot more than he was saying about the night Anita and Norman died. In all those years, I suspected. But when he told me about the will, I thought he was speaking especially to me, you know, like in code. 'I'm going to let you know what really happened, but not till I'm dead and buried.' That's what he was really saying. I knew it. Pansy was with me then, and she knew it too. I could tell."

As Mrs. Rhodis's speech took a sharp turn into the paranormal, Leigh's excitement dragged down to skepticism.

Cara was not so affected. "You had Pansy then? But that must have been eleven years ago!" she said enthusiastically, leaning over to pat the furry off-white lump.

Mrs. Rhodis beamed. "Yes! She was just a pup. But she had the gift even then. Why, I remember one time—"

"Please, Mrs. Rhodis," Leigh broke in as politely as possible, "what did you"—she cleared her throat a little—"and Pansy think Paul Fischer wanted everyone to know?"

Mrs. Rhodis paused. "Why, what really happened in 1949, of course!" she answered in surprise. She looked from Cara to Leigh and leaned forward. "Cara *did* tell you about the murders, didn't she?"

Chapter 10

Leigh turned a hard look on her cousin. "Murders?"

Cara smiled pleasantly. "Now, Mrs. Rhodis," she said conversationally, "you know that the deaths weren't officially ruled as murders. The police determined that Anita's death was an accident, and there wasn't any clear evidence that Norman hadn't committed suicide. Right?"

Mrs. Rhodis pursed her lips and sat back. "There's what the police say—and then there's what I know."

For no apparent reason Pansy let out a sharp, annoying bark. Mrs. Rhodis's face lit up. "Yes, sweetie pie. You know it too, don't you?"

"Would anyone care to fill me in on exactly who died when and how and whether it happened in the bedroom I'm sleeping in?" Leigh asked with poorly concealed annoyance.

"Oh, dear," Mrs. Rhodis said, clamping her hand over her mouth again. "Cara didn't tell me you were superstitious. Perhaps we shouldn't discuss this." The older woman was trying hard to look contrite, but Leigh caught the mischievous gleam in her eyes.

"I'm sure Leigh isn't worried about any ghosts coming back to haunt her," Cara said without conviction. "But not everyone has the stomach for crime that you and I have, Mrs. Rhodis."

Their hostess glowed at the compliment.

Leigh tried to relax. "Please, Mrs. Rhodis," she asked politely. "Tell us what happened. I'm sure no one can recall the details as well as you can."

The flattery worked.

"It happened the night of August 12, 1949," Mrs. Rhodis said precisely, adjusting her ample bottom in the vinyl-seated chair. Bud and I had just got Jimmy to bed when the ruckus started. Yelling and fussing and doors slamming, then the ambulance and the police. I got up and went over, of course. I knew it had to be something with Anita."

Leigh wondered if the older woman had been tipped off by the poodle of the decade, but she kept her mouth shut.

"Well," Mrs. Rhodis continued, "turns out Anita had taken a bad fall down the front staircase. People fall down stairs all the time, but Anita never was the lucky type. Only had the one boy with the good husband, then latched on to that thug Norman without a thought. I told her a hundred times, I said: 'Anita, you don't need another man around just yet. Take some time!' But she never did listen to me. And I was one of her best friends—"

Leigh searched for the least offensive place to break into the rambling. "Are you saying that Anita died after falling down the stairs?"

"She landed smack on her head and broke her neck, so they said," Mrs. Rhodis went on unperturbed. "She was dead when I got there."

Leigh imagined Cara's beautiful front staircase with its carved oak railing. She wondered if she would ever walk up it again without thinking of a broken body lying at its base.

"The boy," Mrs. Rhodis said sadly, shaking her head, "he was in a state. Almost hysterical, I'd say."

"You mean Anita's son?" Cara prompted.

"Robbie, yes," Mrs. Rhodis answered. "He was about fourteen then. Nice boy. I always liked him, though he was a little on the quiet side. That night he was blubbering like a baby, talking gibberish. He just sat there on the floor where she'd fallen. Just sat there. The police couldn't get a thing out of him."

Leigh tried to imagine the scene. It wasn't pretty. "Were the police suspicious of foul play?" she asked.

"They weren't then," Mrs. Rhodis answered matter-of-factly, "but I was." She cradled her chin in her hand and focused on a spot on the ceiling. "Norman told them she'd been carrying two laundry baskets down the stairs and lost her footing." She scoffed. "There were clothes all over the place, so the police weren't arguing about it. They didn't see what I saw, but they were just men; one has to make allowances, you know."

The younger women's eyes flickered automatically to Mr. Rhodis to register his reaction. His head was resting at an odd angle on the chair back, and his eyes were closed.

Mrs. Rhodis took a long swig of lemonade. Finally she patted her lips dry with a handkerchief and resumed her story. "I didn't believe Anita was going down the stairs with those clothes. I looked at them—they were clean. A few were still half folded. Now, what woman you know goes upstairs, loads up two baskets with clean laundry, then brings them down? She might have been taking them up, but how could she fall up the stairs? She was in the family way then, but she wasn't all that big, and she was never the klutzy type. And why would Norman lie about which way she was going? Didn't make sense." Adith Rhodis shook her head with authority. "Just didn't make sense."

Leigh looked at Cara, who appeared deep in

thought. She wondered how much of this story her cousin had heard before. "What do you think happened?" Leigh asked their hostess.

"Well," Mrs. Rhodis answered proudly, "I think she was pushed. Maybe an accident," she conceded, palms held out defensively, "and maybe not." She leaned closer to her audience and spoke in a whisper. "Maybe it was murder."

Leigh wondered if Mrs. Rhodis had ever been an aspiring actress.

"I never believed Norman's version of what happened," the older woman continued in a normal tone, leaning back in her chair. "I'll tell you what I think. I think he threw those clothes around after the fact, that's what I think." With another dramatic pause she blew her nose into her handkerchief.

Leigh wasn't sure she liked admitting it to herself, but what Mrs. Rhodis said did make an eerie kind of sense. She had no trouble imaging that an 1949 police squad might not take too seriously a young neighbor woman's rantings about clean laundry.

"So there wasn't ever an investigation?" Leigh asked.

Cara broke in with a reply. "Well, there was," she said cryptically. "You need to hear the rest of the story. After Anita's body had been taken away and the police had gone, the men got into a fight."

"The men?" Leigh asked.

"I didn't know what was going on," Mrs. Rhodis said, jumping back in with enthusiasm. "I just knew it was loud. I could hear Norman yelling and Robbie screaming, and then the noise just stopped. I finally went to bed, but I didn't sleep too well. Bud was out like a light, as you might imagine."

Leigh and Cara glanced at Bud. He was snoring.

"About two or so the next morning," Mrs. Rhodis continued, "is when I heard the gunshot."

Their attention quickly returned to Mrs. Rhodis. Her eyes flickered down just long enough to take stock of her audience, then went back to the ceiling. "I woke up Bud," she began, "but of course he hadn't heard squat. And afterward it was real quiet. I could see lights going on, and once I thought I heard Paul's voice, but that was it. After a while I decided enough was enough. I called the police back out again."

"It was Norman," Cara broke in eagerly. "The police found him lying in bed with a bullet through his head."

"Suicide, they said," Mrs. Rhodis said quickly, her voice carrying a trace of annoyance at having been scooped. "His hand was still on the gun."

"What did Paul say happened?" Leigh asked.

"He said he was asleep," Mrs. Rhodis answered, not sounding convinced. "He said he didn't know anything."

"What about Robbie?" Leigh probed further.

Mrs. Rhodis's eyes moved to her lap. She took a deep breath and smoothed her skirt again. "Robbie was already gone when the police got there," she said sadly. "And nobody's seen or heard from him since."

Leigh swallowed. "You mean, he just took off? And no one knows what happened to him even now?"

Mrs. Rhodis shook her head solemnly. A morbid silence descended on the porch, broken only by an occasional pant from Pansy. Leigh noticed that the wind had changed, with the fumes from Neville Island suddenly hanging heavier in the air.

It was Cara who broke the silence. "I don't remember asking you before, Mrs. Rhodis," she inquired softly. "Was it Robbie you heard talking to Paul after the gunshot?"

Mrs. Rhodis shook her head. "I don't remember hearing another voice. But you can't hear all that easily from here unless somebody's yelling. I asked Paul about it more than once, but nobody could ever get a straight answer out of him. He just said he was sleeping when it happened, and that after he found his father he couldn't do anything but sit there on the bed. That's where the police found him, anyway."

"Did you believe him?" Cara asked.

Mrs. Rhodis stroked her Adam's apple with a few spindly fingers. "I can't say I did," she answered finally. "I had no reason to think he was lying—he just never struck me as the honest type. His father was a soulless lout, and apples don't fall far from the tree, I always say." She took a deep breath and sighed. "Norman lied about how Anita died. Maybe he pushed her accidentally, then shot himself from guilt. But I can't see that happening. He was a cold bastard—and it wouldn't have been the first time he'd hurt Anita." Mrs. Rhodis's face turned hard. "I saw the bruises. Nobody said much about that sort of thing back then, but I knew. And it got worse once she was expecting, if you can believe that." She paused. "It wouldn't surprise me if he killed her and Robbie shot him. Robbie was a good boy; he loved his mama."

Adith Rhodis stopped speaking for a moment and looked off into the distance. "None of us know what we're really capable of if we get pushed far enough," she said in a dreamy monotone.

Leigh waited for Mrs. Rhodis to say more, but Cara nudged her cousin in the ribs with an elbow. "Excuse me," she said politely, "but I'm afraid Leigh and I will have to go now. Junior here"—she patted her belly—"is telling me it's time to eat again."

"Oh, my," Mrs. Rhodis said dramatically, breaking

from her trance. "Can I get you something, honey?" She quickly rose from her seat.

"Oh, no," Cara said with a smile. "We've taken up too much of your time already. It's been fascinating hearing the story again—thank you."

Mrs. Rhodis chuckled with her cackly laugh. "Now, Cara dear, you know I'd give an arm and leg for a visit by two nice young ladies, especially some with fresh ears for me and my stories!" She tossed her head in the direction of her husband's sleeping form, and leaned toward Cara conspiratorially. "God knows that one's heard 'em enough!"

When Cara put her hand on the arm of the love seat rocker and pushed herself to her feet, an ear-piercing shriek erupted from the floor. The poodle ran circles around her owner's legs, creating noises shrill enough to break glass.

Cara went white with horror. "Oh, Pansy! Did I step on you? I'm so sorry!" She turned apologetically to Mrs. Rhodis. "I'm such an ox these days. I can't see my own feet, much less anyone else's!"

Mr. Rhodis, whose capacity for deep sleep evidently had limits, rejoined the conscious and leaned over to scoop Pansy out of orbit. Once the dog was settled in his lap, the cacophony subsided.

"Don't worry, honey," Mrs. Rhodis said kindly, her arm on Cara's shoulder. "Bud and I step on her all the time, poor thing!"

Leigh tried, but failed, not to be slightly amused. *Psychic, eh?*

Cara offered the poodle a conciliatory scratch behind the ears, and Pansy accepted the gesture somewhat sulkily. Mrs. Rhodis looked at her pet with adoring eyes. "She's a spoiled one, that," she said. "It's a wonder she don't explode with all those table scraps Bud keeps giving her! Why, if she had to live on the piddling amount I feed her, she'd starve to death, poor thing. I keep telling Bud—"

Mrs. Rhodis's voice trailed off as she headed back through the house to lead them out. Cara waved good-bye to Mr. Rhodis and followed.

As Leigh turned to join them, Mr. Rhodis jerked his head and beckoned her closer with a crooked finger. "Pssst!"

Leigh stepped to the side of the old man's chair and leaned down.

"Don't you believe a word she says," he said in a rusty voice, giving Leigh a wink. "She gives this dog two Reese's peanut butter cups every day. Right during *As the World Turns.*"

Chapter 11

Cara lay down on the couch as soon as they returned to the house, and Leigh started worrying. "I'm fine," Cara insisted. "I just need to lie down for a while, that's all. Later we'll search."

"Search?"

"For the will, of course! Or whatever Paul Fischer hid here."

Leigh was silent for a moment. "Aren't you just a teensy-weensy bit afraid to take at face value the word of a woman who thinks her poodle should have its own psychic hotline?"

Cara smiled and shook her head. "Pansy's poor record with the daily number is immaterial. Adith Rhodis remembers every detail of that night like it was yesterday. Trust me."

Trusting people had never been Leigh's long suit. As soon as Cara had eaten and lain back down for a nap, Leigh set out for her old stomping grounds—the University of Pittsburgh main campus.

"Pitt," as it was affectionately called, was in the academic enclave of Oakland, on the opposite side of downtown Pittsburgh. Leigh turned onto Forbes Avenue with a sinking feeling.

What was she thinking? No sane person drove into Oakland in the middle of a weekday. The Cavalier crept along for blocks in bumper-to-bumper traffic, narrowly avoiding the scores of students and white-coated hospital types who jaywalked with impunity. She couldn't help watching the students, backpacks in tow, with a pang of jealousy. Her college days had been good ones. The journalism curriculum had been less than taxing, giving her plenty of time to waste with her two constant companions—Maura the Wonder Cop and Warren Harmon, future President of the United States. They were an odd trio, but they knew how to laugh.

She sighed as she turned—by necessity—into the high-priced museum garage. She and Maura didn't get out too much anymore. And she hadn't seen Warren since—since when? Somehow there was always work to do. She sighed again as she left her car and walked the short distance to the Carnegie Library. At least the grown-up, working Leigh could afford a decent parking spot, she rationalized.

For a while, anyway.

She walked into the library and automatically tilted her head to admire the colorful murals on the arched ceiling. As she climbed to the second floor, her feet sank comfortably into marble steps worn concave by generations of students. She took a right into the microfilm and periodicals room, collected the *Pittsburgh Press* and *Pittsburgh Post* reels for August 1949, and settled in front of a viewer with a smile.

No stranger to the process, she quickly slid in the *Post* reel for the second week of August and turned the crank. The format was cluttered, the writing style antiquated. But in a matter of seconds she found it.

AVALON MAN SHOT DEAD
AFTER WIFE'S FATAL FALL

Woman Breaks Neck; Husband Shot in Bed; Teenage Son Missing

Anita Fischer, 33, died last evening shortly after falling down the staircase of her home at 1133 Ohio River Boulevard in Avalon. Her husband, Norman Fischer, son Robert, and stepson Paul were in the home at the time and were questioned by police. Avalon Police Chief Ronald Reese said that Mrs. Fischer appeared to have lost her footing while attempting to carry two full laundry baskets down the stairs.

Hours later, police were again summoned to the Fischer home after Norman Fischer, 46, was found dead in his bed, a gunshot wound in his temple.

Son Discovers Father's Body

Paul Fischer, 24, stated that he discovered his father's body after being awakened by the sound of a gunshot. He told police that he saw no one else in the home at that time. Anita Fischer's son, Robert, 14, was not present when the police returned after the shooting. His whereabouts are currently unknown.

Wound Possibly Self-Inflicted

Although County Detective Alfred P. Richardson stated that a revolver was found near Norman Fischer's body, he would not speculate as to whether the wound was self-inflicted. District Attorney Ralph Phelps said that no charges relating to the deaths had been filed. Phelps put out a plea urging Robert Fischer to come forward for questioning.

Happy Family

Anita and Norman Fischer, both previously widowed, had been married to each other for three years. The couple and their sons had lived in the Avalon home since the spring of 1946; Chief Reese stated that the Avalon police had had no previous reports of disturbances at the residence.

The article was accompanied by a grainy picture of Anita and Norman standing behind a cake, presum-

ably on their wedding day. She looked young and
happy, a tiny thing with dark hair and eyes. Norman's
light eyes betrayed little emotion, his lips twisted into
a distinctly unnatural smile. Leigh disliked him immediately, though more because of Mrs. Rhodis's accusa-
tions than the picture. Anyone could take a bad
picture. She ought to know.

She flipped the microfilm ahead a few days, but the
story had been poorly followed. A blurb the next day
stated that Robert was still missing; no charges had
been filed. One letter to the editor presumed that a
freaked-out Robert had murdered both his parents,
and that the younger generation's lax standards of dis-
cipline were to blame. Another speculated that the
incident was merely an accident followed by the suicide of a distraught spouse, and that the public should
let the sons grieve in peace. Leigh scanned meticu-
lously through two weeks' worth of news sections, but
found no more. The *Press* had carried a similar story
on the afternoon of the thirteenth, with several short
follow-up articles, but Leigh learned nothing new. Apparently, no charges were ever filed.

She grabbed the reels with the relevant articles and
paid to have them copied. Perhaps Cara's instincts
were worth something. Mrs. Rhodis might be an ec-
centric, but nothing was wrong with her memory.

Cara's front door was blocked by a large package
wrapped in brown paper, and Leigh approached it
carefully. She didn't consider herself paranoid—but in
light of the last two days, caution seemed prudent.
Cara's name and address were clearly visible on top
of the box, along with a smattering of bizarre symbols
and elaborate stamps. On closer inspection Leigh realized—with relief—that the symbols were Japanese
characters. A present from Gil.

So why hadn't Cara answered the door? She wasn't still asleep, was she? Leigh picked up the package, which felt like it housed lead shot, and balanced it on a hip. She opened the door with her key and walked in. Yep. Cara was up. A look at the security box in the foyer told her the system was off, and the buzz of a power tool echoing down the stairs explained the unanswered doorbell.

Aunt Lydie, of course.

She followed the sound to one of the spare bedrooms on the second floor, where Cara stood peering up into a closet. Inside it was the lower half of Lydie Dublin, standing on a stepladder.

Leigh put the package down with a thump. "Should I ask what's going on here?" she yelled from the doorway.

"Leigh!" Cara called enthusiastically. "Did you find out anything?"

"Plenty. But what are you two doing?"

The buzzing noise stopped, and her cousin's answer was interrupted by a voice from above. "There's nothing here, honey!"

Cara swung around to look back in the closet. "Are you sure?" she said, disappointed. "There must something!"

"Sorry, dear," Lydia answered, stepping down. "It's like I suspected. That section only bulges out to cover the vent pipes from the downstairs bathroom. There's nothing up there that shouldn't be."

Cara pouted. Lydie laid down the jigsaw and a flashlight and dusted her hands on her smock. She was the image of Leigh's own mother but with certain significant differences. Her eyes sparkled more than scorned, and her naturally gray hair was—today— cherry red. "Leigh honey, nice to see you! Your mother and I are so glad you're staying over."

"I'm glad too," Leigh said politely. Lydie probably was glad her daughter had company. Frances, on the other hand, was probably just relieved someone would be around to call paramedics if Leigh electrocuted herself with a microwave.

"Mom's been checking out some dead spaces I've found," Cara explained. "No luck so far, but there are plenty of other places we can check."

Lydie looked at her watch. "I'm afraid that's all for today, honey. I've got a class this afternoon, you know."

Cara smiled. "Yes, I know." Ever since Mason Dublin's untimely departure—with another woman—Lydie had worked two and sometimes three jobs at a time to support herself and to pay her daughter's way through school. Now Cara was returning the favor.

Lydie packed up her tools and left them in a corner of the bedroom. "I'll come back tomorrow morning if you want." She gave her daughter a hug. "Are you sure you'll be all right? You know you can always come sleep at the house."

"I'll be fine, Mom. You know how I feel about staying here."

Lydie's mouth twitched, but she smiled and nodded. "I'll let myself out. You take care of yourselves, you hear?"

As soon as her mother had gone, Cara climbed up onto the antique four-poster bed and stretched out on her side. "Are you OK?" Leigh asked.

"As long as I relax, I'm great," Cara answered. "Don't keep me in suspense. What did you find out?"

"Well, nothing you didn't already know," Leigh answered, sitting on the edge of the bed. She handed Cara the copies. "The newspaper accounts from 1949 matched Mrs. Rhodis's story pretty well."

"Of course they did," Cara said smugly. She took

the copies and read them quickly. "Not much follow-up, I guess." She put the papers down and looked at Leigh wistfully. "You know I always thought you should write for a newspaper."

Leigh rolled her eyes. "Don't start with me."

"But you know how well you can write that sort of thing!" Cara insisted.

Leigh shook her head. She liked writing stories, fact or fiction, but the reporter's life was not for her. Crazy hours, incessant phone calls, writing obituaries to pay your dues. She preferred a nice nine-to-five job where all she had to do was make boring products send chills down customers' spines. It occurred to her that she still hadn't told Cara about the layoff, but she was in no mood to get into that now. Instead she diverted her cousin's attention to the box in the hall. "You got a package from Gil."

Cara's eyes lit up like candles, and she sprang to the floor with a bounce. "It's here already?" She gave the parcel a cursory exam, then went to fetch a pair of scissors while Leigh pushed the load down the hall and into the baby's room.

The nursery, which had been evolving into perfection since two hours after Cara saw the plus sign, had little room for a baby. The walls were charming—a bright bluish-lavender tint, with white wainscoting framing a beautifully painted border of a teddy bear picnic. Unfortunately, the walls were barely visible behind the sea of toy shelves and bookcases that covered the snow white carpet. Enough playthings for an army of babies were stashed in every crevice, as were a random assortment of high-tech parental toys like a motorized cradle and complete two-way infant intercom with video. The changing table, Leigh noticed with a sigh, was stashed tidily in the back of the closet.

The toys were an eclectic bunch, reflective of Gil's

itinerary. A Black Forest cuckoo clock held a prominent position over the crib, while remote shelves housed Beefeater dolls and a Peggy Nisbet rendition of Princess Diana. Nearest the front were the Japanese offerings, including a miniature army of samurais, temple wind chimes, and a ornate infant kimono that probably cost as much as Leigh brought home in a month. She shook her head and rolled her eyes. So the guy was handsome, rich, a good husband, *and* nutso about his progeny. He still had no sense of humor.

Cara flew into the room, scissors in hand, and knelt down to cut away the package tape. "I didn't expect it until next week!" she squealed. "I can't wait to tell him it's here." She worked her way through the layers of packaging until a rectangular piece of yellow wood emerged. After setting the shiny lacquered board on its detachable feet, she began to pull out polished white and black stones from a pair of dark lacquered holders. She placed the stones in a geometric design that pleased her, then sat back and cooed in delight. "Oh! Isn't it beautiful?"

Leigh watched skeptically. "It's lovely. What the hell is it?"

Cara laughed. "It's a Go board. Very traditional. Not really for an infant, of course, but Japanese children play simple games with them when they're quite young. It goes beautifully with the house, don't you think?"

The harmony of oriental craftsmanship and Victorian excess was not apparent to Leigh, but she nodded politely. Cara was the artist, after all.

"I don't know where I'll put it," the expectant mother mused. "This room is already full, and it will be so hard to check the closets as it is."

"Check the closets?"

"Of course. Every inch of this house has to be searched. Whatever Paul Fischer left behind, I suspect he hid it well."

Leigh's brow wrinkled. "I know Mrs. Rhodis's story checks out about the deaths, but the bit about Paul Fischer hiding clues in the house is a bit melodramatic, don't you think? Who could possibly care after all this time? I still think the only thing at stake here is money."

Cara sighed. "You would."

"I do. Say Paul Fischer stockpiled a bundle. Maybe somebody ripped off his will to see if they were mentioned, and to destroy it if they weren't. Maybe they only stood to inherit if he died intestate."

Cara shook her head. "But no one did inherit. No heirs were located, remember?"

"So maybe they wanted to keep someone else from getting it. Or maybe we're not talking legal channels. Maybe Paul had something else of value that he wanted to pass on under the table."

"Now who's talking about gold doubloons?" Cara smirked.

Leigh's eyes narrowed. "It always comes down to money. Paul Fischer had something of monetary value, and someone else wants it. For some reason you and I being in this house is an obstacle to that."

Cara's face lit up. "I wonder," she began, "if we're talking about something small—small enough to carry around."

"Why would that matter?"

"The body! Maybe they stole the body because they were hoping he had hid something on his person!"

Leigh scoffed. "A microchip in his dental work? Please!"

"No, no," Cara defended. "Our villain could have been looking for a particular ring or watch, and when they couldn't find it in the house, figured he might have been buried with it!''

Leigh laughed. "O.K., so he pries up the coffin lid looking for a ring. It isn't there, so he takes the whole body. Perhaps for a cavity search? Now, there's a lovely thought! I can see it now—the boring old recluse swallows a bag of diamonds on his death bed, desperate to keep them from falling into the wrong hands. . . .''

Cara sighed and began struggling to her feet. "I don't hear you coming up with a better explanation.''

Leigh gave her cousin a hand. "Give me time. Money is at the bottom of this, one way or the other.'' Thinking about money and power and the people who crave them, she had a sudden flash of inspiration. She snapped her fingers and smiled. "And you know who's going to help me? The Allegheny County Register of Wills!''

"Excuse me?''

"Warren Harmon. He's an old college buddy of mine and Maura's. I helped him get elected, in fact. I don't know what he actually does, but the title sounds relevant. Speaking of Warren, what's for dinner? Do you want me to order something?''

Cara shook her head. "Mom brought over a Mexican casserole. She said it would be ready at five-thirty.''

Leigh smacked her lips. God bless Aunt Lydie.

Warren J. Harmon III's knock sounded on Cara's front door at precisely seven p.m. Leigh checked her watch. If it hadn't said seven, she would have reset it. She opened the door to one of the few men she could count on to come over on a Friday night with two hours' notice.

"Leigh Koslow, Creative Genius!'' He caught her

in a swift embrace. "It's been ages. So glad you called. Take-out cappuccino was exactly what I needed tonight. How have you been?"

She took the paper bag out of his hand and replaced it with a ten-dollar bill. "It's been a hell of a week, actually."

Warren opened his palm and let the bill flutter to the floor. "Please. My pleasure. You know I'd do anything for you."

Leigh smiled. Warren was a politician to the bone. Every word out of his mouth sounded like a part of a state of the union address. It always had, even when they'd been eighteen-year-old freshmen paired off in Tennis 101. He had been on the fast track to the presidency; she had just wanted *not* to be the worst player in the class. When he rescued her by taking that honor himself, she promised to write his campaign literature for free. And a decade later, in his first race for public office, he'd taken her up on it.

"Here." Leigh peeled the plastic lid off the first cup and handed it to him, then took the second cappuccino-in-Styrofoam and led the way into the relatively casual atmosphere of the study. "Make yourself at home. I do."

Warren bent his tall form and sank gracefully into a leather recliner. Leigh watched him curiously. Her tennis pal had been a gawky kid with acne-scarred cheeks and a toothy smile, but this Warren bore little resemblance. It must have been a slow evolution— because she'd missed it entirely. How long had it been since they'd seen one another? "You realize we haven't done lunch since the election?" she asked accusingly. "Big jury commissioner forgets the little people, eh?"

"Don't toy with me," he answered with a smile. "You know I'm the register of wills."

"Just testing you." Leigh grinned, settling in the opposite recliner. "I figure you'll be running for something else before too long."

"Naturally. But the row offices are on their way out, as you should know. Next is the new county council. Then perhaps the state senate. Of course, the earlier I can get a seat in the house, the younger I'll be as governor." Like most politicians, Warren rarely sounded sincere. Unlike most politicians, he usually was. "And as for forgetting the little people, it's you who's been too busy to get together, remember?"

"Oh, right," Leigh said absently, taking a swig of cappuccino.

"But enough about me. I want to hear about this body you found. And I'm curious as to what sort of favor you're angling for. Fair warning: if the two are related, I'm leaving."

"What happened to 'I'd do anything for you?' "

"I stop short at the macabre. And I would never do anything outside the law, naturally."

"Naturally."

"So?"

"So . . . I need some information and I'm not sure how to find it. I need to figure out how much money someone had when he died."

Warren laughed. "Is that all? Good grief, Leigh. You could have come in during business hours for that."

"Really? You mean, anyone can find out what's in anyone else's will?"

"I don't have copies of wills on file, if that's what you mean. But the office keeps inheritance tax returns, which are matters of public record. Did this person die in the last nine months?"

"1989."

"No problem. Give me the name and I'll look it up

Monday. I can tell you who the heirs were, how much they inherited. Is that what you need?"

"Perfect." Leigh smiled. "And what if there were no heirs?"

"Property would revert to the state. The records will show that. What's all this about?"

Leigh took another long drag of cappuccino while she sized up Warren's sense of discretion. *Oh, what the hell.*

She started at the beginning. It wasn't long before Warren was thoroughly engaged. "I'll check out the records for Anita and Norman as well," he offered. "If Anita had family money, it might have been put in trust for her son."

"Great! You can check this out first thing in the morning, right?"

Warren cleared his throat. "Seems like I said Monday."

"Yes," Leigh cooed, "but that was before you cared. Come on, you're the big cheese down there, aren't you?"

Warren studied her as he swished dregs of cappuccino around in his cup. "One condition. You come with me. No—two conditions. We do breakfast first. You buy."

"That's three conditions."

"So be it."

"Deal." Styrofoam cups met with a squeak. There was a soft rapping on the door.

Leigh got up and admitted Cara, who had finished an early bath and was now looking divine in frilly evening wear. "Cara, this is Warren Harmon, Allegheny County's most recent and soon to be last register of wills. Warren, this is my cousin Cara, whose study you're sitting in."

Warren rose immediately and extended a practiced

hand. "Charmed! Leigh has told me so much about you over the years, and you're even lovelier in person!"

Leigh rolled her eyes.

"Why, thank you," Cara answered sweetly. "I didn't mean to interrupt. I just wanted to say hello before I turned in, and to tell you two to make yourselves at home." Her eyes appraised Warren, then threw Leigh a sideways "go for it" as she turned to leave. "I can't hear a thing from my room. You two continue your chat."

The way Cara said "chat," it was all Leigh could do not to slam the door on her perfect behind. When they were alone again, Warren laughed. "So she's the one who stole all your boyfriends, eh? My, my."

Leigh glared.

"Sorry," Warren said, not bothering to stifle his grin. "I see we're still a little sensitive where that's concerned. But on the upside, I'm honored. You appear jealous."

Her eyes narrowed further.

Warren crumpled his cappuccino cup into a ball and dropped it into the trash can. "Don't you worry," he said, dropping a brotherly arm around Leigh's shoulders, "one of these days you'll bring a man home and he won't look twice at her. Then you'll get married and live happily ever after."

"Fat chance."

"Don't be so negative. I'd marry you myself, but, well—you know."

"I know. I'm not first lady material."

"Absolute death. I know just what you'd say: 'Am I getting paid for this? Because if I'm not, I'm outta here!' You'd leave all those foreign dignitaries' wives balancing tea on their laps while you put on sweats and went out for a Diet Coke."

"Damn straight."

Warren sighed. "You'd make a much better president."

Leigh smiled. It was nice to have friends who understood you.

Chapter 12

The next morning Cara watched shamelessly out the window as Warren stepped out of his new VW beetle and started toward the front door. "What do you mean average-looking?" she said to Leigh accusingly. "He's quite attractive, and I know you get along. What's your excuse this time?"

"We're just friends," Leigh answered automatically. Warren had always been her relationship-safe geeky buddy, and she liked it that way. So he wasn't geeky anymore. So what? "I prefer to date men who are—"

"Yes?" Cara prompted.

Leigh faltered. "Um, short. I like to date men who are short."

"Oh, really," Cara asked, amused. "And why is that?"

"No time to explain. See you later!" What had she been going to say? She made a hasty exit, cutting Warren off at the porch steps. "I'm starving," she announced. "How about Eat 'n' Park?"

After Leigh had treated him to a bountiful breakfast of pancakes and bacon, Warren led her into the City-County Building and through a door on whose glass window was painted *Warren J. Harmon III, Register of Wills*. He went dutifully to work, opening and shutting drawers and fingering through yellowed files for what seemed to her like hours. Finally he collected a small

stack of documents and motioned for her to follow
him into his office. She stood impatiently over his
shoulder while he sorted through them at his desk.
"Well? What's the bottom line? Did Fischer have any
money or didn't he?"

Warren fidgeted with the papers some more before
he answered. "If we're talking about Paul Fischer, in
a word, no."

Leigh's face fell. She walked around the desk and
slumped into a comfortable armchair. "Really? But he
had to. I mean, it's the only thing that makes sense."

"The only thing of value he owned was the house,
and it reverted to the state. No heirs could be
located."

"Not even a distant cousin?"

"The search only extends to grandparents and de-
scendants, and then you have escheat. Sorry. No buried treasure there. However, Anita Fischer did have
several thousand in stocks when she died."

Leigh perked up. "Who inherited?"

"Robert Fischer. She had no will either. Ordinarily
her estate would be divided between her husband and
son, but since Norman failed to survive her by one
hundred twenty hours, Robbie got it all. Or at least,
he would have gotten it all."

"Would have?"

"Since he went AWOL, it was held in trust."

Leigh got an idea, and her eyes brightened. "So he
could still claim it?"

Warren shook his head. "Afraid not. We're talking
almost fifty years here. There are notice procedures
that have to be followed, but then it reverts to the
state again."

Leigh exhaled loudly in frustration. "The state sure
made a killing on this one, didn't it?"

Papers continued to flip as Warren searched further. "That's interesting."

"What?"

"I was wondering how Paul Fischer managed to hold on to Anita's house when he wasn't a beneficiary. Turns out it wasn't her house, after all. Our friend Norman had her sign over the deed shortly after their marriage."

The cold eyes in the newspaper picture crept back into Leigh's mind. "Did Norman have any money of his own?"

"Nary a cent."

"It figures. He'd probably already gone through what his first wife left him."

"Paul's mother? How did she die?"

Her head turned. "You know—I don't know."

"What was her name? We could look her up too, if she died in the county."

Leigh shook her head. "I don't know anything about her. But I'm sure I will soon."

After thanking Warren for the favor by agreeing to write all his campaign literature in perpetuity, plus try out the new Chinese buffet on McKnight Road later in the week, Leigh stepped out of his car and walked up the steps to Cara's front door. She was surprised to hear a loud yapping inside.

Pansy?

She opened the door tentatively, but the poodle greeted her happily. Apparently the dog fancied herself more of a butler than a bouncer. Leigh followed the sound of Cara's laughter (and the little dog's waggling rear end) into the parlor. Mao Tse was on top of the secretary, staring daggers.

Cara sat on the couch, Adith Rhodis on one of the wingbacks. Both looked up at her expectantly.

"Well?" Mrs. Rhodis asked loudly. "What did you find out? Paul didn't have a dime, did he?"

Leigh shook her head, explaining how Anita's money was lost to the state.

"So somebody bumped Norman off before he could inherit it," Mrs. Rhodis declared proudly. "And good riddance, if you ask me."

"The hundred-twenty-hour-rule complicates things," Cara noted. "If, for instance, Paul wanted to kill both Anita and Norman so he could have everything, he timed it wrong. But if Robbie wanted to keep Paul from inheriting Anita's money, he timed it just right."

Leigh shook her head. "True. But if Robbie committed murder for money, he overlooked something. Like collecting it."

"Oh," Cara said, deflated.

"Don't forget," Mrs. Rhodis said, finger pointing, "they might neither of them have known about the hundred-twenty-hour law."

Leigh nodded in agreement and sat down. "Let's stick to the facts. One, Norman was an abusive SOB who wanted his wife's house. If they'd stayed married happily ever after, it wouldn't have mattered whose name the house was under. But if she died first, it mattered, because unless she stated otherwise in her will, Robbie might get the house instead of Norman. Two, Norman had another wife who died young. Is there a pattern here?"

Mrs. Rhodis shook her head. "I don't think so, dear. Seems like Anita said Paul's mother died in childbirth."

"Do you remember her name? If she left Norman any money?"

"Oh, Lordy. I don't think I ever knew her name. She wasn't from around here." Mrs. Rhodis sank deep into thought and scratched her chin. "If she did have money, I'm sure Norman spent all that too."

A low-pitched sound echoed in from the side of the house. *"Ad-die!"*

"Just a minute!" Mrs. Rhodis screamed, making Cara and Leigh both jump. "Sorry, girls," she apologized, rising. "Gotta see to Bud. Probably lost his blame glasses again."

She slapped her leg for Pansy to follow, and headed for the front door. "You girls let me know what's going on, you hear?"

They promised they would.

"Where's your mom?" Leigh asked when they were alone.

"She had a class at noon, so she asked Mrs. Rhodis to keep me company till you got back." Cara sighed. "We couldn't find anything on the second floor. But there's still places down here to check. And the basement and the attic, of course. Could you help me search this afternoon? We won't be able to this evening."

"This evening?"

"Dinner at your mom's? Surely you haven't forgotten. I hear she's planning on Yankee pot roast again."

Leigh's stomach rolled. She hated Yankee pot roast. And she had, blissfully, forgotten about the dinner. Not to mention the fact that she was supposed to have invited the Polanskis.

The doorbell rang. Conveniently enough, it was Maura. "Thought I'd be conventional this time." She grinned.

Leigh, also being conventional, invited her into the parlor. Maura entered to the tune of a hiss from Mao Tse, who, having just decided the coast was clear, was now forced to flee to the kitchen.

Cara laughed. "What did you ever do to her, Maura?"

The policewoman shrugged. "I'm a dog person." She squeezed with some effort into one of the antique wingbacks. "I can't stay long, Koslow" she said, looking distinctly uncomfortable. "I'm on duty. But I wanted to see what you two were up to."

"*Library-type* research," Leigh said proudly. "And I'm doing a great job. It's looking more and more like these problems we're having are related to 1949."

"The double deaths?" Maura asked.

Leigh nodded. "You knew about that already?"

"Sure. The Fischer story was legend at Avalon Elementary. With a few variations, of course. The most popular one had old man Fischer throwing his wife down the stairs, then her ghost coming back and shooting his eyes out."

Leigh grimaced. "Charming. Do you know what really happened?"

"Of course." Maura's tone implied the question was ridiculous. "What makes you think there's a link between those deaths and these threats?"

"Mrs. Rhodis"—Cara pointed next door—"says that Paul Fischer told her he had a will." She summarized her neighbor's story, and Maura listened with interest.

"My dad never told me any of that," she said, sounding disappointed. "I wonder if Mrs. Rhodis ever told him about the will, or seeing the other papers." For a moment she was lost in thought. "If Fischer did have a will, and notebooks filled with poems, either he hid them before he died, or someone got to them before the police did. I remember when Fischer's belongings were auctioned off—and there weren't any writings. If there had been, people would have fought over them. A lot of people thought Paul Fischer knew more than he let on."

The room was silent. Maura stood up. "Thanks, guys. You've given me a lot to think about." She headed for the door.

Cara looked at Leigh as if she were supposed to be doing something. "What?" Leigh feigned, annoyed.

"Dinner?" Cara mouthed back.

Oh. Leigh followed Maura to the door. "By the way, my mom wants to invite you and your mom to dinner tonight. You don't have to come if you don't want to."

Maura laughed. "You're a hard sell, Koslow. I'm not sure about Mom—depends on her mood—but I'd love to come. I haven't seen your mom in ages. I don't get off until six o'clock, though. What time?"

"Whenever you can get there," Leigh sighed. "She's making Yankee pot roast."

"Well, hot damn."

"You're a sick woman."

Maura saluted. Leigh shut the door and looked at her watch. She'd better eat a big lunch.

When the doorbell rang at three, Leigh was glad. Ever since lunch she had been climbing and crawling over every inch of the downstairs, knocking on walls and measuring the depth of cabinets while Cara took notes and made sketches. She was bored stiff. Since any visitor could be considered an improvement, she jumped to answer the door. It popped open before she could reach it, however, and a glowing Adith Rhodis pushed her round body inside.

"I've got a lead!" She bustled past Leigh and hurried to Cara. "Irma Sacco," she exclaimed, "on Howden. She may be the answer!"

Leigh had visions of a diabetic cat with a killer left hook. She dismissed them.

"You're going to have to slow down a bit, Mrs. Rhodis," Cara said politely. "Won't you have a seat?"

"No time, my dear! I told Irma we'd be right over. You see, I've been thinking about all this hiding-place business, and it occurred to me that Paul might not have hidden his will in the house itself. He could have hidden it in the furniture."

Leigh looked at the older woman with new admiration. She might be nuts, but she had her moments.

"Anyway," Mrs. Rhodis continued, "everything he had went at auction. I got a few pieces—chairs, nothing special—and I know who bought a lot of the rest. And I started thinking: where would I hide my will? And then it hit me! My writing desk!"

Leigh and Cara exchanged glances.

"Irma Sacco has Paul Fischer's writing desk?" Cara asked.

"Yes, dear. For forty-five dollars. She got taken, but that's not the point. I called her this morning and asked if there was anywhere anyone could have hid something in it, and right away she says yes, there's a stuck drawer she's never been able to open!"

Leigh tried to contain her enthusiasm. A locked desk drawer seemed too easy.

Mrs. Rhodis apparently sensed the skepticism. "Well, come on, then—I've got Bud's toolbox. Let's go see!"

Chapter 13

Irma Sacco must have been waiting for them; her screen door opened the moment Adith's car turned down the street. By the time the women had parked and gotten out, Irma was already deep into a monologue.

"Now, you be careful coming up them steps, doll!" she directed to Cara. "They're slick!"

Why concrete steps should be slick on a dry summer day, Leigh wasn't sure, but she stayed close to her cousin anyway.

"I always wondered what was in there," Irma prattled, continuing the story they hadn't heard, "but I didn't figure it was too much to fuss about. Some buttons maybe. Or coins. It ain't big enough to hold much else. It's got a keyhole in it sure enough, but there never was no key with it, and I figured it just didn't matter, you know."

Irma Sacco was somewhere between sixty and ninety—a birdlike creature with a hook nose and long fingers. Leigh recognized her at once as the owner of a certain obese orange tabby which, though long dead, still made appearances in an occasional nightmare. "Peaches" hadn't wanted her blood sugar taken, and Leigh hadn't wanted a quarter-inch gash across her knuckles. Peaches had prevailed.

Moving quickly but with a slight stoop, Irma led her

guests through an aisle in the floor of the cluttered
living room. Curios, boxed and unboxed, were everywhere. The windows were hung with decorative string
lights—pumpkins here, Holsteins there. Christmas or-
naments abounded, but no tree was in sight; the
most likely location held a foot-high pile of boxed
panty hose. Irma shuffled through a narrow hall
flanked with photographs of unattractive children,
then turned into a bedroom that could have doubled
for a sale bin at Value City. Dolls, macramé plant
hangers, religious figurines, pin cushions, plastic
trinkets, and a wide assortment of light fixtures covered every surface.

"Sorry about the mess," Irma apologized offhand-
edly. "I got a bunch in this week." She turned to the
cousins with a saccharine smile. "You girls interested
in any decorations? Less than half what you'll pay
at Kmart."

"No, thank you," Leigh said quickly. "We really
can't stay long." Her eyes rested on an area where the
debris was roughly rectangular in shape. "Is that it?"

"Why, yes!" said Irma happily, beginning to pick
away at the surface. "I don't really use it for writing,
you know. I was going to paint it up, but I never
did. . . ."

"Here, Irma," Adith announced proudly when the
unearthing was complete. "This is the drawer, right?"

The desk was a heavy contraption of dark wood,
with drawers on either side of a narrow writing surface
and cubbyholes along the back. Most of the cubbies
were open, but three small drawers were solid and
bore tiny keyholes.

"These are open," Irma demonstrated, pulling out
the top two drawers, which, amazingly, were empty.
The fact must have disturbed her—before closing

them she popped a marble in one and a nail file in the other. "The bottom one I've never been able to get to," she said with regret. "Didn't seem worth bothering about."

Cara stepped forward with the tools Adith had brought. "I can see someone's tried before," she said, peering at the stripped hole. "But I think I can get it."

Leigh was confident that Cara would. Lydie was the handyman of the family, and Cara was a good pupil.

"I think it's been broken and jammed," Cara explained. She fiddled with the drawer a few minutes, her belly resting awkwardly on the desktop. "OK, she said finally. "I got it."

Leigh held her breath and pushed forward. The drawer space was small, about an inch and a half wide, and barely an inch deep. It contained a thin gold wedding band, one grimy cuff link, and a folded piece of paper.

Adith and Irma both dove for the jewelry, but Adith was closer. She snatched up the pieces with a look of triumph, then held them close to her face and frowned. "Naw," she said derisively. "Cheap stuff. Probably Paul's mother's ring. And this," she said, tossing the cuff link back in the drawer, "had to be Norman's."

Irma grabbed up the cuff link and nodded her head in agreement. "Garbage. Just garbage." She held her hand out for the ring. Adith handed it over, eyes narrowed.

In the meantime, Cara had carefully pulled out and unfolded the yellowed slip of paper. Leigh looked over her shoulder. It was a small sheet, the size found in a pocket notebook or diary, and it was covered with faint handwriting in pencil.

FATHER

You are gone from this world,
    father of mine.
Never again to smile your crooked smile,
    and tell me of greater things.

I look into your killer's eyes.
    The hate is still there.
For you, for me.
    A hate so vilely nurtured.

Your killer will suffer,
    someday, Father.
The day when
    I see your crooked smile.

"Oooooh, Lordy," Adith exclaimed, reading over Cara's arm. "That's his writing; that's Paul's. He used those same short little phrases in the poem he wrote about Bud."

"What does it say?" clamored Irma, squinting.

Cara read the poem out loud.

Adith clucked her tongue. "Norman didn't commit suicide. See, I told you. Right there in black and white. Or pencil, anyway." She grinned. "And he knew who did kill him too. My, my."

"Yes, that's the way it looks," Cara said, sounding distracted.

" 'The day when I see your crooked smile,' " Leigh quoted. "He means when he dies. He's going to reveal Norman's killer when he dies."

"We suspected that already," Cara said. "But look at this—he 'looks' into the killer's eyes. Present tense." She flipped the paper over. It was not dated. "If Robbie killed Norman," she hypothesized, "he must not have stayed away. He must have come back at some point, when Paul wrote that poem."

"That's the implication," Leigh agreed.

Adith shook her head stubbornly. "Robbie wouldn't have come back. Paul could have turned him in, made terrible trouble for him. There was no love lost between those stepbrothers, I can tell you."

Irma cleared her throat and grinned through cigarette-stained teeth. "Well, I'm glad I could be of service to you girls. And since you seem to like my poem, I'm willing to make you a real good deal on it."

Adith scoffed. "Irma Sacco, you hussy! Nobody's paying you a dime. This is part of an official police investigation. If you don't let these girls turn this thing in, you could be charged with aiding and abetting!"

Irma bristled.

"I think it's withholding evidence," Cara corrected gently. "But Mrs. Sacco has been most helpful." She turned to Irma with a smile. "I'd like to thank you for helping us. Would you accept a Ballasta scissor basket as a gift?"

Irma's eyes gleamed. "With one of them little garter things?"

Cara nodded.

"I'd love it." Irma smiled. "You just take that little paper right on home with you. But before you go, can I interest either of you girls in a pair of panty hose? Only fifty cents a pair—can't beat it."

After declining several other bargains, including a close-out on cat clocks with swinging tails, the women managed to escape with their prize. Heartened by their success, Leigh was even beginning to look forward to dinner. Not only would she have the chance to ask Mary Polanski about 1949, she was going to impress the heck out of Maura.

*   *   *

She should have known better.

"The poem is interesting, but we should be careful not to make too much out of it," the policewoman said calmly, spearing a bite of pot roast.

"What do you mean?" Leigh insisted, irritated. Between the gooey roast and Frances's constant nagging about the foolishness of remaining in the Fischer house, the evening was an unqualified bust. "The poem proves that Paul knew who killed his father, and that the person was still alive."

"Was still alive when?" Maura challenged. "It isn't dated. And there are other possibilities. The writer, if it was Paul, could have blamed someone else for his father's suicide. He could have been looking into the eyes of a picture. He could have been looking forward to his own death so he could avenge the killer in hell. He could have been writing pure fantasy. Who knows?" She forked in the hunk of meat and began to chew contentedly.

Leigh stewed. Were police trained to be killjoys? "What do you think, Mrs. Polanski?" she asked hopefully.

Mary Polanski swallowed a bite of potato and looked up thoughtfully. She was as tall as her daughter, although not as solid, with lanky, angular limbs and a long, sharp nose. If not for her handmade clothes and long gray ponytail, she might have passed for a senior Cruella de Vil. But with her discerning gaze and purple Keds, Mary had a style all her own. "It's quite possible, I suppose," she offered noncommittally.

Leigh tried to conceal her frustration. If getting information from Maura was tough, getting it from Mary was ten times harder, Alzheimer's or no. At least tonight she seemed perfectly lucid.

"I'm curious, Mrs. Polanski," Cara said sweetly, giving it another try. "What do you remember about the deaths that occurred in 1949?"

Mary's intelligent-looking gray eyes turned slowly to her daughter, as if asking permission to answer. Maura nodded.

"I was only thirteen at the time," Mary began calmly, rearranging her napkin in her lap. "Robbie was a sweet boy, and I was a little sweet on him." She smiled, her thoughts far away. "When he disappeared, a lot of people thought he had shot Norman, but I never believed it. My husband and Mr. Mellman were good friends of his too, and we were all very defensive of him. I remember once a bully named Leroy Flynn started taunting Donald—Mr. Mellman—about having a murderer for a friend." She shook her head sadly. "That wasn't a good idea."

It hadn't occurred to Leigh that Chief Polanski and Mellman might have known Robert Fischer better than they knew Paul, but given their ages, it made sense.

"Robbie was afraid of his stepfather," Mary continued. "And with good reason. People didn't talk much about domestic violence back then, but we knew when it was happening. I always believed, and I still do, that Norman was responsible for his wife's death. I think Robbie ran away because he couldn't stand the thought of living with him anymore."

"You don't think Norman killed himself, do you?" Cara asked.

"Norman was a sick man. Nothing he did would surprise me," Mary answered without emotion.

"And what did your father think?" Leigh asked Maura.

Maura sighed and glanced at her mother. "Dad never talked about it. I know that's hard to believe, given how much he liked to gab. But even long after the fact, when it came to the Fischer case, his lips were sealed. If I asked about it, he'd just say, 'The case is closed. Let's let it rest.' "

Mary shook her head sadly. "It was because of Robbie, dear. I told you they were close, and very defensive of him. Neither Ed nor Don have ever been able to talk about that time. It's just too painful for them."

Leigh found it odd that grief over a lost childhood friend should last for four decades, but then, she hadn't lived that long yet. She looked at Maura. "Did you ask Mellman about 1949? What he remembers?"

Maura helped herself to a third serving of potatoes before she answered. "We talked about it this afternoon. Mom's right—it was hard to get anything out of him. He did tell me that he believes Robbie Fischer is dead. He's sure that Robbie would have come forward otherwise, eventually, after the scandal died down."

"And what do you think?" Leigh asked.

"I'm not so sure. We know that someone wants you out of the house. Only a handful of people ever lived there, and almost all of them are dead. If Robert Fischer is alive, I'd say he's my prime suspect."

Mary looked at Maura. "I bet Mr. Mellman wasn't too happy with that theory."

Maura returned a sly smile. "You got that one right. He got pretty hot. You'd think Robbie was some sort of saint."

"He was a sweet boy," Mary defended, "but time can change people. I wouldn't presume to predict his behavior now."

Looking at Mary, Leigh wondered how much crime solving had gone on at the Polanski dinner table as opposed to the station house. Maura had a heck of a gene pool going for her.

Randall Koslow cleared his throat. "I'm sure the Avalon Police Department has the situation well under control. Shall we discuss something else for a while?"

Mary shifted in her seat, suddenly looking uneasy. The only one at the table who appeared happy with the suggestion was Maura. "Sure, Doc," she said cheerfully. "How's the job search coming, Leigh?"

Choking violently, Leigh tried in vain to keep bits of potato from sputtering through her lips. She wiped her mouth and reached for a glass of water, attempting to avoid Frances's gaze. She failed. The beady browns were staring right at her. "You *did* get laid off again, didn't you? I knew it! I told you the advertising business was too risky!" Frances turned scathing eyes on her husband. "You knew about this too, didn't you?"

"Now, dear," Randall answered calmly. "Leigh's a grown woman. She doesn't have to tell us everything."

"Of course you knew!" Frances continued, her hands wringing her napkin anxiously. "You would. All right. Let's think. There's my friend Doreen down at Mellon Bank. She might know of something—"

"Mom," Leigh interrupted, eyes still watering. "I do not need your help finding a job. I'll be fine. Can we talk about something else, please? We do have guests, you know."

Rarely could Frances resist an appeal to her sense of propriety. She cleared her throat and wiped her mouth with her napkin. "I'm sorry. Would anyone like some more coffee?"

"I want to go home."

Mary had stood up at the table, her eyes anxious.

Maura spoke gently, motioning for her mother to sit. "It's OK, Mom. We're having dinner at the Koslows. You haven't had your dessert yet."

"Where's my coat?" Mary pushed back her chair and headed for the door that led to the bedroom.

"I'm sorry, Mrs. Koslow," Maura said, "but I think we'd better be going."

"Don't you dare apologize," Frances said smoothly. "We're just happy you could come at all. Shall I wrap up the leftover pot roast for you?"

Maura nodded, her sad eyes glimmering a little. Within a few minutes, the Polanskis and the pot roast were gone.

"Now," Frances began sternly, "I think it's time for a good, old-fashioned family conference."

Chapter 14

"I can't believe you didn't tell me you lost your job," Cara brooded as they returned to her front door two excruciating hours later. "You know I wouldn't have told your mom."

"No," Leigh defended, "but you would have told *your* mom, and we both know those two can't keep secrets."

Cara grumbled as she turned her key in the lock and walked into the foyer to deactivate the security system. Leigh followed, unable to keep her eyes from fixating on the floor at the bottom of the staircase. A body had once lain there. An accident—or murder?

"Leigh."

The tone made her turn quickly.

Cara's eyes were wide. "Look. The malfunction light is on."

Leigh knew only the basics of how to turn the system off and on, but she was sure that the blinking red light was not anything she had seen before. "What does that mean?" she asked, feeling a need to whisper.

Cara pushed a few buttons, and a message flashed on the display. *Failure to Communicate.*

Within two seconds both women were on the front porch. "I'll have Mrs. Rhodis call the police," Cara said, already walking.

Leigh nodded, but her initial shock was quickly

being replaced with anger. Someone had been in her space, screwing around with her stuff. Who? She wanted to know. "Cara!" she hissed, "Why don't you keep an eye on the front door from Mrs. Rhodis's, and I'll stand in the driveway where I can watch the back? In case someone comes out." Cara nodded without argument.

Leigh walked back to the driveway, keeping her cousin in her line of sight. Cara didn't attempt the stairs, but called to Mrs. Rhodis from below the porch. When their neighbor appeared, Leigh moved farther down the driveway until she could see the back patio.

Her heart was beating against her chest so hard she thought her sternum might crack, but she kept walking. Everything looked normal. Cara's Lumina, tucked carefully against the hedge by the house. Traffic noise from the boulevard as always. Streetlights casting artificial shadows on the low shrubs that lined the drive. Nothing out of place, nothing to frighten. And yet someone had been inside. They must have been. Where were they now?

She walked in the open, giving a wide berth to anything with hiding-place potential. "Stay calm," she told herself out loud. "No one's going to jump you. They've probably already got what they wanted and left. And if they're still here, they'll just want to get out."

"Leigh!" Cara was back out in the front yard. "Stay where I can see you!"

Leigh held up her fingers in an OK sign. She could almost see the back door. When she did see it, her body stiffened. The door was wide open.

She stood still. Someone had broken into the house, that much was for sure. That someone, in all likelihood, had left through the back door. Probably in a hurry.

Leigh's calm logic lasted only a few seconds before the sight of the open door brought out a more primitive sentiment. Maternal instinct.

"Mao Tse!" she cried, and started running, ignoring Cara's calls for her to stay put. She reached the open door and stepped into the kitchen. "Mao Tse? Are you here?" She flipped on the lights, and suddenly felt cold.

The room really hadn't changed—much. The stepladder had been moved to the middle of the room. A yellow beach towel lay crumpled in the floor. None of the cabinets were open, no drawers overturned. But the feeling hung in the air like a disease. A feeling of violation.

Cara stepped into the kitchen behind Leigh. "Come on out," she said sensibly. "The police will be here any second."

Leigh walked into the breakfast nook. The finch cage wasn't on its hook. It was sitting on top of the table. Her eyes scanned its lonely perches. The birds were gone.

A wave of nausea overtook her. Cara walked up softly and put a hand on her arm. "We have to wait for the police—please, Leigh. Come outside."

Leigh shook her arm loose, panic rising. "Mao Tse," she whispered, moving into the family room.

Cara followed closely on her heels. "Wait, Leigh! You can't go in alone. Stop!"

But Leigh wasn't listening. She flipped on the lights, her eyes desperately searching the places she'd seen Mao Tse before—the armchair, on top of the stereo. Nothing.

A siren sounded.

Cara grabbed Leigh's arm with a vengeance, dragged her firmly backward through the breakfast nook, and deposited her in the kitchen by the back door. "Don't you take another step!" she hissed, then called out to the police.

But Leigh's attention was now focused on the dining room, and when Cara released her to meet the officers, she began walking stiffly toward it, turning lights on as she went. Cara's good china and silverware were untouched. The parlor was spotless, except that the kitchen broom was lying in the floor. Had she left in there? Of course not. Had Cara?

"Mao Tse!" She was afraid to raise her voice above a whisper, though she wasn't sure why. She tried to think. A stranger had walked into the house. What would Mao Tse have done? An idea raised a spark of hope. The cat would hide, of course. She fell to her hands and knees and started looking under the furniture. Nothing.

"Ma'am!" An unfamiliar voice, followed by an unfamiliar pair of feet, approached her from behind. "Ma'am? I'm afraid I'm going to have to ask you to step outside until we've had a look around."

Leigh got off her knees and faced an attractive uniformed officer in his early forties. His badge said SCHOFIELD. Had Maura ever mentioned a Schofield?

"Ma'am, I insist. Right away."

Leigh still could only whisper. "My cat . . ."

Schofield took her arm. "You'll have to look for it later." His grasp was gentle but firm. Before Leigh knew what was happening, he had deposited her on the front porch and gone back inside.

Mao Tse. Leigh tried to push away the horrible thoughts swimming in her head. Mao Tse was fine. She was just hiding. No one wanted to hurt her. They wanted something else.

A second officer, who had been talking to Cara, pushed past Leigh and into the house. Cara hurried up. "They've called Chief Mellman; he's on his way. Did you want to call Maura?"

Leigh shook her head dumbly.

"Mao Tse is just hiding somewhere. I'm sure of it," Cara soothed. "You know she wouldn't go near a stranger."

Heavy footsteps and clanking keys announced the arrival of the Avalon police chief. Mellman looked odd in jeans—especially those topped off with an oversized Western belt buckle. But if the sweat on his forehead was any indication, he had jogged the three blocks from his house at a good clip. "Are you girls OK?" he said between breaths.

"We're fine," Cara answered. "We just came home and found the security system down."

"The back door was open," Leigh began, then stumbled. "And my pets are missing."

Mellman's pupils widened. "Did you go in the house?" he asked.

Leigh and Cara looked at each other.

The police chief interpreted their silence correctly, but managed to control his displeasure. "What pets did you have, Leigh?" he asked gently.

A trace of a smile escaped her lips as she remembered Mellman's soft spot for animals. "A cat," she answered. "And two finches."

He nodded, then turned aside and began talking jargon into his radio. Leigh made out "and keep your eyes open for a cat" before he started walking around the side of the house.

The cousins stood in uncomfortable silence. "I should never have relied on that security system," Cara said finally. "This is all my fault, Leigh. I'm sorry."

"Don't be ridiculous. None of this is either of our faults." Anger was creeping back into Leigh's veins.

"We didn't ask for any of this. And this person is going to regret it." She turned suddenly, remembering her cousin's condition. "How are you doing? You're not having contractions, are you?"

Cara shook her head. "I'm fine. Angry, worried—but fine."

After a few more minutes, Mellman appeared in the foyer. "It's all right, girls. Whoever was in here is long gone."

A sudden sense of relief overcame Leigh. In her mind she had seen an officer coming to the door, his face pasty. "Were you the one with the cat? I'm sorry, ma'am, but—"

It hadn't happened. But where was Mao Tse? Where were the finches? She shivered and forced gruesome images from her mind as she and her cousin walked inside the front door. "Leigh, you go with Officer Banks, and Cara, you go with Officer Schofield. Do a walk-through and tell them anything you think is out of place or missing. Try not to touch anything."

Another woman suddenly appeared on the porch, her face flushed to a rosy glow. "What's happening? Is everything OK?"

Leigh thought she heard Mellman sigh. "Were you home this evening, Mrs. Rhodis?" he asked.

"Of course," she said, eyes glittering.

"Then come with me."

Leigh led Officer Banks, who couldn't have been more than twenty-one, up the stairs. *Schofield*. Had Maura mentioned a Schofield? Was he married? Guilt rushed over her at the idle thought. She took a deep breath and started the search. The guest bedrooms all looked normal. So did the nursery and the master. The door to the attic stairway was closed. A bathroom cabinet was open but nothing more. There was no sign of Mao Tse.

Leigh's bedroom was the last stop. "Mao Tse? Are you here?" *Please, be here.*

There was no response.

Leigh looked into the bedroom. One end of a curtain rod had been pulled out of its hook, the curtains dangling diagonally over the window. The closet doors were open. Empty hangers were scattered on the floor.

Afraid to breathe, she dropped to her knees and looked under the bed. A wild-eyed, fifteen-pound Persian looked back at her. And hissed.

Thank you, God. She stood up on weak knees. "She's fine."

"You found your cat?" the officer asked.

Leigh nodded.

"And what's out of place here? Anything?"

Leigh laughed. She was feeling better. "Everything. This is *my* room, not Ms. March's. The closet should be shut. These hangers belong inside, and that is not my taste in window treatments."

The officer dutifully took notes, then examined the window with the crooked curtains. "Doesn't look like anyone tried to open it. Could your cat have pulled this down?"

She nodded. "If she was scared and flipping out, yes."

A high-pitched ranting echoed from somewhere below, and Leigh and Banks scrambled over each other to get back downstairs. When they arrived, Mellman, Schofield, and Mrs. Rhodis were all gathered around Cara in the back hallway. "The nerve!" She was shouting in a voice Leigh seldom heard, and did not want to hear now. "*Nobody* pulls a stunt like this on me!"

All eyes were fixed on the floor at Cara's feet, and Leigh's joined them. Lined up neatly against the wall were two metal gasoline cans, and a box of long matches.

Almost an hour had passed before Leigh had Cara calmed to her satisfaction. The expectant mother lay on the sofa in the family room, dutifully swallowing a pale serving of instant caffeine-free tea. "Nothing was taken," Leigh repeated. "Nothing was damaged. They were interrupted before they could start the fire. Everything's going to be fine."

The hot flush of anger suffusing Cara's face had subsided to a warm glow, but her eyes still shot daggers. "They were going to burn my house down. Mao Tse could have died."

"They didn't. And she didn't. We got here in time. Now drink. Are you having any contractions?"

Cara shook her head, but her mind appeared elsewhere. "We've been wrong all along. They didn't want anything in the house. They wanted to destroy it. Why?"

Officer Schofield stepped into the study, looking apologetic. "I'm sorry to disturb you again, Ms. March. We're almost through here, but I need to ask one more question. Do you remember whether you left any dishes in the sink?"

"I haven't any idea," Cara answered honestly. "I'm a slob about things like that. Leigh, did you notice?"

Leigh remembered the two glasses, peanut-butter-smeared knife, and greasy popcorn bowl she had moved from the counter to the dishwasher earlier that afternoon. "No, I don't think there was anything there when we left. Why?"

Schofield looked uncomfortable. "Thank you." He retreated.

Excusing herself to bring more tea, Leigh traced Schofield to the kitchen, where he was exchanging

muted words and a series of head shakes with Mellman. She looked between their shoulders and into the
sink at the ten-inch-long butcher knife.

The outstretched hands of the officers were not
quick enough to keep her from stumbling backward
over the step stool. The combination of pain in her
tailbone and embarrassment over her clumsiness was
unpleasant. But even more unpleasant was any of the
various scenarios she could imagine for why the intruder had gotten out a knife. "Is it . . . clean?" she
forced out weakly.

"Yes," Mellman answered firmly. "Looks clean as
a whistle. But we're going to check it just the same.
Does it belong to Ms. March?"

Leigh nodded, recognizing the carved handle. Her
cousin kept a matching set of knives in a wooden
block on the kitchen cabinet, and the hole that re-
ceived the ten-inch was empty. She was certain the
knife hadn't been out earlier. She had cleaned up the
kitchen right before they left for dinner—a habit in-
grained by Frances. "Never leave your house a mess,
dear," she had harangued. "You never know who
might pop over."

Who, indeed.

Leigh felt for the stool and sat down. Why a knife?
She glanced at the empty bird cage in the breakfast
nook and felt the last of her nerve crumbling. She
could deal with rude people, even people who made
threats and stole things. But cruelty scared her.

The birds were gone. Where were they? And why?
Why would anyone want her pets? A series of images
flashed through her mind. Disconnected images, random images, suddenly forming a morbid order. With
a jerky movement she clutched the stool underneath
her. It was Mao Tse's stool. The stool she hid under

whenever she was afraid. Just like she hid under the couch, or under the bed. The stool could be moved, but to get a cat out from under the furniture, you needed something else. Like a broom. Or coat hangers.

And then maybe a knife.

Leigh felt a warm lump of bile rise in her throat. She got up to head for the bathroom, and the officers didn't stop her.

Chapter 15

"If you two won't leave," Maura said, sounding defeated, "I'll be happy to sleep over."

Cara poured more decaf. She had calmed down considerably, but the red highlights over her cheekbones betrayed anger still simmering. "Thank you, Maura. But that won't be necessary. Todd is taking care of everything."

Leigh took another long drag on her coffee. A Hampton Inn—even a Motel 6—sounded awfully good. But Cara couldn't be left alone. And Cara wasn't going anywhere.

The clock in the kitchen read 1:00 A.M., and Leigh was exhausted. "When did Todd think he would finish?" she asked, bleary-eyed.

Todd Ford, standing in the doorway to the breakfast nook, answered the question himself. "I'm all done, Cara. The phone line's repaired, and I've got you set up with a radio backup this time."

Cara nodded, annoyed. Todd Ford had been a high school classmate, and one of her many ex-boyfriends. He now owned a security outfit in the neighboring borough of Bellevue. Her "high-end" security system had been foiled, and she was not pleased. "So they cut the phone lines, you said. Is that all they had to do?"

Todd was a strong-looking man, not tall but definitely solid. In front of an angry Cara he withered like lettuce in the sun. "It wasn't just a matter of cutting your phone line," he answered hesitantly. "You have a sophisticated system here. This guy was a real pro." He paused, looking even more uncomfortable, then took a deep breath. "This person knew where your outdoor siren was mounted, and he knew just where to go to destroy the main control unit."

Silence descended. "You mean," Leigh asked after a moment, "he would have had to watch the house for a while—cased it, so to speak?"

"More than that," Todd answered ruefully. "I'd say he's been *inside* your house."

Silence descended again, then Cara shrugged. "That doesn't mean a thing. Half of Avalon has been in this house."

"When?" Leigh asked, surprised.

"We had the place fixed up over a period of years, and the security system was in place most of that time. Construction workers, decorators, carpet installers, cleaners . . . not to mention that gargantuan open house we had last year."

"She's right," Maura said. "Being in the house before doesn't necessarily narrow our suspect list. But expertise with alarm systems—that might."

The women fell silent in thought, but Todd interrupted. "You'll be safe now, Cara. The guards are already outside."

Leigh did a double-take. *Guards?*

"I've arranged for two on at all times, with three shifts. It wasn't easy to contract them on such short notice," he added, rather as a plea. "That OK?"

"It'll do." She answered, then softened. "Thanks, Todd. I appreciate your help."

Todd flushed like a grade schooler and retreated happily. Leigh shook her head.

"I don't like this," Maura said for the sixth time

that evening. "I really don't. Someone tried to burn this place down tonight. Guards or no guards, we can't know what else they might do."

"You're looking at the negatives," Cara said bluntly.

The other women stared at her.

"Would you mind pointing out the positives?" Leigh said sarcastically.

"Of course. First, they *didn't* burn this place down. They failed. *Ha!* Second, the fact that they wanted to gives us insight into their motives. We've been operating under the assumption that something valuable was hidden in this house. Not necessarily an item of monetary value, but something that was wanted desperately." Cara looked at her audience to see if they were following her. They were. "Well, now I've changed my mind. Whatever is hidden in this house, I don't think this person wants it per se. He just doesn't want *us* to find it."

Leigh eyed Maura over her coffee cup. Cara's theory made sense, given what she knew. She had been spared the possible implications of the knife, since Leigh had managed to convince Mellman and Schofield not to tell her about it. After the conniption they had witnessed earlier, it wasn't particularly difficult. Maura had even agreed, at least for now.

Cara continued. "I think that Paul Fischer had a secret—and I think that secret was the identity of his father's killer. Someone wants that secret to die with him." She looked at her audience again. They were quiet. "Any thoughts?"

Leigh wasn't sure what to say. A few hours ago she would have agreed, but now she wasn't so sure. There would be no point in further threatening the house's occupants if the relevant stash was set to be burned any minute. She wondered if the intruder ever in-

tended to strike a match, or if he was merely delivering the last part of a three-pronged threat. If that
was the case, he definitely wanted something in the
house rather than just wanting to destroy it.

"Well?" Cara insisted. "Say something."

"You may be right," Leigh said noncommittally.
"I'm too tired to think."

"Go to bed, then. I am. And I'll sleep well too. The
new security system is rolling, and there are two capable guards prowling about outside. Tomorrow we'll
find that piece of evidence and send this scum to jail
where he belongs." She rose and smiled pleasantly
again. "Good night."

Leigh looked into Cara's determined blue-green
eyes. Her cousin might be a mental case, but she had
a way of getting what she wanted. Maybe she'd get
lucky this time too—maybe they did just need one
more day to find what they weren't supposed to.

Cara left to go upstairs, and Maura looked at her
watch. "Are you sure you don't want me to stay,
Koslow?"

Leigh shook her head. "Thanks, but as much as I
hate to admit it, I think Cara's right that we're safe
for the night. The guards do help. I wish she'd thought
of that earlier."

Maura raised an eyebrow. "Most folks would sleep
better with an armed guard. Not just anyone can afford it."

With the word "afford" the specter of unemployment once again reared its ugly head in Leigh's mind,
but she suppressed it. She could handle only one disaster at a time. The résumés would have to wait a few
days.

Maura took another sip of decaf and fixed her gaze
on the cup rim. She didn't seem anxious to leave, and
Leigh wondered what was bugging her. A thought oc

curred. "Mellman did OK today," Leigh began, fishing. "I mean, he seemed to know what he was doing and everything."

Maura's brow knitted. "I never said he was an idiot, Koslow."

"Well, not in so many words. But when you found out he'd been promoted to chief—"

"Look," Maura cut in dismissively, "I said a lot of things I shouldn't have after my father died. Mellman's no dummy—he's smarter than he lets on."

Leigh was skeptical. "The Columbo thing?"

"Maybe; I don't know. He's always been like that. But Mellman's a follower, not a leader. Chiefs have got to be leaders."

"Like your dad was."

Maura paused. "Yeah." Her eyes turned moist. "God, I miss him."

Chief Edward K. Polanski had died in the prime of late middle age. He was chasing a teenage thief out of a laundromat and into an alley when he collapsed. It was a heart attack, and CPR didn't help. He never came to.

"How would your father have handled this situation?" Leigh asked gently.

Maura sighed and rubbed her face in her hands. "I don't know. That's just it. I'm sure that there are things he would know—about the Fischers—that would help. But he never talked about it. That bugs me more than anything." She stood up suddenly, slammed her cup on the table, and walked to the coffeepot.

Words ran straight from Leigh's brain to her mouth. "You think your father knew something about those deaths in 1949, don't you?"

The anger that flickered in Maura's eyes made Leigh flinch a little, but the fire soon fizzled into something more like guilt. Maura turned away, then refilled both coffee cups and sat back down. "I can't help it," she said solemnly. "It just wasn't like him. You met him—you know what he was like. He was discreet enough when he needed to be, but he loved to talk about old cases, local lore."

Leigh took a sip of coffee and stayed quiet. The early morning hours had always been good for getting Maura's tongue rolling.

"He really shouldn't have—" the policewoman continued, "but sometimes he'd talk about unsolved cases over the dinner table. Mom was brilliant with that sort of thing—and he kidded me about becoming a detective someday. But even when I was a kid, I thought he acted weird about the Fischer case. The most famous crime ever to hit Avalon, and he wouldn't talk about it. He just wouldn't."

"And your mom?"

Maura shook her head. "I've asked her about 1949 over and over, and she insists she knows nothing more than I do—and that Dad never did talk about it."

"But she was there!"

"She was thirteen. How much do you remember from when you were thirteen?"

Leigh could think of a few things, none particularly pleasant, and certainly none with crime-solving potential. "But Mellman was there too. And Vestal—did he know Robbie Fischer?"

Maura shook her head again. "He grew up in Bellevue—different school system back then. He and Dad didn't get to be friends until later. As for Mellman, he's no help. He's pulled all the relevant police files, and he'll talk about the facts of the case, but I can't get anything else out of him. Whenever I ask him anything personal, like what kind of relationship he and my dad had with Robbie Fischer, he looks at me like I'm prying. The whole business seems to make him—well, sad." She let out a long sigh and downed the fresh cup in one motion. "Enough already. Good night, Koslow."

Leigh's eyelids were unbearably heavy, but she hated to lose the moment. "So, Officer Polanski. Who did something naughty in 1949? Who wants to cover it up now?"

Maura stood up and pushed her chair back under the table. "I don't know—and I'm not going to figure it out tonight. I'm off tomorrow, so I'll come by and see if I can lend you guys a hand with the search." She started toward the door but turned around. "If you want to keep brainstorming, think about this. This house sat vacant for years. If Paul Fischer hid anything in it, it's been here all along. But no one wanted it until now. Why?"

Exhaustion, unfortunately, did not ensure sleep. Leigh drifted in and out of consciousness, and nightmares. Her finches were dead, and they were in the house. Their lifeless bodies appeared in the drawer she opened, in the towel she pulled out of the closet, in her cereal box. She would rouse herself to end the dream, only to fall helplessly back into it. Six times she leaned over the edge of her bed to make sure Mao Tse was safe underneath. Only at five, when the cat finally decided to brave life on top of the mattress, did Leigh sleep soundly—her arm loosely cuddling the warm lump of black fur.

At nine-thirty, she roused herself with a yawn and shuffled over to look out the window. The Sunday morning sky was blue, its beauty marred by the white smoke piles of Neville Island, which tilted downstream in the breeze. A tall, lanky man in a blue-gray uniform leaned against a tree near the patio, also admiring the view. Leigh smiled. She could live with a few extra males around the place.

Cara was in the breakfast nook, the table spread with house sketches. She nodded at Leigh and pierced a pickled onion floating in a jar of *giardiniera*. Leigh winced. "That isn't breakfast, is it?"

"Of course not," Cara replied. "This is a mid-morning snack. Some of us got up at a decent hour."

Leigh's eyes narrowed. "Well, none of us got to bed at a decent hour."

"Touché," Cara returned. "I made pancakes earlier. You can heat some up if you want. I'm not going to church this morning. I have a plan."

Leigh didn't doubt it.

"We've done a thorough job with the first floor, and my mom and I took care of the second. It has to be in the basement or the attic. . . ."

Leigh dumped the dirty decaf filter, filled a fresh one with regular, and poured already hot tap water into the back of the coffee maker. Her cousin's elaborate plan of attack drifted in one ear and out the other as she held her cup impatiently in the spot where the pot should be. Drip. Drip. Drip.

Her brain began to function as she fed it one swallow's worth of caffeine at a time. "Why now, Cara?" she interrupted, remembering Maura's question. "Why does someone want us out now? Couldn't they have searched this house themselves anytime since Paul Fischer died?" Having had a cup's worth of swallows, Leigh replaced the pot and sat down to wait for more.

Cara fished out a pickled hunk of cauliflower with her fork, and Leigh quickly replaced the bottle top. An empty stomach could take only so much.

"I've thought about that," Cara answered, smacking her lips. "The house was vacant for years, then Gil and I were in and out. We had a lot of redecorating done. We stayed here over weekends and holidays. But no one cared about that. The first inkling of a problem was the body. Which arrived, as you'll recall, the same time you did."

Leigh didn't care for the implication. "So what is that supposed to mean? You think somebody doesn't want *me* in this house?"

Cara looked apologetic. "No, no, that doesn't make any sense. Not really. Why would you be more of a threat than me, or Gil? Or better yet, all those workmen who were puttering around in here?"

It seemed as though, if Leigh thought about it hard enough, an insult was implicit in that statement. She chose not to think about it. The fact was, the body had shown up the day after she had moved in. The date of her arrival had hardly been publicized. Wouldn't it take time to plan such a stunt?

Leigh banged her forehead with her palm. "Of course!"

Cara looked up expectantly.

"The cash box! Didn't you find the box right before I moved in?"

Cara's eyes widened. "Last Sunday. Two days before."

"And a lot of people knew about that, right?"

"I suppose so. I reported it to the police. The family knew. And Mrs. Rhodis—"

"I.e., the whole city of Avalon, probably."

"Probably. So . . . you think our culprit heard about the money stash, and then began fearing that other hiding places might exist?"

"It makes sense, doesn't it?"

"Yes," Cara answered, "it does. There was plenty of time to search this house after Fischer died. Someone could have determined then that there was nothing here to worry about."

"Or," Leigh mused, "they could have thought they got it all out."

Cara's face lit up. "I bet it wasn't the money, after all. I bet it was the book!"

"The book?"

"The blank book I told you about. It was one of those write-in books people use as personal journals. It didn't have a word in it, but it had label tape on the front that said 'summer 1989.' What if that's what made somebody worry? Worry that there were other journals and that Fischer had hidden them too?"

"It would make more sense if they were worried about a will being hidden," Leigh insisted.

"No, it wouldn't!" Cara argued. "A will is worthless if it's not found soon after the writer dies. If Fischer had hidden the will, even with the cash box, the house would have reverted to the state long before his wishes were known."

Leigh knit her brow. "So you think Fischer left his will in a drawer or a box or somewhere, but kept his journals locked up?"

"Why not?" Cara continued excitedly. "Maybe he had always hidden his journals—since before 1949 even—when other people were living here too. Maybe whoever took the will and the other writings didn't know about the journals, or maybe they found some and thought that was all. But now that he or she knows Fischer liked to hide things . . ."

Leigh's racing thoughts were interrupted by the doorbell. She got up to answer it, wondering if there were enough pancakes for both her and a guest. The peephole showed an older, less fit security guard than she had seen out her bedroom window. Next to him, if she looked down at just the right angle, was a balding head. She opened the door.

The caller was about five feet four or five inches tall, and easily surpassed Cara in the belly department. He wore tired-looking dress pants with suspenders, and a white shirt with ink stains on the pocket. Leigh remembered him well.

"You OK with this man?" the security guard said brusquely. Leigh nodded, and the guard retreated from the porch.

"Hello, Ms. Koslow," the bald man began, all business. "Bob South, the *Post*. How've you been? I heard you had a break-in last night. Any relation to the body you found?" He stood expectantly, notebook and pen in hand.

She smiled. "Hello, *Bab*. We meet again. Call me Leigh. That's L-E-I-G-H."

The reporter looked at her uncertainly. "Uh-huh. I'll make a note of that. About the break-in?"

Instead of inviting him in, Leigh stepped outside. She didn't want Cara to start blabbing, and she didn't want to delay her breakfast any longer than strictly necessary. Avoiding his eyes, she wondered what to say. If she didn't tell all, would he find out anyway? He obviously hadn't checked on the autopsy report. The press would have jumped on that. And the fish . . . she supposed she had inadvertently covered that up by going to the station in person rather than calling. No scanner messages to intercept. So what was she supposed to say now?

"Why would you think there was a connection?"

But Robert W. South was no fool. He smiled impatiently. "Ms. Koslow, I've done my homework this morning. I've seen the autopsy report. I know about the threats—the note on the body, the fish. This break-in was another one, and you don't have this guard here for ambience. Somebody wants you two out of that house pretty bad. Any ideas why?"

Leigh ground her teeth. *Think, think, think.* What was police record was police record, but she didn't want her investigations into the 1949 deaths public. It was irrational, but now that they were so close, she didn't want anyone beating her team to the punch. Let him write another dry story with just the facts from the police, she decided—she'd get her name in the paper some other way.

"You know as much as we do, then. The police aren't being much help." As soon as the words were out, she winced. If that got quoted, she'd be the main course at the next Polanski table. She recanted. "I suppose you could talk to Officer Polanski. She's been doing most of the investigative work and really is very helpful. But she's off duty today."

South dismissed the suggestion with a wave of his hand. "Polanski's at the station, but she wouldn't talk to me. The whole department's in chaos over some old person that wandered off. Could I speak with Mrs. March, please?"

"Mrs. March is having some health problems and can't be disturbed," Leigh answered distractedly, wondering why Maura would be at the station. Did she know the missing person?

"Did anyone else see or hear anything else last night? Neighbors?"

A chill swept up Leigh's spine. Mrs. Rhodis! "No," she said adamantly, "no one was home. None of the neighbors around here pay much attention—you know, they're all pretty old and everything. I'm sure they were already in bed." She uncrossed her fingers behind her back and smiled. "Sorry."

South smiled back, but something in his expression

made Leigh doubt her acting skills. "Thanks," he said flatly. "I'll be talking with you again, I'm sure."

"Fabulous. Good-bye!" Leigh walked backward into the house, then scurried over to a front window to see if South was leaving. Cara was already there, watching him.

"What did you tell him?" she asked.

"Nothing," Leigh answered, "but he knows most of it. And I have a bad feeling . . ."

South, after having briefly rummaged in the backseat of his car and shared a few words with the guard, began walking across the front lawn. Leigh stamped her foot.

"Damn! He *is* going to Mrs. Rhodis's."

"So what?" Cara asked calmly. "It will all become public eventually. Maybe that will be a deterrent."

Since Leigh had no sound reasons for her actions, she decided not to defend them. She headed back out the door to intercept South, but didn't get far. Before she reached the bottom of the steps, Maura's car rolled up the boulevard and pulled into the only available spot, the grass on the other side of the driveway. Leigh went to meet her, a bad feeling in the pit of her stomach.

Maura stepped out of the car. She looked dreadful. Her skin was pale, and she was sweating too much, even for a hot summer morning.

"What's wrong?" Leigh asked, shaky.

"It's Mom," came the weak reply. "She's gone."

Chapter 16

"What happened?" Leigh breathed.

"She wandered off sometime last night." Maura leaned back onto the hood of her car and rubbed her hands over her face. "When we got home from your parents' house, she said she was tired, and she went upstairs. I didn't hear any more from her, and I assumed she was asleep." She paused. "When the call came about the break-in, I told my aunts I was leaving, and I took off. Whenever I'm out, we open the connecting doors in the duplex so they can listen for her, but they didn't hear anything last night. This morning she was gone."

So she could have been gone all night. "Has this happened before?" Leigh asked softly.

"She's wandered off in the day a few times, but never at night. And"—her voice cracked slightly—"never for very long. She's never gone more than a few blocks before either somebody recognized her or she recognized a house."

They were no longer alone, Leigh noticed. Cara, South, and Mrs. Rhodis were clustered at her elbow, and the guard was listening too—albeit at a discreet distance. "I'm so sorry," she said. "Just tell us what we can do."

Maura glanced furtively at Cara, then turned back to Leigh. "If you could help spread the word, I'd ap-

preciate it, but other than that, I want you to watch
out for yourselves. You have your own problems to
deal with." Leigh began to protest, but Maura raised
a hand to stop her. "The guys on the force are being
great. They're all out looking for Mom—most of them
on their own time—and Vestal is organizing volunteers at the Episcopal church. We're bound to catch
up with her soon."

"Is Vestal at the church now?" Mrs. Rhodis asked.
Maura nodded.

The older woman stepped over to the car and
pressed her wrinkled hands over the policewoman's
thick ones. "Don't you worry, hon. Mary Polanski's
as tough as they come. We'll find her."

Maura smiled appreciatively, and Mrs. Rhodis
headed off.

"Are you sure we can't do more?" Cara asked
gently.

"You need to find that evidence, if that's what it
is," Maura answered flatly. "The sooner the better."
She stood up. "I need to get to St. John's. I'll keep
in touch."

Leigh and Cara saw her off sadly. South had already
left, without a word. The women walked back in the
house and closed the door. There was work to be
done.

By late morning it was evident that South's renewed
interest was the tip of a media iceberg. He hadn't been
the only reporter in the city to connect the break-in
with the body, and once the story was out, it was way
out. A decade-old body, the threat of arson, and a
hint of mystery were excellent fuel for a dull news day,
and every television crew in the city wanted visuals of
the March house. Leigh did her best to fend off the
masses while Cara was content to stay inside, making

phone calls. The timing wasn't all bad—none of the news crews left without promising to run a picture of Mary Polanski on the next broadcast.

After the major locals had come and gone, and Cara had asked every Avaloner she knew—and many she didn't—to keep an eye out for Mary, lunchtime was declared. Leigh told the guards to shoo away any stragglers, turned off the phone ringer, and dug her answering machine out of an unpacked box. "We'll check it for important messages," Leigh explained as she plugged it in, "but we won't have to keep answering it while we search the house."

After scarfing down several rather excellent pimento cheese sandwiches, the women got a second wind. Cara went to get her maps of the house, and Leigh went to make sure the answering machine was working. It was already blinking.

She pressed the message button and turned up the volume. The voice was all too familiar. "Leigh dear, this is your mother speaking. Are you there?" There was a pause. "You weren't in church this morning. I'll assume you've been helping Maura. We'll be looking for Mary ourselves this afternoon. I called to tell you that we heard about the fire. Lem has to work until five, but as soon as he's done, we're getting his pickup and we're coming over to get your things. Please be ready. Cara will be staying with your aunt Lydie until Gil can come home. Your father agrees. See you at five-thirty."

Leigh cursed. "Too bad," she said out loud, rewinding the tape with a flourish. "I guess it isn't working after all."

"Any messages?" Cara asked, maps in hand.

"No good news, sorry."

Cara sat down and spread out the plans. "We're going to settle this, Leigh," she said firmly. "Paul's little legacy must be either in the basement or the attic. As soon as we find what this person is after, we'll make it public, and that'll be the end. By the time Gil gets back, it'll be like nothing happened." She was lost in thought for a moment. "Although I daresay he won't be pleased with me when he finds out I've kept all this from him."

Leigh tended to agree, but she knew Gil couldn't stay mad at Cara for long. It was Leigh he would blame, probably forever.

"Well," Cara announced cheerfully, "I'll deal with that when the time comes. Right now, we can't waste a moment."

It didn't take long to rule out the basement as a hiding place. The concrete-block walls were clammy, even in the middle of August, and conditions for long-term storage hardly seemed ideal. Furthermore, there were no obvious spaces unaccounted for.

The cousins walked back up the basement stairs, Leigh following Cara in case she slipped. "Why did Paul Fischer have to make this thing so damned hard to find, anyway?" Leigh griped. "Didn't he want it to be found?"

Cara reached the top of the stairs and turned around, her hand on her abdomen. "We've been over this before. He wanted to leave evidence that would be found only after his death. If he hadn't hid it, it would be too easy for Norman's killer to steal it."

"Maybe he already did."

"A negative attitude will not help!" Cara snapped.

Surprised at the change in tone, Leigh looked at her cousin's face closely. "You're having contractions again, aren't you?"

Cara looked away. "It's just the damn steps. Starts them off every time." She walked into the kitchen and poured herself a large glass of water. "I've got to lie down for a while. Will you start mapping out the attic?"

Leigh sighed. If the contractions got any worse, she was going to call Gil herself, and that was that. In any event, she had a strong feeling that neither of them would be in the house much longer. Not that she planned on allowing herself to be dragged off to her parents' place. A tent city maybe, but not her parents' place. She looked at her watch. She had about three hours before something hit the fan, one way or the other.

She was just about to start upstairs with the drawing supplies when the front doorbell rang again. Fairly certain the guards wouldn't let any of the press on the porch, Leigh went to answer it. It was Lydie.

"I told you my daughter lived here!" she said to the guard indignantly.

The younger guard that Leigh had admired out her window that morning merely smiled. "Just doing my job, ma'am," he said politely, then gave her a wink and turned away. She started. The only winks she got were from men who were either over sixty or capable of firing her. She watched his departing form with a new sense of appreciation. *Beats the detectives.*

"Leigh!" Lydie insisted, tapping her arm. "I asked where Cara was."

"Oh, sorry," she answered, closing the door reluctantly. "She's in the family room."

Cara, who was relaxing on the couch, sat up a little when she saw her mother. "Is there any word on Mary?" she asked.

Lydie shook her head.

A strong wave of guilt spread over Leigh. She should have asked that question herself the moment Lydie walked in. Curse the guard and his wink! "How's Maura holding up?" she offered meekly.

"She's a strong girl," Lydie answered sadly, "but the more time that passes, the more we all worry. Mary didn't take her car, which means she must have wandered off on foot. You'd think she couldn't get too far that way, especially with everyone looking. But with no sign of her at all, I just wonder—"

"You think she's had some sort of accident?" Leigh asked tentatively, her heart pounding faster at the thought.

Lydie shook her head. "Who knows?" She sighed. "But what else could have happened? She didn't get on a bus—the PAT drivers that were around have all been questioned. Plus, she didn't take her purse." Lydie was quiet for a moment, then looked at her daughter. "But I didn't come over here just to talk about Mary. I know about what happened last night." She struggled to keep the anger out of her voice. "Why didn't you girls call us? Why did we have to find out about it through the grapevine?"

"I'm sorry, Mother," Cara answered, sounding tired. "I didn't see the point in worrying you in the middle of the night. We're fine, and with the guards we're perfectly safe."

Lydie looked at her daughter with the shrewd appraisal only mothers can perfect. "The contractions are worse."

Cara didn't answer, but her eyes betrayed an anxiety neither woman could miss.

"What does Gil say about all this?" Lydie demanded. Cara looked away and took another drink. Lydie's eyes widened. "Oh, no, honey. Don't tell me you haven't told him!"

"I update him every day about the contractions," Cara said defensively. "It's just—"

"Just what?" her mother prompted.

"I'm afraid that I'm going to end up on bed rest.

When I called the doctor this morning I got an ultimatum. If the contractions get regular, I'm down for the count."

"Well, that's it, then," Lydie said decisively. "You're coming home where I can pamper you appropriately." She stood up. "I'll stay and help you pack some things. This snipe hunt is too stressful for you, and it's got to stop. Leigh and I can keep searching during the day if it makes you happy. But you've got to get away from this—physically and mentally—for the baby's sake."

Cara sat quietly, looking at her drink. Both women expected a protest, but none came.

Lydie began packing, and Leigh supposed she should too. After all, she'd wanted to get out of the house for days; the only thing holding her back had been responsibility for Cara. So why didn't she want to leave now?

The doorbell rang. Leigh skidded past Lydie and opened it. The young guard was there, as hoped, and his eyes were a brilliant shade of blue. Unfortunately, he failed to wink as Leigh acknowledged the man that brushed past him and barged inside.

Warren looked nothing like a politician. His hair was still wet, his jeans had holes in the knees, and his faded black BEAM ME UP, SCOTTY T-shirt had shown only marginal taste in its prime. Leigh's eyes widened. "No offense, but I feel I ought to warn you—there are reporters and cameras all over the place."

Warren looked briefly over his shoulder, then recovered. "Never mind. Are you OK?" He put his hands on her shoulders and studied her closely.

"Of course," she said, puzzled. "Why shouldn't I be?"

He exhaled, then released her. "I know about the break-in. And Mo's mom."

"You saw it on TV?"

Warren shook his head but didn't elaborate. He took Leigh's hands and pulled her over to the parlor couch. "Sit down. There's something you need to know."

Leigh's heart rate started climbing. She'd had enough shocks in the last few days and didn't care for any more. "Like what?" she snapped, pulling her hands away.

Warren, well versed in her tendency to shoot the messenger, took a deep breath. "When I got out of the shower this morning, there was a message on my answering machine. It was a fake-sounding voice—either a woman or a man trying to sound like a woman. They said—" He paused. "Well, the intention was to threaten my girlfriend."

Leigh looked at him as if he'd gone mad. "Since when do you have a girlfriend?"

He sighed. "They were talking about you, Leigh. I think someone has been watching the house and saw me come over—saw us leave together."

Her brow furrowed. "That's ridiculous. How would anyone know who you were?"

"I'll try not to take that as a subconscious insult," Warren said steadily, grinding his jaw. "You do remember that my mug was prominently displayed all over the county last fall?"

"Oh, right," Leigh said absently. "But I'm not your girlfriend."

"If you'd quit fixating on that, you'd realize that it doesn't matter how the caller got my number," he said irritably. "The point is, he or she did. And I wasn't happy with what they said."

She looked up expectantly.

"The caller said: 'If you want your girlfriend to keep her pretty face, you'll get her out of my house.' "

Leigh looked away. A generalized order to vacate was one thing. This threat was personal. Her hand rose automatically to her cheek.

Warren pulled it down. "I've already taken the tape to the police station, and they're on top of it. Nothing's going to happen, Leigh. That's what you've got Brutus for anyway, right?"

She looked up, perplexed. "Who?"

"Brutus." He tilted his head toward the door. "Mr. Macho."

"His name is Brutus?" she asked, distressed.

Warren frowned. "I don't know what his name is. Shall I ask him for you?"

Leigh ignored the sarcasm. "Cara hired the guards last night." She did her best to explain the night's events without sensationalizing, but that was a difficult task. Warren took it in uneasily.

"I assume you two are leaving now."

"Well," she answered hesitantly, "Cara is."

His voice rose. "What do you mean 'Cara is'?"

She stood up and began to pace. "Look, I've been ready to cooperate with this creep from day one. He wants me out, I'm out. But Cara wouldn't go. She held her ground, and believe it or not, I admire her for that. And now she's buckling, not because she's afraid of getting hurt herself, but because the stress is putting her baby in danger. You know how that makes me feel? It makes me mad as hell. I think this guy is a bully, and a coward! Why can't he threaten me in person? Why does he call you? I may be the world's biggest wimp—but right now I'm mad enough to choke the life out of this jerk myself!"

She took a deep breath. "It's hard to explain. I know that even if Cara isn't here, she's going to worry about this thing. If only I can find 'it' today and settle this, she won't have anything to worry about anymore, and maybe it will help the contractions."

Warren was not convinced. "If she's like you, she'll just find something else to worry about. You both need to let it go."

Leigh folded her arms over her chest. He studied her for a moment, and his steady gaze unnerved her. He always could read her like a book.

"I'll give you the afternoon," he said finally, rising. "I'm going to go find Mo's mother. If you're still here when I get back, I'm going to drag your sorry butt out myself." He headed for the door. "And don't think you're fooling me. You want to solve this thing for *you*."

Leigh's mouth dropped open. "Meaning what, exactly?"

He walked back over to her and put his hands on her shoulders. "Some free advice from an old friend. This isn't a game, Leigh, and you're not a contestant. Don't try to be a hero. You'll live longer that way."

He released her and started walking to the door, unaware that the back of his T-shirt made a nice post-script. THERE'S NO INTELLIGENT LIFE DOWN HERE.

"Warren?"

He turned. "Yes?"

"I thought you got over the Captain Kirk thing in college."

He gave her a reluctant smile. "Forgive me, friends, for I am a trekker. It has been six months since my last convention."

Leigh grinned as she watched him go. Maybe she *was* trying to be the hero. Maybe she did want to be the one to find all the answers. But wouldn't everyone be better off once this mess was cleared up?

She picked up her drawing supplies and headed for the attic.

Chapter 17

Leigh pushed Mao Tse's already flattened face with her toe and backed her out of the attic doorway. "Sorry, girl. I can't let you roam around up here. You might fall through the insulation or something." She pulled the thin wooden door closed, only to feel Mao Tse scratching against the other side. *Knock yourself out, cat.*

The naked lightbulb overhead turned on with a tug to its hanging chain. With windows on every side, the attic wasn't as dark as it could be, but a little extra light wouldn't hurt. She walked the length of the attic and back. The ceilings were high in all but the farthest corners, and the space could easily have been finished into a comfortable third floor. She wondered if that had been part of the original plan. Unfortunately, Anita's family, and the Fischers after them, had only gotten smaller with time.

Leigh ran a sleeve over her sweaty brow. The attic was hot and stuffy, but she tried not to dwell on that. She stationed herself at the far end and began sketching the layout, taking measurements of the walls and looking carefully at the floor for signs of a section that was moveable. After almost an hour of steady but fruitless work, she flipped over her sketch to see if taking notes could help organize her brain.

Paul Fischer
1949. Witnesses deaths. Knows who killed his father.
Doesn't say who. Why? Co-conspirator?
1980s. Writes will, perhaps naming father's killer in
it. May have other incriminating writings around too,
but hidden.
1989. Dies.

She made a second column and began in bold
letters.

VILLAIN
1949. First crime: Murders Norman Fischer.
1989. Second crime: Steals Paul Fischer's body from
funeral home. Why? Also probably steals will and
other papers from house.
Now. Starts to worry when hiding place is found?
Plants body on our doorstep. Threats: Fish, phone,
arson setup. Animal

She put down her pen, the nausea rising again. Why
would anyone want to hurt her pets? The finches were
gone. She had put their empty cage in her closet, and
no one had mentioned them since. But every time she
opened a drawer or a closet door, she flinched a little.
He had used fish before. What if—

She shivered and put the pen back on the paper.
There was no point in dwelling on what he intended.
The finches were dead, of that she was fairly certain.
And if they were dead, at least they weren't suffering.
She had had birds die before. Dozens, in fact. She had
killed two herself once by putting the cage outside
and letting their seeds get moldy in the rain. As for
Mao Tse, she was fine, and that was all Leigh cared
to contemplate.

She looked at the questions she had written, but she
couldn't answer any of them. No matter how hard she

wanted to forget what happened at the break-in, it mattered to the case. Did he really want to burn the house down? If so, why the knife? Wouldn't burning everything be enough?

But if he was only posturing in an effort to get the women out, he must be looking for something worth keeping. She made a third column with the title *it*.

IT
Evidence of Norman Fischer's killer, maybe Anita's.
Money/family heirloom

Her pen tapped over both possibilities, pockmarking the paper. She had been convinced that money was the root of all evil, and she still was. But there was no evidence that any of the Fischers had ever owned anything valuable, at least not since Norman squandered Anita's family money. Or did he? Perhaps he squirreled away more than just the deed to the house?

Leigh's heart beat faster for a moment, then slowed. If Paul Fischer had anything valuable, what good did it do him? He spent his whole life working as a clerk, and he was hardly a big spender. What, or who, would he have been saving it for?

She underlined the first theory again. Half of Avalon thought at least one of those deaths was murder. It made sense that Paul might know what really happened but didn't want it public. Perhaps he was involved himself. Perhaps he wanted the truth to come out only after it couldn't hurt him.

What if he just wanted to hurt someone else? Leigh frowned. She didn't care to participate in a petty scheme of revenge. On the other hand, if the person who was going to get it was the same one who hurt her pets, she didn't really give a damn.

Looking back up at the first lists, she realized she

was getting nowhere. If the killer wanted to avoid
being exposed, he should have burned the house down
at the first opportunity—there was no point in harass-
ing them further by hurting the pets; they were just
innocent bystanders.

A thought occurred to her, and her heart started
beating fast again. What if the person who wanted
them out didn't know what they were looking for?
What if they just wanted to know what happened in
1949? Wheels in her brain started turning steadily. The
person would have to search the house himself, so no
one else would find the evidence. The threats would
make sense—they had to stop Cara and Leigh from
finding "it" first. Were they worried that Fischer
would incriminate them? Perhaps even unjustly? Or
were they trying to protect someone else?

Leigh turned over the sheet and began to scribble.

GOAL
To find the evidence before we do.

THREATS/BARRIERS
Body
Fish
Fake arson attempt
Pet—

She stumbled over the word again. She couldn't
bear to print the one that came into her head. It was
silly, but she just didn't want to look at it. She wrote
"Pet harassment," then skipped to the next line.

Threat on "boyfriend's" answering machine
Mary

The word stared Leigh back in the face, and her
eyes widened. She wasn't sure why she had written it.

Mary's disappearance was certainly one in a series of stressful events, but it could hardly be blamed on this villain.

Or could it?

The attic was sweltering, but Leigh suddenly felt cold. Maura had been planning to help with the search today. All the police had been on alert. But since Mary's disappearance, Maura had been occupied, and the entire city of Avalon was distracted. Coincidence?

The walls of the attic suddenly seemed steeper, lower. The corners had grown darker. Threats were one thing; action was another. She shivered. What if *he* had Mary?

Deciding to think no more, she collected her things and headed for the stairs. Only after opening the door did she step back in to turn off the light. Mao Tse was asleep at her post, and Leigh scooped her up and jogged down the stairs. It was time to get out of this place—guards or no.

Back downstairs, by the light of the afternoon, everything seemed normal. Cara was asleep on the couch in the family room, an empty glass of water on the floor by her side. Lydie had several suitcases packed and was on her way to the door. "I'm glad you came down," she said in a whisper. "Can you stay with her while I take a load over? I'll come back again and pick her up before supper."

Leigh nodded.

"Thanks, honey." Lydie smiled. "You've been good to her. I know neither one of you wants to go back with the old folks, but under the circumstances it's best."

"I'll be happy to come keep Cara company," Leigh replied, "but I won't be staying at my parents. I'm—" She thought for a moment. She didn't know where she was going. "I'm going to crash with a friend."

Lydie studied her and smiled, squeezing her arm. "Good luck, my dear." The last part of the phrase hung unspoken in the air. *You'll need it.*

"*Leigh!* Leigh? Are you here?" Cara's high-pitched voice carried from the family room to the bedroom overhead, where Leigh was packing an overnight bag. She rushed down the stairs in two and threes, swung around the banister, and hurried down the hall.

Cara was lying on the couch, feet tucked up like a child, her hands on her belly. Her voice was quieter. "Leigh. Good. You're still here."

"Of course I'm still here."

When they were children, Leigh had been the one who spooked easy. Cara was never frightened of anything. Spiders, snakes, triple daredevil hot sauce, dates with older boys—all were taken in stride. She got concerned occasionally, anxious very rarely, but never, ever scared.

Until now. The pitch of her voice had warned Leigh; now the look in her eyes confirmed it. Cara was terrified.

"Tell me what's wrong." Leigh's adrenaline surged, but she made herself stay calm. "The contractions? They're regular now?"

Cara nodded. "Almost every five minutes."

Leigh was on autopilot. "Tell me where to find your doctor's number."

The call to the doctor confirmed what Leigh already knew. She had to get Cara to the hospital. She moved mechanically, helping Cara to the door, grabbing whatever necessities her cousin asked for. The middle-aged guard now stationed out front insisted on carrying Cara to the car, and his offer met with little resistance.

Leigh drove down the boulevard, past The Point,

and back into Oakland, where she swerved into the entrance of Magee Women's Hospital, taking a temporary detour over a poorly placed curb. After a seemingly interminable delay in the registration area, Cara was finally wheeled into an exam room off the labor suite. As Cara changed into a gown, Leigh took her purse and wandered out to the pay phones in the main lobby. The time had come.

She fumbled around in Cara's purse, looking for a wallet. She found one. A policeman wandered down the hall, and Leigh smiled at him nervously. This isn't illegal, she told herself, it just feels that way. Cara's wallet contained the usual—pictures of family and friends, mostly Gil, very little cash and a whole lot of plastic. Before long she had what she wanted: Gil's number. She picked up the phone and hesitated. She'd never made an international call in her life. She'd certainly never charged one. Collect? No. Gil would have a heart attack before she ever got to talk to him. She looked at the sheaf of plastic cards before her. One had to be a phone card.

No. She felt guilty enough already. She fumbled around in her own purse and pulled out her phone card. It was the least she could do.

After five minutes of clicks and pauses, a phone began to ring on the other side of the world. She wondered if it was a cellular. A happy, husky voice answered on the second ring. "Gil March."

No words came out of Leigh's mouth.

"Hello? Hello?"

"Gil, it's Leigh," she blurted. "Don't worry, Cara's fine."

"Leigh? What's wrong? Why are you calling?" the voice demanded. Gil was no idiot; he knew placation when he heard it.

Leigh chose her words carefully. "Cara wouldn't

have wanted me to call you, because she's fine and she doesn't think there's anything to worry about, but I thought you'd want to know that she's having more of the contractions."

There was a short pause. "Where is she?"

"We're at Magee, just as a precaution."

There was a longer pause. "I'm coming home, Leigh. Tell Cara I'll be there soon." The background noise had increased, and she pictured him packing as he talked. "I appreciate your calling."

"Sure. I'll tell her."

"And, Leigh?"

"Yes?"

"Tell her I love her."

Leigh swallowed hard. She was building up to a good cry, and she hated that feeling. "Will do," she squeaked, and hung up.

When she returned to the exam room several minutes and a few local calls later, a student resident was just leaving. Cara was still pale, but her face was somewhat brighter. She hadn't even noticed her purse was missing.

"I'm not dilating," she explained breathlessly, "so I'm probably not in labor. Not yet. The baby's heartbeat is strong. Hear?" A steady whooshing sound came from the machine next to Cara's bedside, which was connected to two wide straps around her abdomen.

Leigh's mood quickly deteriorated to panic. The baby's heart sounded wrong. She leaned closer to the monitor. It was the same "washing machine" murmur she'd once heard in a tiny Maltese puppy that tired easily. Her father had explained that a vessel outside its heart—which had allowed the unborn pup to borrow its mother's blood supply—hadn't closed after birth as it was supposed to. The pup had needed radical surgery . . . Leigh's own heart seemed to stop. It was too much.

"What is it?" Cara asked, worried.

Suddenly Leigh erupted into nervous laughter, and her heart started beating again. "Nothing, I'm just being an idiot. I thought your baby had a PDA—I forgot it hasn't been born yet!"

Cara had only a passing familiarity with veterinary medicine. She had avoided the clinic like the plague ever since passing out in the surgery at the age of seven, and she saw no humor in the present situation. She looked as though she'd been struck.

"Honestly!" Leigh answered, relieved and mortified at the same time. Could she possibly be any worse at this? "It sounds exactly like it's supposed to," she said firmly. "It's wonderful. Fabulous. Perfect. Just like this baby's going to be, when it's born. In eight weeks."

Cara smiled faintly. "Well, anything over six and a half would be fine," she said, rubbing her belly gently. "They're moving me to labor and delivery. They're going to get me started on an IV and monitor me for a while, just to make sure everything's OK."

"That's good news," Leigh said, trying not to sound stiff. It wasn't easy. She took a deep breath. There was no point in dragging the whole business out. She'd kept enough secrets. "I called Gil. He said he loves you, and he's coming as soon as he can."

Cara's eyes widened, then turned moist. "I'm glad, Leigh. Thank you."

Leigh's stomach tightened. Cara was afraid. Really afraid.

Chapter 18

Leigh stretched her sore neck and stood up from the recliner that had been her bed. At least this room had a window, and she knew it was morning. The prenatal floor was a definite improvement over the windowless labor room where she and Cara had spent most of the night.

Cara was sound asleep, and deserved to be. When the IV fluids hadn't done the trick, the doctor had started her on Ritodrine. The drug hadn't agreed with the patient, and after Leigh ran out to the nurses' desk screaming that Cara's heart rate was 165 and climbing, the orders had been changed. Unfortunately, the magnesium sulfate that was the doctor's second choice proved less than a miracle drug. The contractions, albeit not as frequent, had kept coming. For twelve long hours Cara remained upbeat while the drug made her face burn and kept her eyes from focusing. Only after Leigh had told every lousy joke she could think of and had offered Cara her ninety-fifth cool cloth did the doctor stop the medication and release them from the labor suite.

The contractions had never stopped completely, but according to the doctors, Cara wasn't in real labor. Her 33½-week-old baby was still in danger, however, and no one was inclined to take the situation lightly. She wasn't going anywhere soon.

Leigh stretched her legs and contemplated stepping out for a cup of coffee. She was about to get up when she heard a gentle rapping at the door, which was slowly swinging open. Two very similar-looking faces peeked tentatively around the edge. Leigh put a finger across her lips, and the women came closer on tiptoe.

"How is she doing?" Lydie whispered.

"Fine," Leigh answered. "She's been asleep since I called you last. They'll probably want to keep monitoring her really closely, though."

"That's just fine by me." Lydie smiled, moving closer to her daughter.

Frances sidled up to Leigh. "And how are you holding up, dear? I was so glad you could stay with Cara last night. Is Gil here yet?"

"No, Mom." Leigh yawned. "I suppose it takes awhile to get here from Tokyo." *He'll be here today if he has to hijack the Concorde.*

"Well," Frances continued, "Lydie is here to stay today, and I'll be in and out too, so you'll have plenty of time to pack."

"Pack?" With too little sleep and no coffee, Leigh's brain was in a fog.

"Yes, of course. Pack. I noticed you hadn't made much progress by the time we got there yesterday. Of course, I understand—with Cara's problems . . ."

Leigh's thoughts drifted. What day was it? Monday? She turned to her mother. "Maura's mom is OK, right? They found her?"

Frances rubbed her lips together, a nervous habit. "No, dear. There's been no sign."

"Two nights now. Maura must be frantic," Leigh thought out loud.

"Half of Avalon is out looking for her," Frances continued. "Your father was up at the crack of dawn taking a shift. But you need to concentrate on your

own situation. I brought you something." She fished
around in a giant purse sporting a red sequin cardinal
and pulled out a folded section of newspaper. "With
everything that happened yesterday, I figured you
didn't have time to look at this yourself."

Leigh snatched the paper, wondering how bad the
media blitz had become. She looked down and sighed.
It wasn't the Monday news page. It was the Sunday
classified section, marked up with red ink. She scanned
it briefly. The first two circled jobs were secretarial.

She put the paper on the floor and got up. "I'm
going to take a walk, Mom. I'll check back later." She
exited hurriedly and took the elevator down to the
main floor. Some fresh air would do her good.

The elevator doors opened to reveal the kind of
face that inspired sculpture. Square jawline, full lips,
heavy lashes framing hazel eyes, and a full head of
sandy blond hair. Unfortunately, the man connected
to the face looked as though he had just completed a
transoceanic migration. Which, in fact, he had.

"Hi, Gil."

Cara's husband had only one thing on his mind.
"Hello. Is she all right?"

Leigh delivered the most accurate, yet most inspir-
ing report she could muster, and Gil hastily boarded
the elevator. She walked on through the revolving
glass door to the parking lot, stopped, and took a deep
breath. Cara wouldn't be needing her anymore. But
Maura certainly did.

The surface of Officer Polanski's desk was not visible, nor was Officer Polanski. According to the young
woman at the front desk, Maura was not officially on
duty, but would probably be in and out. Leigh returned to her Cavalier in the parking lot and tried to
think what she should do next. It was cloudy, and

pleasantly warm inside the car. Her body made a suggestion, and her brain took it. She fell asleep.

She awoke some time later to the unpleasant sound of her stomach rumbling. The fact that it was past lunchtime was irrelevant, since she hadn't had breakfast. The nap had been refreshing, although it hadn't done her neck any favors. She tossed her head in small, painful circles and cursed herself for not being smart enough to lie down on the backseat. On the fourth toss, she noticed something—a small piece of notebook paper stuck under her windshield wiper. She cranked down the window and collected it. "Looking for me?" the scrawl read. "I'll be inside." Leigh smiled and hauled herself out of the car.

Maura sat slumped over a mound of paper, her chin resting on a propped-up hand. "Rise and shine, Koslow." She smiled weakly. "I thought about waking you, but I figured you could use some shut-eye. No safer place than the police lot, I suppose." She looked awful. Her face was puffy and her eyes bloodshot. "How's Cara doing? I heard she's at Magee."

"She's fine. No labor—they're just watching her."

"That's good. And how are you? Warren told me about the call."

"I'm fine," Leigh answered quickly, not wanting to think about it. "How can I help you? Gil's home, and I'm off duty. Just tell me what you need."

Maura's eyes moistened a bit. "I wish I knew what more to do, Leigh. I've made a hundred phone calls; people everywhere are looking—volunteers, police." She rubbed her chin with her palms.

Leigh could tell she wanted to say something but wasn't sure she should. "Out with it."

Maura hesitated at first, then finished in a rush. "It's just that—I can't believe she simply wandered off, or we would have found her by now."

The words echoed Leigh's own uncomfortable thoughts. She said nothing.

"Mom's never been gone this long without getting her orientation back, and once she did, she'd get back home—I know she would. She's a smart lady." Maura hesitated again. "It's almost as though something, or someone, is keeping her away."

The words seemed to usher an icy draft into the small room. Leigh hunched up and rubbed her arms unconsciously. Somehow saying the thought out loud made it more likely to be true. But what could she say? She couldn't admit her own worst fears. Instead she stalled. "What do Mellman and the others think?"

Maura waved the question away. "No one knows what to think. Mellman's a mess over it—his migraines are back with a vengeance. He gets out of sorts whenever anyone gets hurt in his borough, but I think he's taking my mother's disappearance personally—like he's failed my dad or something. He's been doing his best, though. Everybody has." She reached for a Styrofoam cup near her elbow but stopped, seeing it was empty.

Jumping on a chance to help, however small, Leigh picked up the cup and filled it, along with another one, from a pot two desks over. She wanted to help more, but she wasn't sure how. Was her idea a worst-case scenario, or was it a lead? She returned with the cups and sat back down. Perhaps mentioning it could help, after all. "Have you ever wondered if your mother's disappearance could be related to the problems at Cara's?"

Maura held the coffee cup close to her face, as if she too had felt a chill. Her words indicated the thought was a new one, but her face said otherwise. "What makes you think that?"

"Nothing concrete. Just a feeling."

Maura considered. "It's far-fetched, Koslow."

"I know that."

Silence ensured.

"So, did you do any more searching in the house before—well, before you went to the hospital?" Maura asked.

"We ruled out the basement. Only the attic is left." Leigh considered the implication. The attic had spooked her, but she could rally herself for a good cause. "If you think there might be some connection with your mother's disappearance, I'll keep looking," she announced. "If not, give me something else to do."

Maura ran a large hand through hair that hadn't been washed in a while. "Frankly, Leigh, we've got the bases covered right now. Your looking around the attic can't hurt, as long as the guards are still there. Maybe there is a connection." Her voice cracked slightly. "At least it would give us something."

Leigh had never seen despair in Maura's eyes, and the look she saw now was as close as she cared to get. She stood up. "I'm gone," she said. "Call me if you need anything."

That something would be blocking Cara's driveway when Leigh arrived was not surprising. The story had no doubt come out in the Monday paper, waiting to enlighten any holdouts who might have missed the Sunday night telecasts. But of the various vehicles whose presence at the house could be easily explained, a full-sized moving van wasn't one of them.

Leigh pulled the Cavalier hastily into a parking lot down the boulevard and ran up, her blood boiling. "What the hell is going on!" she yelled at the two muscular men who were maneuvering the parlor couch through the front door. They managed to ignore her completely—only after the piece was loaded in the truck did one of them deign to acknowledge her.

"Is that your cat upstairs?" the chubbier of the two croaked.

Leigh breathed in. "Yes!" she answered sharply.

"Well, get her in a cage or something. We shut the door up there, but we got to go in and out, and I don't want to get yelled at if she runs off."

Someone tapped Leigh's shoulder. She whirled around and faced a security guard she didn't recognize. "Miss Koslow?"

She nodded, fuming.

"I'm Henry Torman with Ford Security. The boss got a call a little while ago from Mr. March. He's having the contents of the house shipped to a mini-storage, and we're off duty as of this afternoon."

"Mini-storage?" Leigh's head was spinning. "He can't do that! My stuff's in there!"

The thinner of the two movers walked up to Leigh with a clipboard. "Are you Ms. Koslow?"

She nodded again.

"You need to mark your stuff separately from the rest as soon as you can. We started with the fancy stuff, so that's already packed. Haven't got to the bedrooms yet, but we will soon."

"Who told you I was going to mark my stuff?" Leigh said, disbelieving.

The mover looked bored. "Mr. March." He flipped a page on the clipboard. "Your stuff's going to 625 Ridgewood in West View."

The Koslow residence. "The hell it is!"

Both men shrank back, looking at her as though her medication were overdue.

Leigh cleared her throat. "Um, sorry. But there's been a mistake. My stuff is most definitely not going to West View." *I'll live with it in the mini-storage if I have to.*

The mover shook his head. "Talk to Mr. March. We're following his orders until we hear otherwise."

Using a few expletives whose meaning she wasn't entirely sure of, Leigh stormed inside, threw her essentials back into the boxes they had only recently come out of, and coerced a panicked Mao Tse into her carrier. If Mr. International Bigshot wanted to throw his weight (and money) around, there wasn't a hell of a lot she could do about it. It was, after all, not her house.

Either Gil had read the morning paper or, more likely, Frances and Lydie had spouted off the whole story. In any event, he would not be pleased with her. When the consulting opportunity had come up in Tokyo, Gil had first refused it. He hadn't wanted to be away from Cara so late in the pregnancy. But Cara had insisted, saying he couldn't pass it up—that he needed time off *after* the baby was born, not before. He had agreed only when Leigh had promised on a stack of Bibles to move in with Cara and watch her like a hawk. And now—this.

She pictured his California-tanned face turning to an angry mauve. He had probably hit the roof and vowed that no one would set foot in the house again.

She sighed. He was efficient, she would give him that. Not just anybody could produce a moving van and crew within hours. Gil had a way with a cell phone. And a checkbook. But he hadn't been thinking clearly, or why would he have fired the guards? Her anger returned. Gil's motivations didn't matter. Nobody manipulated her—or her stuff.

She mumbled and grumbled through eight or nine trips to her car, then started the engine. Mao Tse rubbed her face on the metal grid at the front of the carrier, protesting with her usual grating tone. "Sorry, girl," Leigh answered, rubbing the cat's protruding nose. "You can blame your Uncle Gil for this one." She had a sudden urge to go throttle her cousin-in-law posthaste, but resisted it. Better to cool off first. And to find a roof to sleep under.

Chapter 19

As Leigh had a tendency to do in times of crisis, she soon found herself in the parking lot of the Koslow Animal Clinic. She lifted Mao Tse's carrier and toted the unwilling cargo through the back door. The kennel room was packed, but eerily quiet, as it tended to be on surgery afternoons. The only alert residents were a bored-looking cat on an IV line and a beagle with a brace on its neck, and neither were inclined to waste their energy announcing a visitor.

Leigh popped open the largest cage on the top row and set it up with litter pan, food and water dishes, and a soft, folded-up towel. She opened the carrier door and nabbed the ball of black fur inside just as it sprinted out. "I know you hate it here, Mao," Leigh said sympathetically. "But you can't stay in the car—and I don't know where I'll be tonight." She plopped the cat into the cage and closed the door, then poked her head into the hallway outside the surgery to see what was going on.

The associate, Dr. McCoy, was juggling a double load of patients while Randall dealt with an emergency—a Doberman with an intestinal obstruction. His eyes were trained intently on the surgery table, but his peripheral vision caught Leigh like a snake with a heat sensor.

"Leigh—scrub up. I need you."

Somewhat glad for the distraction, she did as she was bidden, and soon found herself retracting some unhealthy-looking abdominal contents.

"Whose dog is this?" she asked.

"New clients," Randall answered, in the ever so slightly stilted conversational tone peculiar to surgeons. "From McKees Rocks. Dog got into the kid's room and chewed up a bunch of toys. They waited too long to bring him in."

"Hmm," Leigh responded. It was a familiar tale. "Dad?"

"Yes," he replied, making a neat scalpel cut over a swollen piece of intestine.

"Did you ever meet Paul Fischer?"

His eyes met hers briefly over their face masks. "No, I don't believe I did. He didn't have any pets, you know."

Leigh sighed. "I wonder if anyone really knew him."

"Catch that loop of bowel," Randall chastised.

She did.

"Someone knew him well enough to hate him."

Leigh looked up sharply. "What do you mean?"

He shrugged. "To not allow his body to be buried, but to keep it—doing who knows what with it—until it became useful. That sounds like vengeance, not just lunacy."

Randall wiped his brow with the front side of his shoulder. He had opened the intestine and pulled out the dog's problem—a mangled green and white piece of plastic. He held it up for inspection. "What do you think? Teenage Mutant Ninja Turtle?"

Leigh shook her head. "Wrong decade, Dad. The turtle lovers are into body piercing now."

"Power Ranger?"

"Warmer." She looked at the plastic closely. "My money's on Buzz Lightyear."

"Hm." Randall went back to work, cutting out the dead tissue around the swelling. "OK, finger-clamp the ends for me. That's right."

Leigh held the cut ends of intestine impassively. "Do you really think that's likely?" she asked.

"I've never heard of Buzz Lightyear."

"No! I mean this person hating Paul Fischer."

Randall waited a moment before answering, then spoke while he sewed. "Perhaps you should look at why someone might hate him."

She nodded. "It keeps coming back to Robbie. Mrs. Rhodis insists he was very close to his mother. If Paul was in some way responsible for her death, Robbie would hate him. But maybe he couldn't publicly accuse Paul of anything because Paul in turn would accuse him of Norman's death."

"They had a mutual hold over each other," Randall said, trying out the thought. "Plausible enough. But answer this. Why would Robbie care now if Fischer's papers revealed his guilt? He's already AWOL. The police can't imprison him if they have no idea who or where he is. What difference would it make?"

Leigh sighed. "I don't know. Every theory I come up with has a hole you could drive a truck through."

Randall finished sewing the intestines back together and prepared to close. "Thanks, Leigh. That's all I need."

She peeled off her gloves and dropped them in the trash can, then took off her mask and gown. Randall rolled the dirty surgery drapes into a ball, disconnected the dog from the anesthesia machine, and rolled it onto its side. "I assume there's still no word about Mary," he said, removing his mask and throwing it away with the drapes.

"I'm afraid not."

"And no change in Cara's condition?"

Leigh shook her head. "Not that I've heard. I think I'll head back over there now and check on her." *And tell her husband he's being an ass.*

Randall touched the corner of the Doberman's eyes to make sure it could blink, then rolled back a thick black lip to reveal healthy pink gums. He patted the dog's back absently. "Will I be seeing you at the house tonight?"

"Sorry, Dad," she answered sincerely. "I can't deal with being almost thirty, unemployed, *and* living with my parents."

Randall smiled. "Isn't sponging off the old folks supposed to be hip nowadays?"

She snorted. "I've never been very good at the generation-X thing. I'll be staying with a friend."

"Who?"

A part of her resented the question. Did he think she didn't have any friends? The truth was, she really didn't have that many friends she could impose on with impunity. As delighted as she would be to announce to her mother that she was staying with Warren, his apartment had only one bedroom, and his mod couch/sofabed was a chiropractor's dream. She'd tried it once when her apartment was being painted, and her spine still hadn't recovered. "I'll give you the phone number as soon as I'm settled," she answered evasively.

The Doberman made a gagging sound, and Randall pulled the endotracheal tube out of its mouth. "Could you fix a cage up on your way out?"

She readied a spot in the kennel room for the semiconscious dog, and Randall carried in the seventy-pound dead weight and laid it down. He removed the IV bag from between his teeth and hung it on a hook outside the cage. "I'll be here all afternoon," he said, breathing a little heavily. "Keep me posted."

Leigh returned to her jam-packed Cavalier and drove to the hospital in Oakland. She picked up a badge at the visitors desk and approached Cara's door cautiously. No sounds were coming from inside. She knocked softly.

After several seconds Gil opened the door. She looked past him to where Cara lay on her side in the bed, her eyes closed.

"She's asleep," Gil said stiffly, pushing Leigh backward out into the hall. He followed her and shut the door. "And we need to talk."

Leigh avoided his eyes, which resembled the sparklers she and Cara used to play with on the Fourth of July. She decided to strike preemptively. "I gather I'm being thrown out of the house."

Gil ground his teeth, a gesture only he could make look attractive. "I trusted you, Leigh. You said you'd keep her in line, make her rest. And now I find out that since last Wednesday . . ." He took a breath. "If you were a man," he said simply, "I'd deck you."

Leigh had no response to that. She was all for women's rights, but she wasn't an idiot.

"How dare you let Cara stay in that house! You knew it was dangerous. You're not stupid!"

Leigh rankled on her cousin's behalf. "Are you saying your wife is?"

A low growl escaped from Gil's throat. "You know what I'm saying. Cara is impetuous. It's one of the many things I love about her. But she gets wacko ideas, and she lets them override her common sense. And she's pregnant. You know how those female hormones screw up a woman's thinking."

Leigh's eyes narrowed. "No, I don't believe I do.

Perhaps we should ask Cara about that. I'm sure she'd entertain the topic of her own mental incompetence."

The sparklers turned into Roman candles. "You should have known better. You should have called me."

He had struck a raw spot, but Leigh held her ground. "I was planning on it," she confessed. "But Cara convinced me that you would be unable to resist your own hormonal inclinations to protect her, and would screw up your job in Tokyo. She didn't want that to happen."

Leigh decided that the veins standing out in Gil's neck were not so attractive. He made more guttural noises, but kept his voice down. "I could have protected her, and the baby, and the house. It was my job. I had a right to know."

"Would you have rushed back here?"

"Of course I would have!"

"And would your taking off have stalled the project? Made you miss the deadline? Would you have had to go back to Tokyo even closer to the due date, or after the baby was born?"

He blinked.

Aha. "Perhaps a few extra days did make a difference?"

He paused and looked away. "The project is finished. We wrapped it up shortly before you called."

Leigh smiled slyly. "Well. Congratulations."

Gil looked uncomfortable. "Thank you."

Relaxing a little, Leigh decided to push the envelope. The irony of her defense of Cara's independence did not escape her, but she was on a roll. "Your wife is a grown woman. She has her moments, I'll grant you. But she's not stupid. And she can take care of herself. Not telling you about the threats was her decision, not mine. And I respected that. Maybe you should respect her judgment too."

Gil's eyes turned angry again. Leigh looked at the clenched fists that led up smooth arms to broad shoulders. That familiar little twist in her gut was back. A subject change was in order.

"Can I stay at the house until I get another place?"

He looked at her as though she had asked to bungee jump off the roof. "Of course not! It isn't safe."

"Well, not now that you fired the guards, anyway!"

Something flickered in his eyes, but she wasn't sure what. "Your stuff is at your parents' house. You can do whatever you want with it. Cara and I will be moving into a rental as soon as she's discharged. I have a realtor looking now. As for the house, I don't care what happens to it."

"That's good," Leigh retorted, "because it'll be burned to the ground within a week."

"Great!" he said sincerely. "I can use the insurance money. God knows no one will buy that mausoleum now. We'll find a new house. In Franklin Park. Or maybe Seattle."

Leigh decided to stop fighting. In a way, she agreed with him. She wouldn't mind seeing the house burn down, considering all the trouble it had caused. But certain questions had to be answered first. And if the house burned, they might never be.

She supposed that was the idea.

"Gil? Leigh?" The sound of Cara's voice drew them both inside quickly. "What are you arguing about?"

Leigh sat down on the edge of Cara's bed. "We weren't arguing. Just one of my typical trademark animated discussions."

Cara eyed her suspiciously but let it go. "It looks like I'll be in here a few days," she said, resigned. "Are you going to be OK at the house by yourself?

I'm sure it's perfectly safe with the guards, but don't feel like you have to stay there if you don't want to. Gil can get you a temporary apartment until you find one you really like."

Leigh resisted the urge to glare at Gil out of the corner of her eye. He could be the one to tell his wife her dream house was soon to be ashes. It was his fault, anyway.

"Don't worry about me. Everything's under control. You just worry about yourself and the baby. On second thought, strike that. Don't worry at all."

Cara smiled. "I'm trying. Everything seems better now." The look of adoration she gave Gil made Leigh feel queasy. "But my treasure-hunting days appear to be over, at least for now. Just promise me you'll tell me if anything else happens." She looked at Leigh purposefully. "I'll be dying of curiosity, you know, and bored to death in this bed."

Gil walked over and put his hands on Cara's shoulders. "No one's going to let you get bored. I have at least six weeks' worth of stories to tell you about Tokyo."

"I'll bring you some library books," Leigh said, ignoring him. "Did you find that one by Irma Sacco, the one about the ghost that returns to avenge his father's death?"

"No." She smiled. "I never did."

"You'll like it. It has a happy ending. At first the heroine's boyfriend is kind of a stick in the mud, but then the ghost puts a spell on him."

"Oh, really?" Cara grinned. "What kind of a spell?"

"He thinks he's Miss Marple."

Cara laughed heartily. "Wonderful. Bring it in."

Leigh got up to leave, and Gil hastened to open the door. "I suppose a little light reading might do her good," he said. "Thank you, Leigh. Good-bye."

Leigh let him close the door behind her, and smirked. Her original assessment had been right. He had no sense of humor.

She decided to make herself useful at the volunteer search headquarters, and perhaps seek inspiration about whose friendship she could impose on. St. John's fellowship hall was buzzing with activity—about a dozen people milled about talking on cell phones, arranging stacks of flyers, and making maps. Vestal Fields sat imperiously behind a long folding table, a lit cigar in one hand, a lengthy printout in the other.

Leigh noted that he had, miraculously enough, escaped undue persecution by the media. His skills as a spin doctor were not to be sneezed at: a body had been stolen from his establishment a decade or so ago (before security measures were tightened)—he regretted the incident, but was grateful for the chance to properly reinter the deceased. Patrons could be reassured that their loved ones would be treated with only the greatest of respect . . . yada yada. He had been wise, she supposed. Dealing with this now was far better than dealing with a necrophilia scandal back then.

"Hello, Mr. Fields," she said sweetly, remembering her previous persona. "You're so wonderful to be doing this."

If Vestal held grudges against manipulative women, he didn't show it. He smiled broadly. "Nonsense. Mary's like a sister to me. Have you come to help?"

"Yes," she answered with a blink. "Whatever you need."

Vestal walked her over to a table set up with two fax machines. "We've sent pictures of Mary to all the hospitals in the area. Now we're widening the field.

Can you send the flyer to this list of places in West Virginia?"

Leigh nodded, but pretended ignorance of the fax machine. Vestal offered a demonstration, and when he was thoroughly buttered, she went in for the kill. "We've moved out of the house, you know. It was foolish, our staying there. We should have listened to you." She couldn't remember whether he had ever suggested they move out, but it didn't matter. He would take credit for it anyway.

Vestal's cheeks reddened. "I'm just glad you girls are all right. Nasty business, that."

"It's all so confusing," she continued, "especially the part about 1949. Just out of curiosity, did *you* know Robbie Fischer?"

The right buttons had been pushed, but Vestal couldn't deliver. "Sorry," he said sincerely. "I knew about him, of course, after the fact. But our paths never crossed."

Leigh must have looked disappointed. Vestal's eyes lit up for a moment. Then he smiled in satisfaction and leaned close to her ear. "I did help embalm his parents, though, God rest their souls."

She leaned away as a reflex. "You did? But how old were you?"

"Seventeen or eighteen, I suppose." His face shone with pride. "I was doing some myself by then. I don't remember them all, but no one could forget the Fischers. Huge scandal, you know. Huge. And him with a bullet hole in his head."

It was ghoulish to care, but she couldn't help it. "You saw the actual bullet wound?"

Vestal nodded solemnly.

"Did you think it was a suicide?" Leigh pressed.

He looked at her curiously from behind an ill-formed smoke ring. "I'm a funeral director, my dear, not a coroner. I do remember hearing that there were powder burns on his hand, and that his prints were on the gun. Sounded pretty open-and-shut. The rest was just a lot of tongues wagging, I always thought."

"Oh," Leigh said, somehow disappointed. She decided to try another angle. "Do you remember Chief Polanski ever talking about Robbie's disappearance?"

He considered, then shook his head. "I don't think so. Not something he or Mellman ever liked to talk about."

Leigh sighed. She was getting tired of hearing that.

"No, wait! Chief Polanski did mention Robbie once."

She was all ears. Vestal beamed at the captive audience and proceeded. "A ways back, maybe twenty years ago, there was a real tragedy in Avalon. A thirteen-year-old boy beaten to death by his father. It was a horrible thing. The whole town was disturbed by it, but the chief and Mellman—they took it really hard. Being police, you know, they're used to most things. But this kid got to them. At first I thought it was because of Mellman's past."

Leigh's brow furrowed. "His past?"

Vestal looked at her with surprise. "Ever wonder how he got that W. C. Fields schnoz?"

She shook her head.

"The same way as W.C. Dear old dad."

Leigh felt a wave of pity for the new chief. Evidently Robbie wasn't the only one who had grown up in a troubled home.

"Bill Mellman was a first-class bast—uh, rascal. Drank too much, got mean. Used to beat up on Ethyl—his wife—pretty bad. Finally got himself stabbed to death in a bar brawl." Vestal paused and shook his head.

Apparently Chief Mellman's dad didn't deserve a "God rest his soul."

"Anyway," Vestal continued, "I thought that's why they were so upset about the thirteen-year-old being killed, but it was more than that. Polanski told me the kid looked a lot like Robbie Fischer."

Leigh's head began to swim. "Like Robbie?"

"Physically. You know. A certain resemblance. Chief Polanski said that Robbie had been abused as well, and that the kid's death brought up a lot of bad memories."

She considered. "Bad memories of Robbie's abuse, or bad memories of his disappearance?"

Vestal shrugged. "Bad memories, period, if you ask me. The three of them were tight, so I suppose they had some good times, but it sounds like their fathers—except for Polanski's—made their lives pretty miserable. Things were really bad for Mellman especially, when his father was alive—then Robbie took off without a word and never came back. Eventually the boys had to face the fact that the three musketeers were now two, and that Robbie was dead, God rest his soul."

"But was he?" she wondered out loud.

His eyes twinkled. "Romanticizing a bit, aren't you?"

She was offended and apparently looked it.

"I don't mean to burst any bubbles," he said apologetically, "but the poor boy was fourteen, and he was alone with no money in a big city in 1949. The odds weren't good."

"But not impossible."

Vestal grinned. "You really want to believe that boy is alive, don't you? May I ask why?"

Leigh didn't have an answer. Maybe she did want Robbie to be alive and well. And maybe she didn't.

*   *   *

Somewhere in the middle of Leigh's forty-second fax transmission, Maura checked in, looking worse than ever. She exchanged a few words with Vestal, then sat down on the hard tile floor beside the fax desk.

"Haven't you slept at all?" Leigh asked, concerned.

"I got a few hours in earlier today," Maura said dismissively. "Sleep deprivation I can do. How are things at your end?"

"I'm a faxing wizard, as you can see," Leigh answered, working as she talked. "As for the contractions and the search, they're both slowing. Gil has sicced the dogs on me—I'm no longer allowed in the house. He's had everything moved out."

Maura whistled softly. "Cara's husband is the protective type, eh?"

"You could say that. And Cara doesn't know—she thinks I'm still staying there."

"You need a place to stay?"

Leigh had hoped for an invitation. "As a matter of fact, I do. My stuff is all at my parents', but I'm afraid if I go back there, I'll never come out."

Maura grinned tiredly. "I can picture that. Your mom would be happier with you under lock and key."

"Polanski?" The women looked up at an officer Leigh didn't recognize. "We've got a Jane Doe."

Maura scrambled up off the floor, then looked into his eyes. Her huge frame sagged like a dishcloth. "You mean a body," she said flatly.

The officer nodded.

Chapter 20

"Beaver County Sheriff's Department pulled a woman's body out of the Ohio a half hour ago. Near Shippingport. She's on her way to the medical center in Beaver."

Not a muscle in Maura's body moved, and the officer squirmed a little. "We don't know much else, Maura. They said Caucasian female, approximately six feet tall. It could be anybody. But we knew you'd want to check it out."

Maura nodded. "Appreciate it," she said tonelessly. "I'm on my way."

The officer looked uncomfortable. "Do you want me to drive you? I'm on duty, but I could get—"

"No need." Maura waved him off. "I'm gone already." She withdrew a set of keys from her pocket, gave them a shake, and headed for the door.

Leigh hastened to catch up. She had to do something. "I'm driving," she said firmly.

Maura's blue eyes were weary, but the fire was still behind them. "I'm queasy enough already, Koslow. You're not driving me anywhere. But if you want to come . . ." She paused. "I'd like that."

A smile and a nod sealed the deal. Leigh looked over her shoulder at the small gathering of volunteers, who had ceased working and were watching the conversation in earnest. "The officer will fill you in," she announced, and followed Maura out the door.

They spent most of the trip in silence. Maura drove in her usual law-abiding, safety-conscious manner, but for once Leigh didn't complain. The fingers that held the wheel in a precise ten and two o'clock position were white as snow, and Maura's broad brow was dotted with clammy beads of sweat.

Leigh rehearsed a few lines of dialogue in her head, but none passed muster. She had no idea what to say. But she should say something, shouldn't she?

"I've never been to this hospital before." The words were out before she could decide against them. A stupid comment. But it would have to do.

Maura didn't respond.

She tried again. The direct approach this time. "This isn't your mother, Maura. I know it isn't. Mary is safe, somewhere. I have good instincts about this sort of thing. Really, I do."

A ghost of a grin broke the eerily calm facade, but only for a second. Leigh slumped back into her seat. Perhaps silence would be best after all.

They were spared the indignity of asking directions to the morgue by a local officer who spotted Maura in the hospital parking lot. "Polanski?" he asked.

She nodded.

The officer waved them over and began walking away from the front entrance and toward a side door. "I'll take you down." The women followed, descending from the friendly mauve hues of the patient areas to the more sterile-looking white hallways beneath. The officer swung open an unmarked set of metal doors and ushered them inside. He pointed at a cubicle with a short row of vinyl-covered chairs. "You might want to have a seat for a minute," he suggested.

Leigh began to sit, but Maura stood and shook her head. "Let's just do it, OK?"

The officer nodded sympathetically, and tilted his head in the direction of another metal door. "I'll tell them who you're here to see." He slipped through the door quietly and gave muffled instructions to someone within. In a few seconds he stuck his head back out. "They're ready," he announced.

Maura's pause was short. She pulled herself to her full height and opened the door with a strong motion. Leigh followed.

Before them, a human form covered with a paperlike sheet lay still on a steel gurney. The sheet bulged over a probable forehead, belly, and feet, but its stiff texture hid further detail. Leigh swallowed the bile that kept rising in her throat. Not counting her most recent encounter, she had never seen a body before, except at a funeral. Paul Fischer she hadn't known. The people she had known were laid out nicely, ready for the most discerning viewer. This body had been pulled out of a river. She tried to envision the face of her friend's mother, waterlogged and staring. She couldn't. It wasn't going to happen.

She moved close to Maura's side as the white-jacketed attendant reached for the sheet at the body's head. She could feel Maura take one long, shuddering breath before the barrier was removed.

Leigh hadn't intended to look. But she couldn't help it. What had once been a face was puffy, grayish skin, misshapen and eroded at its protuberances—a feast for the wildlife of the Ohio. Leigh's eyes froze on the corpse involuntarily, her thoughts halted with horror, her stomach lurching. She might have stayed that way indefinitely if not for the viselike grip that squeezed the blood out of her right arm. She looked up into Maura's face, which reminded her of the positive aspect of the cadaver.

It wasn't Mary.

Leigh felt a blow to her lungs, which were flattened inside her straining rib cage, and for a moment her feet didn't seem to be on the floor. Eventually she realized Maura was hugging her. She smiled and, as soon as it was physically possible to do so, took a long breath. "I told you so," she croaked.

"That you did," her friend conceded easily. "This woman is not my mother," she announced, her police voice back again. "But I wish you luck identifying her."

With that, Maura exited the morgue posthaste, with Leigh at her heels. An escort out wasn't necessary.

"Are you sure it's not much trouble, my staying at your house?" Leigh asked, feeling guilty. She had picked up her Cavalier at St. John's and stationed it, and half of her belongings, on the street outside the Polanskis' modest duplex.

"If it were, I'd tell you," Maura insisted almost cheerfully, leading her up to the open porch. "Honestly, Koslow, the house is too damn quiet. I can't stand to be here anymore. And I need to get in a few hours' sleep before my shift tonight."

"Tonight?" Leigh asked, disbelieving. "You have to go to work?"

Maura shrugged and opened the front door with a key. "Mellman's letting me search for Mom on the clock, but I've been using my own time so far. In fact, my weekend just ended. If you don't mind, I thought I'd grab a bite and sack out until eleven."

"Don't worry about me," Leigh said, entering. "I can fend for myself. In fact, I can fend for you too.

What are you hungry for? I can make anything that comes in Styrofoam and requires a tip."

Maura didn't answer, but turned her back and walked into the small kitchen that bordered the L-shaped living/dining room. She returned with a purple flyer. "Beijing Gourmet," she said with a smile. "Moo goo gai pan, if you please."

Leigh smiled back. "Done."

The cartons were cardboard, but the tip was gratefully accepted. Leigh looked around the tattered house, wondering where her friend usually ate. Since the dark wood table in the dining area was home to a computer, she suspected the tiny metal drop-leaf against the kitchen wall. She was looking for a rag to wipe the jelly stains off its plastic top when Maura collected her food, a fork, and a can of Mountain Dew, and plopped down on the couch. Leigh followed.

The garlic chicken was the best she ever had, but unfortunately, she could only pick at it. The image of the mauled face remained before her eyes, and Maura, though she ate like a starving woman, seemed suddenly depressed, more so with every bite. Leigh turned anxious when the policewoman wadded up her fortune and threw it against the wall.

"Bad news?" she queried softly.

" 'You reap what you sow,' " Maura scoffed. "Thanks a hell of a lot, China. I needed that."

Being a master of the emotion, Leigh knew guilt when she saw it. She put down her food and faced her friend squarely. "This is not your fault."

"The hell it isn't!" Maura roared, jumping up from her seat and beginning to pace. "I didn't check on her, Koslow, did you know that? I let her go to bed right after we got home. Then when the call came about the break-in, I ran out. I didn't check on her then, and I didn't check on her when I got back! I just assumed my aunts would hear her if she left. What was I thinking? She could have been gone all night Saturday, not to mention last night. How could I be so careless?"

"Now, you listen to me," Leigh began calmly. "You are the best damn daughter in the whole world, and if you say another derogatory word about yourself, I swear I will slap you. Who was the model child? The model student? Who fulfilled her father's every expectation and more? Who gave up her independence, a job she loved, and a place of her own to come back and take care of her mother? Who answers the same questions fifty times a day without ever losing her cool? Who reads books like this"—she held up a paperback from the coffee table—"so they know just the right way to manage a parent with Alzheimer's?"

Maura swallowed.

"*You* do, my dear. You're such a better daughter than me, I don't even like to think about it. Your mother's wandering was not your fault, and whether or not you noticed right away is immaterial. You've done everything you could for her, and you still are. End of discussion."

Her appetite returning, Leigh took another mouthful of chicken. Maura sat back down beside her, rubbing bloodshot eyes. "I'm afraid, Koslow."

The chicken burned its way down Leigh's throat. Guilt she could deal with. Having her personal fortress of strength be afraid was another matter.

"I'm glad the woman from the river wasn't her," Maura continued in an unsteady tone, "but a part of me just wanted to know. Do you know what it's like, not knowing what's happening to her? Whether she's hurt, or sick, or frightened?"

Leigh could only guess. She remained silent, and Maura went on.

"The worst part is, I don't believe she just wandered off. You don't believe it either. I know that, even though you won't say it. She didn't meander down Elizabeth Avenue and into oblivion without a single soul seeing her." She took a deep breath. "Her disappearance has something to do with the Fischer family."

Leigh's appetite was gone again. When Maura said it, the theory became reality. And the reality was scary as hell. "But why?" she asked softly.

Maura shook her head and sighed. "Either she knows something about the murders, or someone thinks she does."

One word stuck out at Leigh. "You said 'murders.'"

"Yeah, I did. Stuff like this doesn't happen over accidents and suicides. Mom was only thirteen, but her mind was a steel trap. She knew something. I think they both did."

A new thought drove its way into Leigh's brain. Both of them? Suddenly she could see what kind of torment her friend had been facing.

"I don't believe Robbie Fischer ran away hysterical and died," Maura continued. "I think he killed his stepfather, probably in retaliation for his mother's not so accidental fall, then took off. And what's more, I think he's been back in Avalon. More than once."

Until tonight Leigh hadn't been able to imagine how Robbie Fischer could show his face in Avalon without everyone in the city finding out about it. Now she saw a way. "If Robbie Fischer did come back, he must have been trying to hide. And if he was innocent, he wouldn't have any need to."

Maura nodded grimly.

"But he could have talked to some of his old friends. Friends who would help him stay hidden. Right?"

The wrinkles in Maura's brow deepened. She looked miserable. "My dad was the chief of police!" she blurted out suddenly. "If Robbie had a reason to hide, then Robbie was covering up a crime—a crime without a statute of limitations."

"Then your dad couldn't have known," Leigh said quickly, having no desire to slander the idol of the world's most honest person. "Neither of your parents knew. There must be some other explanation." She tried hard to think of one. "Maybe Robbie didn't kill Norman. Maybe it really was a suicide, and Paul blamed him unjustly."

Maura shook her head. "He'd have no reason to stay hidden once the death was actually declared suicide. Paul's official statement was that no one else was in the house that night—if he recanted his story, it wouldn't be worth crap. And even if Paul Fischer continued to threaten to 'expose' Robbie, he's been dead for a decade. Why be afraid now? If Robbie is back and trying to destroy evidence that he once committed murder, I have to believe it's because that evidence is damned good."

Leigh considered the argument. "But that evidence would have to say more than just 'Robbie Fischer' did it. No one knows who 'Robbie Fischer' is. If he's afraid, it must be because the evidence identifies him *now*."

Maura looked at Leigh with respect. "I agree. Robbie Fischer is back and worried about exposure at least, prosecution at worst. Of the people Robbie Fischer knew best as a child, none will talk about him." She took a deep breath. "Don't you see? It all points to the same thing. My mom knew something. Maybe she's on his side and maybe she's not. But somehow she got herself into trouble."

Something Mary had said at the dinner rose up in

Leigh's mind. "Time can change people. I wouldn't presume to predict Robbie's behavior now." Wise words from a wise woman. Perhaps she did know more than they'd given her credit for.

Leigh sat, silent in thought, but Maura headed for the staircase. "I've got to get some sleep. You can have the daybed in the sewing room upstairs, or the couch if you like—it's probably more comfortable. You'll find sheets and blankets in the closet next to the bathroom. Anything else you need?"

Leigh shook her head absently, her gaze falling on a stack of old albums piled on one of the chair seats. "Wait," she called. "Would you mind if I looked through those albums too? They're hers, right?"

Maura looked even more tired. "I thought I might find—well, something. I didn't. There is a picture of Robbie, if you want to look at it."

"Thanks," Leigh answered, her eyes lighting up. "And thanks for letting me stay here."

Never comfortable with gratitude, Maura simply nodded and kept climbing.

After unearthing a nearly full can of Café Vienna in the pantry, Leigh allowed herself the indulgence of settling down with a steaming mug and the dusty pile of albums. She loved old things. There was an aura about them that attracted her—they had experienced things she never would. Who had held them? Where had they been? What corner of the world, what moments in whose lives, had they witnessed?

None of the albums were dated on the outside. Leigh ignored the vinyl ones with the plastic-covered stick-on sheets, more interested in those that were leather-bound and filled with brown paper. They weren't stacked in any discernible order, yet Mary was clearly a historian, of sorts. One album focused solely on Chief Polanski's career, beginning with a photo of him and Mellman as teenagers graduating from the police academy and ending with a carefully laminated obituary. Other albums were more general, full of yellowed newspaper clippings from weddings, funerals, births, and graduations.

Leigh opened each and flipped through quickly, trying to establish its time frame. She couldn't help learning quite a bit about Mary—she was fond of local theater, enjoyed regional history, and was proud as a peacock when Maura tried out for the seventh-grade football team.

But where was the picture of Robbie? Leigh concentrated on the most decrepit of the books, and opened one to a black-and-white picture of a family in front of a new clapboard house. A girl of nine or ten, clearly Mary, smiled from ear to ear as she posed with a small spotted dog. A younger boy had turned his head the second the picture was taken. The couple looked young and full of life, and Leigh wondered if Maura had known her grandparents.

This album was mostly pictures—family, friends, the spotted dog. The photographs didn't seem to be in any particular order age-wise, as if they had been transferred from a pile without much sorting. Some showed Mary as a child, others as a young woman. Never handsome, but always with an air of dignity, her strong spirit shone through in all. Leigh could see why someone like Maura's dad could fall for her. She was a rock even then.

Suddenly noticing a bright yellow bookmark sticking out from farther back, Leigh flipped ahead. *Well, duh.* On the left-hand page was a large black-and-white photo of a school class lined up in front of a brick building. Mary was in the back row, surrounded by boys. On the right-hand page were three smaller

pictures. One of Mary's father standing by a car, one
with a corner ripped off—a teenage girl riding a horse,
and a tiny photograph of an adolescent Mary with
a boy.

Leigh peered at it anxiously, then pulled it from its
paper corners and looked at the back. ROBBIE, it said
simply, in pencil. She flipped it over again. Mary
looked gangly and awkward but certainly not shy. She
had her arm draped clumsily around her beau, who
was at least six inches shorter. His face was sweet and
childlike, that of a boy just short of puberty. Soft-
looking, wavy hair framed dimpled cheeks and kind
eyes. "Jeez, Mary," the expression said, "you're embarrassing me."

Leigh replaced the photo and shut the album with
a smile, for once letting her gut instincts override
logic. She would almost bet her life on it. That boy
had never killed anybody.

Chapter 21

According to the information desk at Magee, Cara March was no longer on the prenatal floor. She had been moved back into labor and delivery in the middle of the afternoon, and no incoming phone calls were allowed. Leigh's heart sank. She hung up Maura's phone and called home, praying that Randall would answer. She was lucky. "Cara's contractions picked up again, so she's being treated with more of the magnesium sulfate," he answered calmly. "As I understand it, there still aren't any other signs of labor."

Leigh breathed a sigh of relief. "So she'll be down there through the night again, probably."

"Probably. Are you OK?"

"I'm fine. Maura had a scare, though." She told her father about the trip to Beaver, leaving out the gory details. Not that the description would bother him, but she didn't want to think about it. "I'm staying with Maura for now. Tomorrow I'll start apartment hunting. And tell Mom that I'm working on the job too."

"Are you?"

"It's better you don't know that, Dad."

"Gotcha."

Leigh finished the call and started up the stairs. She had no idea what or where the sewing room was. She had had dinner with Maura and her parents a few times in the old days, but had gone upstairs only as far as the bathroom. Not that it mattered what the sewing room was like. Even the basement was preferable to moving back with her mother, or sleeping in a house known for mysterious deaths. Those two were a wash.

The narrow steps were covered with a worn green and gold shag carpet. Leigh smiled. Following fashion didn't appear to be a Polanski trait. The stairs opened up to a small foyer, where the carpet changed to burnt orange. A small bathroom and linen closet faced the top step, and a door off to the side, presumably the one to Maura's bedroom, was closed. A narrow hall led off toward the front of the house, with two open doors on one side and a heavier closed door, which appeared to connect the duplexes, on the other. Leigh walked past the first doorway and stopped, surprised.

Women's clothing was strung out over every surface—dresser top, bed, chairs, windowsill. The dresser drawers were open, with stray pieces of underwear hanging over the sides. She walked in for a closer look, wondering if this could be the sewing room, yet knowing that it wasn't. A brassiere dangled precariously from a drawer pull, and she unconsciously lifted it and put it back in its place. 42A. This was Mary's room. So why the mess?

"Oh, dear. We really should have tidied up, shouldn't we? Mary doesn't need to come home to this!"

Leigh whirled to face a stooped elderly woman who leaned precariously on a wooden cane. "I'm sorry," the woman said pleasantly, "I didn't mean to scare you. You must be a friend of Maura's." She extended a wrinkled hand. "I'm Charlotte Pratt, from next door."

The kindly eyes dispelled Leigh's alarm, and she

took the bony hand in hers. "Hello. I'm Leigh Koslow. You must be one of Maura's aunts?"

"Technically," Charlotte answered with a twinkle, "I'm her first cousin once removed. My mother and Chief Polanski's mother were sisters. But nobody bothers about such things anymore. 'Aunt' is fine."

The older woman's warmth was contagious. Leigh dared say she would be less accommodating if she found a stranger snooping in her cousin-in-law's underwear. "Maura's asleep—she was kind enough to offer me the sewing room for a few days," she explained. "I guess I'm in the wrong place."

"I'm surprised you didn't run in terror," Charlotte giggled. "Clothes thrown everywhere, scary old hag sneaking up on you . . ."

Leigh began to protest, but Charlotte dismissed her sputtering with a wave of a hand. "Don't bother telling me I'm beautiful, Leigh Koslow. I'm old, but I'm not stupid." She laughed again. "I am sorry about the mess. When we realized Mary was gone, Maura asked Judith and me to see if we could figure out what she was wearing. We were frantic, and a bit reckless—obviously. I never even thought about cleaning up."

Leigh remembered the descriptions she had faxed. *Wearing white cotton blouse and blue jeans with flowers embroidered on the back pocket.* "I guess you figured it out," she commented.

"Yep," Charlotte answered proudly, beginning to fold and put away the clothes. "We've been living side by side for eleven years; I don't imagine she owns a stitch we wouldn't recognize. She makes almost everything herself, you know."

Leigh nodded. Having this friendly woman to chat with set her detective sensors on. She cleared a spot on the bed, sat on its edge, and began to help fold.

"Where do you think Mary might be?" she asked tentatively.

"To be truthful," Charlotte began easily, "I can't think of a thing that could have happened that makes any sense at all. The Alzheimer's is getting worse, no doubt. But Mary's never been continuously incapacitated." She looked at Leigh out of the corner of her eye. "I was a nurse, you know. I'm not just prattling."

"I didn't think you were," Leigh answered honestly.

Charlotte appraised her. "Good. Too many people nowadays think a woman over seventy shouldn't know any words with more than three syllables, much less have a valid medical opinion."

"They're incognizant."

Charlotte guffawed. "He-he! I like you, Leigh Koslow."

"Likewise." Leigh smiled. "You have a theory about Mary?"

A pause followed as Charlotte took a deep breath. "I'm afraid to say what I really think. At first, when she disappeared, I thought she'd just wandered. Judith drops off at seven and sleeps like the dead, but I'm a night owl—and a light sleeper to boot. I've heard Mary get up and leave the bedroom before. I still don't see how she could get out of the house completely without me hearing her, but I can't say it's impossible. Especially if she was trying to be quiet."

"Would she do that if she was confused?" Leigh asked, confused herself.

"Unlikely," Charlotte answered knowingly. "When she's out of it, her wandering seems innocent enough. Like she's trying to get somewhere, not get away from something. But I couldn't swear she wouldn't sneak out for some other reason—while in perfectly sound mind. Maybe she got confused later . . ." She faltered. "I'm just guessing like the rest of them."

Folding the clothes gave Leigh a new idea. "She was wearing street clothes, but Maura thought she had gone to bed."

Charlotte touched a finger to her nose. "Right-o. Either she never went to bed, or she changed out of her nightgown sometime before the next morning. We found it on the chair, right there." She pointed down at the chair she had just cleared, then returned to sorting the clothes on the bed. Leigh was about to ask another question when Charlotte's expression transformed into a puzzled frown.

"What?" the older woman muttered, shuffling around to the closet. She opened the doors and examined the clothes she had put away a few moments before. Then she turned again, quickly enough to set her off balance for a moment, and sorted through the garments left on the bed. "Did you put anything away in the drawers?" she asked.

Leigh shook her head. Charlotte drifted about the room twice more, looking in the closet, the drawers—she even had Leigh check under the bed. Finally she sank down on the chair, her curved spine pitching her head away from its padded back. "I'm not sure I believe this," she said dryly.

"What is it?" Leigh asked, sitting forward herself.

"The pink shirt with the embroidered roses," came the low response. "And the T-shirt with the hummingbirds, and two pairs of white pants. And I'm not certain, but probably some underwear."

"What about them?"

"They're gone, Leigh Koslow. And they were here before."

Since the words made no sense whatsoever, Leigh had a moment of doubt. Perhaps this woman wasn't as sharp as she seemed.

"I'm not making this up," Charlotte snapped, quick to read her mind. "I know Mary's clothes, and those things aren't here. Now, maybe Maura did something with them—I don't know. But if she didn't . . ."

"Then what?" Leigh asked, still confused.

"Then someone came and got them. And I can't see why anyone would need Mary's clothes except Mary."

Light dawned, but it was dim. "Are you saying she came back here?"

Charlotte didn't answer. "No more speculating. I'll wake Judith and see if she did anything with the clothes. You ask Maura." She sprang up, somewhat faster than would be expected, and shuffled off toward the connecting door.

Leigh remained seated—why, she wasn't sure. Perhaps it had to do with those rare occasions in her college days when she had attempted to rouse Maura from a sound sleep. The memories were not pleasant ones. Once she had got her jaw clipped when a semiconscious Maura dreamed she was being shaken by a thug. Another time, when she had tried the remote approach with her rape whistle, Maura hadn't spoken to her for days.

She rose with a sigh and crept down the hall to the closed door, wondering if Charlotte's assignments weren't as arbitrary as they seemed. Judith might sleep like the dead, but Leigh, given the option, would rather wake her—sight unseen. She opened the thin door into a pitch-dark room, shoving debris along the carpet as she pushed. The hall light cast a shadow on Maura's form, sleeping peacefully on top of an unmade, oversize twin bed.

Leigh took a deep breath. "Maura?" she asked softly, from a distance. There was no response. "Maura?!" she repeated, louder.

"What? What is it?" Maura leapt up in one fluid

motion, landing heavily on the floor in front of Leigh. Leigh stepped back, but it was too late. The toes on her left foot were crushed by a heavy heel, and her nose was bumped by an elbow. "Koslow!" Maura thundered. "Damn! Why are you hiding there in the dark? What is it? Is it Mom?"

Leigh rubbed her nose and balanced on one leg. "I didn't mean to alarm you," she said diplomatically, albeit in a nasal tone, "but Charlotte sent me to ask you something important." *Let* her *take some of the rap*.

Maura waited.

"She's taken another look at your mom's clothes, and she thinks some things are missing now that weren't missing on Sunday. We need to know if you've moved anything—"

Maura was gone. Leigh hobbled off in pursuit, and caught up with all three women on the other side of the duplex. There was no time for introductions, but she presumed the sleepy-looking woman in the worn nightgown was Judith.

"Of course I'm sure!" Maura bellowed. "If you two didn't touch the clothes, nobody did." She pushed past Leigh and went back through the door toward Mary's room. Leigh hobbled after her again, catching a ghost of a grin on Charlotte's face as she did so. Her own eyes narrowed.

Maura was sifting through the clothes herself, quickly returning the room to near its previous state. "You're right!" she exclaimed. "They're gone. And they were here. I know they were."

She sank onto the bed, a wide grin on her face. Leigh looked at her questioningly. "Don't you see, Koslow?" She beamed. "Somebody got those clothes for her. She's all right! She's hiding somewhere, or

she's being hid, but either way she's being taken care
of. Someone brought her a change of clothes!''

Leigh tried to catch her friend's enthusiasm, but her
pessimistic side ruled. Did they really know Mary's
wardrobe that well? She couldn't begin to catalog all
the crap in her own closet, and she considered herself
an organized person. Mary's captor stealing clothes
from the house of a police officer? It was nonsense,
and Maura should know better. "But how could anyone get in here?'' she asked mildly.

"There's a key hidden on the porch,'' Maura said
dismissively. "Mom could tell them exactly what to
do.'' Her eyes lit up even more. "Heck, she could
even have gotten them herself! If she was careful.''

Leigh's skepticism remained. Maura was usually the
one who held back—who was cautious. The role rever-
sal was unsettling, at best. "But why would she be
hiding from us?''

Maura sprang up from the bed. "Who cares?! Don't
you get it, Leigh? This proves she's all right! *She's all
right!*'' Maura pushed past her silent aunts. "I'm going
on down to the station. The guys are going to love
this!''

Leigh looked at the faces of the two older women.
Judith looked confused first off, concerned second.
Charlotte looked thoughtful, and less than enthusias-
tic. Did they see what she saw? An overtired daughter,
a little too desperate for a good sign?

"Do you think she's OK?'' Leigh asked quietly.
"Maura, I mean?''

Judith looked at Charlotte; Charlotte sighed. "She's
been through a lot. A little hope won't hurt her. After
all, she could be right, you know.''

The sewing room turned out to be a small room
with an orange-upholstered daybed, a sewing machine,

a black-and-white television, and a rowing machine without dust. After noting a conspicuous dip in the middle of the daybed, Leigh grabbed a pillow and blanket and returned to the downstairs couch. She sank quickly into a light, fitful sleep, but was interrupted by the piercing shrill of an old-fashioned dial telephone.

"Hello!" she barked automatically, her mind still hazy. The shrill sound came again. Leigh cursed at the fist she was holding to her ear and picked up the phone. "Hello! What is it?"

There was a pause. "Leigh? Is that you?"

Leigh sank back down into the couch with the phone. "Yes, it's me. What is it, Warren?"

"What do you think? I'm checking on you. Is everything all right?"

"Well, we're out of the house, aren't we?"

"That's not what I asked. I know Cara's in the hospital—I sent flowers already—and I know you and Mo had a rough afternoon. Are you really OK?"

"I'm fine."

"No . . . new developments?"

Leigh paused, seeing through his question. "Out with it, Harmon. What happened? You get another call?"

"No . . ." he began reluctantly.

Her pulse began to quicken, but she fought it. She was tired of getting scared. "Then what?" she asked irritably.

He sighed. "It's the Channel Five news. I have a friend who's a cameraman there, and I'd asked him to keep his ears open for me. He just reported some unpleasant rumors about the piece planned for eleven o'clock."

Leigh waited.

"A reporter researching the house dug up the 1949

story. He seems to feel there's evidence implicating Mary Polanski as a suspect in the arson attempt."

"What?" she said, incredulous.

"I know it sounds ridiculous to us, because we know Mo. But it looks bad. Mary did disappear the same night as the arson attempt, and hasn't been seen since. If she simply wandered off, she'd almost certainly have been located by now. And being an Avaloner isn't her only connection to the Fischer house—she knew Robbie Fischer as a child. Her husband was the chief of police, and her daughter is currently on the force; she's a prime candidate for special treatment. And she's known to be mentally unstable."

Leigh's blood boiled. "She's not insane; she has Alzheimer's! Don't those idiots know the difference? And the rest of those facts don't add up to squat!" She couldn't help but think of the facts they didn't know. The puppy love. Chief Polanski's refusal to discuss the case. The missing clothes.

"There's still a good chance they'll back off it," Warren said hopefully. "Sometimes editors balk at these things. I just wanted to warn you—and Mo."

Leigh thanked him, assured him she was safe and sound with the door bolted, and put the phone in its cradle. She picked it up again to call Maura, but a glance at the clock stopped her. It was 10:59 P.M.

She settled herself in front of the Polanskis' aged television, switched on the dial, and adjusted the antenna. By the time the tube had warmed up and she had gotten rid of the snow, the story had already begun. Visuals of Cara's house, looking quite respectable in the daylight. There were shots from across the street, close-ups of the front door, and a side-angle view from the Rhodis's front yard. She held her breath as the reporter sensationalized the house's bloody history.

Mary's name wasn't mentioned.

She breathed a sigh of relief, but as the story wrapped up, her attention was drawn to the side view. Something didn't seem right. The picture was quickly replaced with one from the police station, where an officer made a bland statement about the Jane Doe in Beaver. A mug shot and description of Mary followed, with the innocuous lead-in of "Also, in Avalon . . ."

Leigh walked over and switched the television off. She stood for a moment, eyes focused on nothing in particular, her brain replaying the side view of the house. Something was wrong.

Chapter 22

She stood a few moments, her brow creased in concentration. Her sketches. Where were they? Vaguely remembering stuffing them into a box, she grabbed her keys off the counter and walked out to the Cavalier. She found the folded papers in a box next to her answering machine, stuffed up on the ledge inside the back window. Settling into the front seat, she spread them out over the steering wheel under the car's dim overhead light.

Her fingers traced the crude outline of the inside of the attic. There were eight windows in all. Two flush with the wall and six dormers. She frowned. Had she drawn them right? She had only managed to closely investigate the floor and two of the four walls when she had gotten spooked. If only she had finished . . .

She exhaled in a huff and folded up the drawings. She was stupid to have quit. The nonsense would end when the house's secret was uncovered. And the sooner the nonsense ended, the better for everybody.

She tucked the drawings in her back pocket, grabbed the flashlight out of her glove compartment, and started walking.

Like many of the narrow brick streets in Avalon, Elizabeth Avenue was steep enough to slide down on a snowy day, but on a warm evening in June, the trek merely made one's insteps sore. The Polanskis' duplex was just a few blocks from the boulevard, and after one had crossed that busy thruway alive, only a few more paces were required to reach Cara's door.

Leigh skirted the entrance and walked around to the side facing the Rhodis's house She pointed the flashlight up toward the roof, and her breath caught. She hadn't been seeing things, after all. Only one window on the west side of the house was a dormer. The other was tucked inside a triangular gable, protruding from the main roof with its own set of eaves. That window was flush with the wall.

She pulled out her drawings. There was no doubt about it—she had made a mistake. Either she had misdrawn the interior sketches, or she had been fool enough to quit searching too soon.

Which was it?

She had to know.

Leigh put a hand over the keys in her pocket. She could get in, all right. No problem there. And if someone saw her? Well, what difference did it make? She had every right to be there.

She marched to the front door and twisted her key in the lock. The door swung open easily, and she walked into the foyer and punched in the security code. She smiled as the unit acknowledged her. Gil wasn't so smart. He could have at least changed the code. She locked the front door behind her and turned on the lights. Would Mrs. Rhodis see them on and call the police? No matter. By the time they arrived, she'd have everything all wrapped up for them in a nice little package.

Unemployed Copywriter Solves Fifty-Year-Old Mystery.

Leigh smiled to herself and started up the stairs, flipping lights on as she went. *Offered Six-Figure Ad-*

vance and Film Rights for Book Proposal. The smile was still on her lips when she reached the attic door.

She swung it open and stepped in to pull the light chain. After dark, the single one hundred-watt bulb didn't accomplish much in the huge space. She shone her flashlight on the west bank of windows.

Her sketches weren't wrong. The windows were both dormers.

When she ran her fingers carefully along the walls flanking the far window, she was looking for something subtle. Some loose panel that might be pried away to access the dead space—the triangular spaces on either side of the window that had to be at least a foot and a half deep. What she found wasn't subtle at all. A rectangular outline in the wall near the floor, where the original wood had been cut out and replaced. She pressed gently on each edge. The top junctions split apart, but the panel didn't move. Sticking a fingernail in the exposed wood along the rectangle's top edge, she pulled. The door top popped out easily, folding down on flimsy hinges to rest at her feet.

The beating of Leigh's heart rattled her rib cage as she aimed her flashlight into the still compartment. At first she saw only more of the floor. Then the light reflected a tall object, with horizontal stripes. She stuck her head deeper into the opening. It was a stack of books.

Wedging her shoulders through the door, she was just able to reach it. Thinking that Paul Fischer must have been a small man even before he shrank, she pulled the bottom of the pile toward her. The stack promptly collapsed—with books toppling onto her arms and a cloud of ancient dust exploding upward.

She pulled her head out of the hole, coughing, and shook the dust out of her hair. One book had fallen

near the door, and she snatched it up hastily. The fine
gray-brown powder on its cover matched nicely with
her newly decorated forearms. She opened the cover.

It was a journal dated SPRING, 1968. She flipped
through the pages quickly, seeing the same stilted
printing she remembered from the poem. It was
Paul's. Paul Fischer's journal.

> All anyone talks about anymore is the war. On the
> bus yesterday, I tried to tell a man about how writing
> was a dying art. He told me I was foolish to think
> about art when young men were dying every day on
> foreign soil. I told him I'd almost died on foreign soil
> myself, at Normandy. He believed it, but it didn't mat-
> ter. He said that all war was wrong. We stopped talk-
> ing then. How can you talk with someone like that?

Leigh's brow furrowed. She agreed that writing was
a dying art, but as far as she could tell, Paul had little
to contribute to it. Unless, of course, being prolific
counted for something. She read a few more snatches
that complained about the war-obsessed society, then
put the book down and dug deeper into the cavity.

The journals were out of order now, if in fact they
had ever been in order. She wasn't having luck with
that sort of thing. The books were all neatly dated on
the front, either with ink or label tape, but she had to
pull each out and dust it off before she could read the
inscription. Not all the books were the same. Some
spanned only a few months, others years. A few plain
notebooks had been thrown in, several in pencil and
barely legible. She feared at first that the notebooks
were the older ones, but they were dated at random—
perhaps Paul had used notebooks whenever his current journal ran out of space, and before he bought
another. She could see now why summer 1989 was

downstairs in his bedroom. He had not yet started it when he died.

Leigh found a book dated 1943 and squealed in delight. How old would Paul have been then? Eighteen.

> I'm happy about it—why shouldn't I be? Father says he's worried about what everyone will think, but I doubt he cares, really. He doesn't want me to leave him, I know that. I'm all he's got.
>
> He told me maybe I should tell people another reason, like that I have flat feet. But I don't see why being underweight is any worse than walking like a camel. The Fischers have never been big men. If it saves my hide and keeps me whole, I've got no problem with it. Let the others get shot at. I'll hold down the fort on this side of the ocean. Somebody's got to. God knows we can't leave it all to the women.

Any simpatico Leigh had felt for Paul as a fellow writer quickly dissolved. He was self-absorbed and small-minded at eighteen, and hadn't changed by forty-three. She slammed the book closed. When had Norman married Anita? It didn't matter. What she needed were the journals from 1949. Where were they?

She put her head and shoulders back into the hole, then froze. Sounds filtered in the hole around her waist and echoed up to her ears. She pulled her head out and sat quietly. The squeaking wood couldn't lie. Someone was walking up the attic stairs.

Her breath seemed to catch in her throat. Who was it? She hadn't been afraid—not really—not since seeing Robbie's face. The lights were on. It was probably just the police.

But there were no sirens, no sounds from farther below. Just the steady creaking. Step. Step. Step. The person's progress was maddeningly slow. If it was the police, why weren't they calling out? Leigh took a quick glance around the attic. There was nowhere to hide, even if she had time. The hole in the wall taunted her. If only she didn't have such damn big hips!

Step. Step. Step. Leigh's heart beat violently against her rib cage. There was no point in thinking—she was going to meet this person, and she was going to do it with a dusty book or two and a lightweight flashlight. No way around it. She grabbed the flashlight and switched it off, then flattened herself in the corner of the dormer.

Step. Step. Heels creaked as they swiveled on the landing. The attic door was open. A flashlight beam appeared and shone through the doorway at the opposite wall of the attic, making sweeping arcs. Someone called her name.

"Leigh?"

She swallowed as the figure stepped into the light of the lone bulb. It was the blue-eyed security guard.

"I'm over here," she said, exhaling. "I, um, I forgot some things."

The flashlight beam swung around and caught her in the midst of the pile of books. "You scared me," she chastised.

The guard smiled. "Sorry," he apologized in a soft baritone. "I would have guessed you didn't scare easy. Are you crazy, coming back here by yourself at night?"

"Probably," Leigh answered honestly. "But I needed something." A thought struck her. "So what are you doing here? I thought Mr. March cancelled your contract."

"That's what we're supposed to say," he said matter-of-factly. "Your cousin-in-law's no idiot. He figured maybe somebody'd try something else if the house was unguarded."

"And that's a good thing?" Leigh said sarcastically. Gil was on her bad side, and she wasn't inclined to give him the benefit of a doubt.

"If we catch him, it is," the guard said logically.

Leigh humphed. "Well, why don't you tell Mr. March his security has been breached?"

The guard smiled again. "I already did—when you came in the front. He told me to find out what you were doing and then shag you outta here."

Leigh's face burned. "Well, you can tell him I said, 'Go to hell,' and that's a direct quote."

The security guard leaned back against the door frame and grinned, clearly enjoying himself. "I think it'd be better if you told him that yourself. In the meantime, please get what you need and come on out. It really isn't safe."

"Why not?" Leigh insisted. "You're guarding it, aren't you?"

His grin increased. "I guess you've got me there." He looked at the pile of books scattered at her feet. "I'll give you a couple minutes to get those together. Then you'll have to leave, I'm afraid. Do you want help?"

"No," Leigh answered quickly, "I just want one or two. Thanks."

The guard winked at her and left. She got back down on her knees, which were more than a little shaky. Fear, anger, and lust in quick succession could certainly wreak havoc on one's nervous system.

Determined to bring all the books out into the light, she put her torso back into the hole and shoved them out one by one. The bottom of the door had been poorly sanded, and she cursed at the scratches criss-

crossing her stomach. It was a good thing she preferred one-piece swimming suits.

Coughing and sniffling, she pulled the books away
from the dusty hole and began rubbing off each one.
Fall 1961. Spring/Summer 1954. Spring 1947. Had Paul
Fischer been a more interesting person, she might have
liked to read them all. As it was, only one mattered.

And after she had cleaned and stacked about two-
thirds of the journals, she found it.

Summer, 1949. The stilted letters jumped out of the
dust, reverberating in her brain like winning lottery
numbers. She opened the book gingerly and turned to
the first page.

June 12, 1949

I think he regrets it now—like I knew he would.
All day long she does nothing but snivel around, whining about how I need to get married and how I never
help out around the house. Father doesn't put up with
that nonsense, and he shouldn't. He needs me around,
and he knows it.

They need me around in the office too, but Klausen
doesn't see that. He has no idea what a mess things
would be without me—

Leigh skipped ahead, having already read all the self-
obsessed whining she cared to read. Unfortunately, the
entries that described events were few and far between,
most of the journal was more of the same. Paul clearly
resented both Anita and Robbie, and fantasized about
living alone with his father again. It was hard for Leigh
to remember she was reading the words of a twenty-
four-year-old man and not an adolescent.

July 18, 1949

It's laughable! Here Anita would love nothing better than to marry me off, while her own son has more

of the opposite sex than he can handle. I saw her hanging all over him again today. Poor little guy hasn't got a clue what to do with her. But then again, who would? Such an ugly thing—gangly, with those big bug eyes. Downright sinister-looking, if you ask me. Pulling him around like he was a puppy dog. God! And people wonder why I'm not in a hurry to get married!

Leigh curled her lip in distaste. Sinister-looking? Mary? Perhaps that was how Paul Fischer interpreted intelligence in a woman.

August 2, 1949

Father split Anita's lip open yesterday. She deserved it, of course, but it's hard on everybody when she looks so bad. I heard the neighbor woman hassling her about it outside. She should just stay in when she looks like that. At least with Robbie, he can say he was fighting with kids at school. I'm amazed bullies don't beat him up more often anyway. He's such a mama's boy.

Rage bubbled up in Leigh, and she slammed the book shut. But it was a pointless rage. Paul Fischer was dead—long dead. Which was just as well.

She heard the guard moving around downstairs, and the sounds comforted her. The house was seeming evil again, if only because Paul Fischer had lived in it.

She took a deep breath and reopened the book. She wasn't reading any more of his nonsense than was absolutely necessary, but she had come here for a reason, and she'd gone too far to quit now. She flipped page by page until she found what she wanted. The first entry after the fateful night.

August 14, 1949

Everything's changed now. But that's OK.
I'll write to you now, Father.
I'm sorry. You're gone, and life will never be the

same for me. But everything's going to be all right. In a way I know you're still here with me—in this house. My house now.

I'm so, so sorry. But I did all I could, you have to admit that.

I kept my cool, I used my brain. And all should be well from here on out. You'll keep your good name. I'll see to that.

It was bound to happen sooner or later—the whole thing. Anita just kept on making you angry. She wasn't what you thought when you married her—I understand that. She was a silly, spineless woman who didn't deserve a man like you. I don't blame you. But you could have gone to prison for it. I saved you from that, Father.

I was clever. The police were completely convinced, and why shouldn't they be? I knew you were proud of me. Dirty laundry would have been better, but it didn't matter. No one listened to that blabbermouth idiot Adith anyway.

A chill crept down Leigh's spine. She had suspected that Norman killed Anita; they all had. But seeing it spelled out in Paul Fischer's cold phrases turned her stomach. She wanted to stop reading, to throw the book at the wall, but she couldn't. The information she had wanted for so long was right there in front of her, and it just kept coming.

If Robbie hadn't acted like such a child, it would have ended there. But no, he had to argue about it, to actually strike you! It was his own stupid fault for falling against the marble. He wasn't hit that hard. I've taken plenty worse.

But they were weak, both of them. You were blubbering then, Father, and don't deny it! I was the one who came through for you—I was the one who didn't panic. I knew no one would miss Robbie. They would just think he ran away. Which he probably would have if he'd had a chance.

Leigh heard footsteps on the attic stairs again, but they didn't concern her. The guard could cool his heels until she was done.

My plan was a good one, and it would have worked. It did work! I tied the block on good—he went straight to the bottom and he's not coming up. I rowed way far out, where it's deep. I've always wanted to live on the river!

The footsteps were more rapid this time, and heavy. Leigh continued to read.

How could I know that damn kid was spying on me? I was cleaning up your mess—I couldn't stay with you too. It wasn't my fault. You know it wasn't! I did everything I could for you, Father.

But he got to you, and you were wimp enough to let him. So now I've got to think of myself, Father, for once. I could go to jail instead of you, for conspiracy, withholding evidence, there would be something. And I'm not going to prison. I'm not. Not for you or anybody.

The footsteps stopped, and a flashlight beam flickered over Leigh. She ignored it.

It will be OK. Because I'm a fast thinker. We have an understanding. If we both keep quiet, we'll both be OK. If one talks, we both suffer. That won't happen.

But don't you worry, Father. Justice will be done in the end. He'll get what's coming to him someday. I'll see to that. And everyone will know that he's a murderer.

I wouldn't have thought it of him. Such a mild-mannered kid. Ash gray, he was, standing there by your bed. Blood splattered on his clothes. He looked like he didn't even know what had happened. But he did know. He saw me at the river and he went after you.

He knew you killed Robbie. And he murdered you. Murdered you in cold blood. But he'll pay someday. Do you hear me, Don? Someday, you'll pay.

Leigh jumped as the guard touched her shoulder. She hadn't even noticed him walking over. She jerked her head up.

It wasn't the security guard. It was Chief Donald Mellman.

Chapter 23

"Are you crazy, girl? You've got to get out of here! The whole damn house is on fire!"

Leigh looked into the face of the police officer she'd known since her childhood. Reserved yet loyal; soft-spoken yet firm, always calm. She stared at his twisted nose, the grayish hair falling into his eyes, and the beads of sweat forming on his broad forehead.

Later, she would realize how differently things might have turned out if she'd simply gotten up and gone with him. He had come to save her, to get her out. He was still the benevolent chief of police. The house was burning; his goal was accomplished. Or so it seemed.

But she didn't. She couldn't.

The pudgy fingers burned a hole in her shoulder, but her body didn't respond to her brain. She couldn't move.

"Leigh?" he asked, growing more agitated. "What's wrong with you?"

She looked up into his pale gray eyes. A boy, only fourteen years old. Beaten and disfigured by his father. A facade of calm. A core of rage.

"Leigh!" he shouted, grabbed her arm and pulling her to her feet. "Let's go!"

She should have dropped the book. She didn't even want it. But the filthy journal was stuck inside the death grip of her frozen fingers, and as he pulled her up, it came too.

Mellman grabbed at it, then paused. He lifted her wrist and scanned the open page.

Leigh watched his eyes grew wide, and felt a tremor pass through his giant frame. Then he shoved her wrist roughly toward the floor and stepped away from her.

Still, she couldn't move.

"That bastard!" he screamed. It was a loud, gut-felt scream. The kind of scream whose very tone made the listener's own adrenaline surge. Before her eyes his whole countenance changed. Gone were the dull, lackluster eyes, the easy half smile. His face was fire-engine red, his pupils dilated, his muscles taut; his huge chest heaved with the effort of each breath. Leigh made her first motion. She stepped back.

He shook his head, a rattling motion, and pointed a finger at Leigh. "He won't win! I won't let him!"

She wanted to speak, but her throat produced no words.

He continued in a voice now deathly calm. "You don't know what he did. He tied Robbie's legs to a block. Did you know that? Tied him to a block and dumped him in the dirty river—just dumped him in. *Like garbage!"*

She swallowed. Mellman began to pace as he talked, gesticulating wildly.

"Paul wasn't a kid—he was a man. He could have stopped it. Norman beat Robbie, hit him, over and over, and Paul didn't care. He didn't do it, but he might as well have. Let Robbie's mother die, let Robbie die, and *didn't even bury him! God!"* He swung around to the wall behind him and smashed it violently with a fist. The wall shuddered, but Mellman seemed oblivious to the pain.

He turned back to Leigh, his voice suddenly calm again. "Paul didn't deserve to be buried either."

Leigh inhaled sharply, understanding dawning in her stressed-out brain. It was Mellman. Mellman who had avenged his friend's murder by shooting Norman Fischer. Mellman who had spent the next forty years hating the stepbrother who'd let Robbie die. And Mellman who'd stolen the body.

She watched as he stared down at the floor, scraping his foot slowly from side to side. His hand fidgeted over his gun belt.

"I never meant to hurt you girls," he said softly. "I like you."

"I know . . ." The words came out hoarsely, and Leigh swallowed and repeated them. "I know you didn't."

He looked up at her. "Robbie was my best friend. My best friend in the whole world. He never hurt anybody. He didn't deserve to die."

"Of course not," Leigh soothed. But her calm facade was only voice deep, because her nose and ears had convinced her that what she'd hoped was a bluff was real. Alarms in the ceilings below her feet beeped in chorus, and the smell of smoke hung thick in the air. "We need to get out of here," she said, shaky.

Mellman drew his gun.

"Paul wanted to ruin my life, you know," he continued calmly, caressing the gun's barrel. "He wanted me to go to jail. That probably wouldn't happen. But he knew I could never keep being a policeman. And that's all I have."

Leigh watched without breathing. She had never even seen a loaded weapon, other than tucked away safely in someone's gun belt. Her eyes fixed on it in horror as he began waving it aimlessly in the air.

"Nobody knew. Just me and him. That stupid will

of his—he should have known better. I got that before
the son of a bitch even died." He glanced at the journals littering the attic floor, aimed, and fired. Leigh
jumped and threw her hands pointlessly over her ears.
A book jerked, sending a cloud of dust to join the
smoke already swirling around the junction of floor
and rafters. Mellman erupted into peals of laughter,
the gun tracing wild motions as he convulsed in mirth.
Somewhere below, glass was breaking.

Leigh's legs, thankfully disconnected from her terrified mind, began moving her toward the door.

"Freeze," Mellman said forcefully, training the gun
on her. Then he began to laugh again. "Sorry. Didn't
mean to scare you. Old habit."

Leigh stood still. She imagined that the floor was
growing hot under her feet as Mellman's laughter dissolved into sobs. He laid his head in his hands.

"We have to leave now," she said as firmly as she
dared.

"I never wanted to hurt you, Leigh," he repeated,
wailing loudly. "You know that! Hell, I never even
wanted to hurt your damn cat! If it hadn't kept running away from the doors—"

She stared at him in amazement. "You—"

"I only wanted to burn what Fischer left. Don't you
see? Nothing had to suffer. It hurts to be burned, you
know." He stood solemnly now, one hand rubbing a
scarred elbow, the gun hanging limply from the other.

She took another step toward the door.

"No!" He was alert again, the gun trained, his eyes
wild. "You can't leave. If you do, everyone will know.
They'll think I'm a killer, and I'm not! He was a
devil—you can't be blamed for killing a devil, can
you?"

Leigh had no answer.

"Well, can you?" he thundered, walking toward her, the gun pointing from his outstretched hands.

"Uncle Don?"

A meek, childlike voice drifted to them from the attic door. Mellman froze, then turned. It was Maura.

"Uncle Don, it's me, Maura. I need your help."

The woman Mellman turned to see was almost as big as he was, but from the look of his eyes, he appeared to see a child. "Maura, honey, you need to go back downstairs," he ordered in a gentle, paternal tone.

"I won't go without you, Uncle Don, and my friend. You'll come with us, won't you?"

Sweat rolled off Mellman's face, which seemed to register increasing confusion. His hands held the gun frozen on Leigh, but his attention was diverted to Maura, who moved slowly toward him. "Don't show your gun to my friend, Uncle Don. You're scaring her."

Mellman blinked. He looked at Leigh, then back at Maura. "I don't mean to," he said softly.

"I know you don't," Maura soothed, now only a few feet away. "But she's afraid of guns. Can she go now?"

Mellman slowly lowered his pistol, looking at Leigh apologetically, but speaking to Maura. "She won't tell anybody, will she?"

"Of course not," Maura responded firmly. She had managed to step in between Leigh and Mellman, and now she gestured to her friend behind her back. The implication was clear. *Move toward the door, slowly.*

For once, Leigh saw no point in arguing. She made slow, sideways movements toward the stairway as Maura shielded her from Mellman, who had started to cry.

"I didn't do anything wrong!" he babbled. "I never meant to hurt anybody. Norman pulled the gun on me, you know. Right out of the nightstand. But he was so puny, and even then I—"

Maura issued low orders to Leigh as Mellman's speech gave way to racking sobs. "Stay low. Crawl down the stairs—don't open the hall door. Just climb out the window onto the roof. The glass is broken."

Leigh reached the attic doorway and immediately dropped to her knees. Black smoke seemed to fill the stairway at all but its lowest points, and more and more of the noxious haze was streaming up and curling into the rafters of the attic. They didn't have much time.

She looked back at Maura. "You've got to hurry!" she called.

Mellman was babbling again, and though Leigh couldn't understand what he was saying, Maura's hushed call was deathly clear. Even on her cockiest day, Leigh wouldn't have considered defying it. *"Go. Now."*

Leigh swung her legs out in front of her and down the stairs, then lay on her back and edged down. The smoke in the staircase was thick enough to burn her lungs, and her whole body felt hot. She coughed and sputtered as she slid over the last half of the stairs and belly-flopped onto the square landing at the bottom. She was lying on broken glass, but that didn't seem important. She just wanted to breathe.

Thick smoke rolled under the door separating the attic steps from the upstairs hall, and Leigh took Maura's advice not to open it. Her odds of reaching the main staircase at the other end did not look good.

Instead she hooked her fingers over the windowsill, dimly aware of a stabbing pain, and pulled herself up. The heat seemed unbearable, and for a moment she was certain she would faint. But as the cool night air touched her face, and the wail of sirens assaulted her ears, she found renewed strength. Thanks to the abundance of gables on the old Victorian, a stretch of angled roof lay just below the window ledge. She threw a leg out and onto the roof, banging her head on the side of the window in an effort to stay low. Head down, she pulled her second leg through and released her hold on the piercing sill.

"Quick! Over here!" a voice called. It was exclamatory yet soothing, and comfortably familiar. Feeling a sudden rush of relief, Leigh rolled over to get her bearings, but discovered she had none. Her chest heaving with coughs and her limbs heavy, she rolled helplessly down the gentle incline. As her legs plunged forward into nothingness, her scrambling hands caught on a thin rim of metal. The gutter held only for a moment or two, but it was enough. When Leigh's blood-smeared fingers lost their hold, she plunged down into waiting arms.

As to what the sobbing mass at her feet was babbling about, Maura could only guess. What she did know was that every second that passed made the air hotter, the smoke thicker, and their chances of a safe escape even more remote.

"Uncle Don," she continued, her voice as meek as she could force, "would you put down your gun please? I'm afraid too."

There was no response other than the pained sobbing of a man whose mind had lost control of his emotions. A wave of guilt spread over her. The signs had all been there. If she'd only been paying attention. But she hadn't, because she was too close. She'd lost her objectivity, and now she was paying the price.

She reached down and gently touched the hand that

cradled the pistol. But Mellman's wide fingers only clutched it tighter, and he looked at her, more lucid. "I can't face it, Maura. I can't. You go on. It's all over for me, anyway."

The smoke curling up from around the attic floorboards joined that wafting up the stairwell, the two swirling in concert to increase the sinister haze above. Maura dropped to her knees, coughing.

"*No.* It's not over. You didn't do anything wrong. Everyone knows that. Everyone knows what a good police chief you are."

Mellman turned red-rimmed eyes to her and talked through a wheezing cough. "You think so?"

"Of course!" She swallowed. "My dad was the greatest, but you're giving him some stiff competition."

The trembling lips turned into a smile, the face calmed. "I'll quit now, then," he said serenely, scooting away. His arm lifted the gun to his head as he nodded. "Now's the time. They'll remember me fondly then."

It was a reflex, she would claim later, nothing more. Maura sprang at her adopted uncle with catlike quickness, her outstretched hands targeting his forearm. At impact, her heavy body rolled over his, one deafening shot blasting in her eardrums.

"Dale!" a man shouted. "We need the oxygen over here!"

Fuzzy figures buzzed around Leigh as she fought her way back to consciousness. She was lying flat on the ground. Her arms, fingers, and back throbbed with pain, and every breath brought daggers to her chest. "Maura?" she choked, bringing on a violent bout of coughing.

"Don't try to talk," the uniformed man beside her

insisted as he bandaged her bleeding right arm. "Just lie still. You're going to be fine."

A second figure came into focus, sitting beside her on the grass. She looked up into the concerned face of the blue-eyed security guard.

"Thank God you got out all right," he said with relief, his voice hoarse from the smoke. "I'd have never forgiven myself." He looked up at the house, which no longer puffed out billows of gray ash as much as tongues of flame. "I still probably won't."

A bandage was swathed around his head, and when he turned, Leigh could see that the dark hair on the back of his crown was clumped with dried blood. She raised her already bandaged left arm and pointed. "Yeah, I know," he replied, embarrassed. "Stupid, huh. Never saw it coming. Who'd have thought—"

Leigh's eyes widened in horror as she noticed that the window she had come out of was now no more than an outline in a glowing sea of red. She sat up, her throat raw, and croaked, "Maura! You have to get her out!"

The uniformed man pushed her back down, and the arriving paramedic quickly covered her face with an oxygen mask. "Take it easy," he said firmly. "The firemen have everything under control. There's nothing you can do now except make yourself worse. Now, breathe."

Tears formed at the edges of Leigh's eyes, burning their way down her cheeks. Her lungs felt as though there were fire inside them, and the plastic mask made her claustrophobic. Nonetheless, the fogginess in her brain began to clear. She looked at the blue-eyed guard. Remembering the strong arms that had broken her fall, she pointed at him, then at the window. It was a question.

Understanding, he smiled a small, sad smile. "Wish

I'd been that useful. But until just now I've been lying here unconscious myself."

Her brow furrowed as she heard footsteps approaching behind her head. A fourth figure dropped to its knees behind her and gently brushed the hair from her forehead. "She's going to be fine," the blue-eyed security guard assured. "Thanks to you. That was some catch, for a woman."

Leigh craned her neck up, and Mary Polanski's ash-blackened face smiled back at her.

Chapter 24

As Maura rolled off Mellman, she saw the first lick of flame fighting its way up the attic staircase. Before she could move, another arose from nowhere and attached itself to her pants leg. She pulled off her shirt, buttons flying, and suffocated the orange tendrils against the dusty floor.

Holding her body off the hot floor as much as possible, she crawled close enough to run her fingers over Mellman's bloodied head. His hair was damp and sticky, but her fingers found only a shallow track across the back of his skull. He would live.

If, of course, she did.

Flames now leapt unencumbered through the attic door and against the nearby walls, and Maura turned her attentions to the nearest window. She had already heard sirens—the firemen were probably there, and ready. Though it seemed like hours since she had stepped into the burning house, only a few short minutes had passed. She didn't have many more; the heat alone would soon be unbearable.

Mellman stirred, then began to thrash and howl in pain as the scalding boards underneath him singed his prone body. Maura drew her gun from its holster and heaved it, with every ounce of strength she had, at the nearest pane of glass.

The sound of the separating shards falling to the

roof ledge outside was followed by that of several
voices shouting. The rush of oxygen into the steamy
attic gave the nearby flames a temporary rally, but as
Maura lay with her face covered, an ax pounded
through the remainder of the window, and she was
promptly drenched with a thick stream of water. She
smiled and looked up.

A man in a heavy yellow suit jumped through the
opening. Maura tried to move toward him but instead
doubled into a coughing spasm. Two pairs of heavily
clad arms hoisted her up and over the window ledge,
where a third man waited. He held her down on the
roof ledge while she caught her breath, then led her
carefully to a ladder. She couldn't remember how far
up she was, but she didn't care. The ladder led down,
and that's where she was going.

Mary touched the deep cut on the side of Leigh's
forehead. "You should look at this too," she told the
paramedic. Then she smiled again at Leigh. "Maura's
going to be fine, dear. They just put her in the
ambulance."

Leigh's heart warmed. Maura was all right. Mary
was all right. But how—

Mary shook her head at Leigh's confused expression. "Everything's going to be all right now, dear.
Don may even make it if he's lucky."

"But where—" Leigh sputtered barely recognizable
words into the oxygen mask.

"Shhhh." Mary corrected, her finger to her lips.
"Don't talk. You're wondering where I've been? No
wonder. Apparently everyone did." She sighed. "I
suppose I wandered again. I've been told I do that
from time to time. I've no idea when or why I left
home, but I do remember being out walking, and coming to Donald's front door. I said hello and asked if

he could remind me how to get home. But then I got even more confused. It happens sometimes, as you know. People tell me things, and they just go out of my mind.

"Anyway, Donald told me that Maura and Judith and Charlotte were all sick, and that I had to stay with him for a while. I didn't remember their being sick, but I figured I had just forgotten."

She sighed again and moved out of the way as the paramedic leaned over to treat Leigh's bleeding scalp. "I tried to call home, but the phone was dead and the door was always locked. I mostly just sat tight and enjoyed the chocolates and Chinese food Donald kept bringing me. It was only a couple of hours, I guess." She smiled slightly. A sad, bittersweet smile. "He didn't mean any harm."

The blue-eyed security guard watched Mary in amazement. "You were at Mellman's? How did you get away?"

She smiled again, this time proudly. "Donald always did underestimate women. The phone was dead, and I finally got tired of it and decided to try to fix it myself. The plug was just out of the jack, is all. I plugged it back in and called home. Judith answered and went hysterical."

Leigh surprised herself with a chuckle. It hurt her chest, but it was good for her soul. "OK, men," said an authoritative voice in the distance, "let's take her in the next one. Go ahead and get her on the stretcher. Ma'am? You come too."

Mary followed the stretcher without protest. Strapped on safely and covered with a blanket, Leigh looked up at the bugs circling the ambulance's blinking lights. They flitted about energetically, apparently uninterested in the more dramatic glare of the burning house. Leigh thought of her finches and smiled. Now at last she knew where they were. He had let them go.

Never one to obey silly rules, especially those delivered by militia-like emergency room nurses, Leigh pulled off her oxygen mask, swung her legs over the side of the hospital bed, and shuffled into the next cubicle. Maura, unfortunately, was not so mobile. She had minor burns on her hands and legs, and was lying restlessly with an IV line feeding into her arm. Mary sat in a chair beside the bed, her own arm wrapped in a sling.

Leigh looked sadly at Maura, then, seeing Mary's state, drew in her breath, horrified. "Did I do that?" she whispered.

"It's just a hairline fracture," Maura answered hoarsely, "but yes, you did. I told you to go on the roof, not roll off it."

Leigh smiled at her friend's brusque attempt at humor. Maura looked well enough, albeit understandably irritable. "I owe you both a lot," Leigh said softly.

Maura tried to wave her hand, but only succeeded in making a small jerky motion. "I was only doing my job. It's Mom you owe. She says you were heading right for the concrete patio. You'd have broken both legs, or worse, if she hadn't been there."

Leigh preferred not to think about that, but she thanked Mary profusely, offering a silent prayer to the rowing machine in the sewing room. "So spill it, Leigh," Maura interrupted suddenly. "Why the hell were you up there in the first place?"

A blank stare was all Leigh could return as she tried to figure out what Maura already knew. "To get the journals," she said finally.

"What journals?"

"Paul Fischer's journals. Specifically, the one that said what happened in 1949."

Maura's eyes grew wide. "Then there *was* something hidden in the house?"

Leigh nodded, then looked incredulous. "Don't you know all this already?"

"How could I?"

"You were there."

Maura rolled her eyes. "I got a frantic call at the station from my aunt, screaming that Mom was at Mellman's place. I busted down his damn door getting her out, and then she started telling me some crazy story about how she was staying with him because we were sick. I didn't know what was going on, and I still don't. I want to know why Mom was at Mellman's, why he lost it in the attic, and, most especially, why he was holding a gun on you. Now, are you going to explain or am I going to rip out this freakin' IV line and beat it out of you?"

Leigh looked at Maura in amazement. "But how could you just walk in there and . . ." She trailed off. "What made you go to the house, then?"

"I got a message from Cara's husband," the policewoman explained slowly, with visible restraint. "He wanted to let the department know that you had broken into the house and were screwing around with something in the attic. He said that the security guard had been instructed to boot you out—but I knew that with you, that meant trouble. I was on my way over there when Charlotte called. After I talked to Mom, I got more than a little nervous about what might be going on. And with good cause. The guard was passed out on the patio, and I could hear Mellman ranting and raving up above. Now . . ." her restraint broke, *"spill it!"*

Leigh sat down on the foot of the white-sheeted bed and explained the story of 1949—or at least Paul

Fischer's version of it. Maura listened with fascination; Mary was visibly disturbed.

When Leigh had finished, Maura looked up at her mother. She tried to keep her voice steady but was not completely successful. "Did you know, Mom? When it happened?"

Mary, who had been pacing restlessly most of the time Leigh talked, narrowed her eyes at her daughter. "Of course not," she snapped. "You think I'm so far gone I'd let all this nonsense happen without saying a word?"

Maura shriveled. It was an effect Leigh did not witness often.

"No, Mom," she soothed, "I just thought maybe—"

"You thought I was protecting Donald? Ridiculous. Not that I blame him for killing Norman Fischer. That man had to be a monster—even more so than I thought. But I wouldn't put my daughter's safety in jeopardy to protect anybody. I always knew that Donald suffered horribly as a child; I knew that he had some emotional problems from time to time. But if I thought for one minute that he was capable of killing another human being— It scares to me to think about it."

Maura breathed deeply. "Do you think . . . did Dad—"

"Don't even ask that!" Mary raged, her eyes flashing. "Your father would never let a man he knew was guilty of murder serve on his police force. No matter what the circumstances. Do you understand me?"

Maura nodded quickly. "I'm sorry, Mom. We're all a little stressed out here. I think maybe it would be better if we got some rest. Could I get somebody to take you home? Charlotte and Judith are dying to see you."

Mary's temper cooled. The word "home" seemed

to strike a chord with her. "Yes," she said softly, "as long as you're all right. I'd like to go home."

After a thorough chastisement from the hospital staff, Leigh was escorted from Maura's cubicle and discharged into her parents' care with several prescriptions and a laundry list of do's and don'ts, tediously collected and penned by Frances. As Randall pulled their car around to the exit, Leigh pleaded a bladder emergency and slipped away long enough to find the room Maura had been moved to for the rest of the night.

"Did you see Mellman down there?" Maura asked without greeting.

Leigh shook her head.

"He's burned pretty bad," she said dully. "They had a hell of a time getting him off the roof."

Leigh was anxious to change the subject. "I'm being discharged into the care of nurse Frances," she said. "Are you going to be all right? Really?"

Maura knew her friend wasn't asking about the burns. She took a deep breath. "It bothers me that I might never know for sure. What Dad knew. But since I won't, I'm going to choose to believe that he never knew what really happened. He might have suspected—I can't believe he didn't—but he couldn't have known unless Mellman told him."

Remembering something, Leigh jumped in quickly. "Mellman told me that no one knew but him and Paul."

Maura looked up, her eyes brighter. "Really? He said that?"

Happy that lying wouldn't be required, Leigh nodded again and smiled.

The policewoman relaxed back into her pillows. "Mellman always was good at keeping secrets," she said thoughtfully. "Abused children are like that sometimes. That child went through hell and back, and no one seemed to pay attention. How could the man be healthy? It was a long time ago, but how could anyone really forget? The guilt of having taken a life? The fear of being found out? God, as if the abuse weren't enough. It was a miracle he functioned as well as he did." She was silent for a moment. "It makes you think, doesn't it?"

Leigh didn't want to think. Thinking only brought up images. Images of Robbie's fourteen-year-old body sinking into the mud at the bottom of the Ohio. Images of Mellman sleeping peacefully while Paul Fischer's body lay stiff . . . where? She shuddered, trying to shake the thoughts out of her head. "I'm just glad your mother's OK," she repeated. "I can see why he wanted to make the most of her disappearance. I mean, it certainly got you off the Fischer case, but I'm scared to think what he was going to do with her. She couldn't stay there forever."

Maura shook her head. "I'm not a psychiatrist, but I really don't think he ever planned to hurt her. He didn't kidnap her—she just showed up on his doorstep. Literally. Then I guess it occurred to him that distracting the rest of the force could buy him time. He took good enough care of her." She snorted. "Even brought her a change of clothes!"

Leigh wasn't convinced. "But what if he had succeeded in burning the house without being suspected? What would he do with her then?"

Maura shrugged. "Honestly, Koslow, I wouldn't be surprised if he hadn't thought that far ahead. But it wouldn't be impossible. He could return her at any time and say she just wandered up, or that she had been sleeping in his tool shed, or whatever. With the Alzheimer's, people probably wouldn't believe her if

she disagreed with him. And she might not disagree
with him. I still can't convince her that she was gone
for a full forty-eight hours."

"But she was so sharp at the fire," Leigh protested.
"She was lucid the whole time. She watched for me
at the window, told the firemen you were going to
the attic . . ."

"Alzheimer's is a bizarre illness," Maura said matter-
of-factly. "I had no idea if she would follow my instructions or not. But we were all lucky she was
there."

Lucky, indeed. A pause hung in the air, and Leigh
knew she should probably let Maura rest. But one
thing still bothered her.

"Paul Fischer's body," she asked quietly. "I still
don't get it. Why?"

Maura shrugged. "Revenge, I suppose. Control.
Fischer held the power when he was alive. In death
the upper hand was Mellman's. He could hide the
body easily enough in that big old house of his—half
the rooms stayed locked up anyway."

"But why put it in the hammock?" Leigh persisted.
"Do you think that when Cara found the blank journal, he figured there might be more?"

Maura nodded. "I bet he thought a body in the
backyard would clear the little women out fast." She
chuckled softly. "He didn't know *you two*."

You mean he didn't know Cara, Leigh thought. She
thanked her friend a few more times, wished her a
good night's sleep, and headed back toward the waiting car. She didn't want to think anymore. She wanted
to take her painkiller, drink a cup of tea, and slip into
a comfortable bed with clean sheets.

A few nights of her mother's pampering wasn't
looking so bad, after all.

Epilogue

Two months later, and a full two weeks after Cara's due date, Leigh walked up the brightly lit postpartum corridor at Magee Women's Hospital, a spring in her step. She located Room 2834 and knocked loudly on the door.

"Come in!" shouted a happy voice.

Leigh smiled at the sight of her cousin, beaming from ear to ear and holding a tightly wrapped bundle in her arms.

"Come and meet your new nephew," the radiant mother ordered. "Mathias Luke," she said proudly, turning the little face around, "say hello to your auntie Leigh."

Leigh looked approvingly at the perfect round face, framed by a soft halo of reddish-brown hair. His eyes, veiled with thick lashes, were peacefully closed. He was perfect. Of course.

"I guess he's a bit tired at the moment," Cara said unapologetically. "But you can see his eyes later. They're the prettiest dark blue!"

Leigh gave her cousin a hug and stroked the baby's downy cheek. "Technically," she said, quoting Charlotte, "he's my first cousin once removed. But nephew is fine by me," she grinned. "Are you feeling OK?"

"Never better," Cara answered cheerfully. "The birth was a breeze. Incredibly ironic—my needing pitocin after all those contractions—but the doctors say it happens sometimes. And nothing matters now that Mathias is here and healthy as a horse."

A quick glance around the room told Leigh that Gil had been busy. She'd been less mad at him since discovering his covert plans to trap the arsonist, but his other irritating traits remained. The sin of excess, for example. The room was packed from floor to ceiling with fresh flowers of a hundred different varieties, balloons, candy, wrapped packages, teddy bears, and an extremely large donkey with an Uncle Sam hat. Her brow furrowed. "What the hell is that?"

"Shhh!" Cara laughed. "No cursing in front of the baby! I thought maybe you'd know what it was. It's from your friend Warren. The note says something about raising the baby right."

Leigh chuckled. "I think he means left."

"Speaking of friends, how's Maura doing?" Cara asked, concerned.

"Great. Her burns hardly bother her anymore. She was really lucky. We both were."

Cara's eyes saddened. "I can't tell you how sorry I am. If I hadn't been such a romantic . . ."

Leigh waved the sentiment away. "Don't be ridiculous. You and Gil"—she cringed at the admission—"had us safely moved out. I went back in of my own idiocy. If anybody should apologize, it's me, for getting Maura into it."

"You haven't said . . ." Cara asked tentatively, "what will happen to Mellman?"

There was a pause as Leigh sighed, tired of the topic. "His burns are healing, so physically he'll recover. Emotionally is another story. I expect he's looking at early retirement and a hell of a lot of counseling, at the very least."

"The evidence—"

"There is no evidence. Paul's journals burned. All that's left of them is my recollection, and if you ask me, I'll say it's fuzzy. Not to mention that it was hearsay to begin with. 1949 won't cause him any problems. 1999 is another story."

Cara's face had lost its shine, and Leigh found that unacceptable. "Look!" she cooed, pointing at the tiny face in the blanket, "he's waking up!"

Mathias Luke March stretched against the wrapping with tiny fists until one plastic-banded arm escaped. He yawned, then returned to somnolence.

"Isn't he precious!" Cara exclaimed, all traces of melancholy gone. "Gil says he looks like me, but I say he has his father's chin."

"Where is the proud papa, anyway?"

Cara laughed. "Out to lunch, and probably the mall. Our credit cards will never recover."

Leigh doubted that. "I'm glad you two—I mean, you three—are so happy."

A thoughtful smile passed Cara's lips. "This whole business has taught me something, you know."

"Oh? Don't get involved in half-century-old mysteries?" Leigh said lightly. She hated when her cousin got mushy.

"No, silly. Don't hold back things from people you love, even if you think you're protecting them. I should have told Gil about the threats from the beginning. He probably could have helped."

Leigh looked skeptical.

"And *you*," Cara said accusingly, "should have told me that you were worried about that butcher knife."

Leigh sighed heavily. "How was I supposed to know you were the one who got it out?"

Cara rolled her eyes. "For heaven's sake, Leigh, I was holding it right behind you the whole time you were looking for Mao Tse! I thought you saw it. You might be foolish enough to confront an intruder without a weapon, but I'm not!"

"Well," Leigh said, reluctant to apologize, "it's over with now. Let's think about more pleasant things. Like little Mathias here."

It was a guaranteed ploy. Cara looked down at the sleeping infant and kissed his red head tenderly. "Oh!" she said suddenly. "I almost forgot to tell you. We bought a farm!"

Leigh blinked. "A what?"

"A farm!" The new mother beamed. "Snow Creek Farm. Six acres right in the middle of McCandless! It's beautiful—you're going to love it. It's got an old farmhouse and a big empty barn, and there's a pond with turtles. Won't that be great for Matt? And there's even a log cabin by the creek—"

Leigh laughed out loud.

"What's so funny?" Cara smiled.

"Couldn't you just get one of those nice new mansions in a Franklin Park plan, complete with a wooden swing set and a fence?"

"How perfectly boring," Cara teased. "I would die. Did I mention that the farmhouse is supposed to be haunted? And that the field in front is a flood plain?"

Leigh promptly exploded into laughter, and was pleased to notice that her lungs no longer ached with the effort. "I give up!" she said. "You're hopeless."

Cara laughed with her. "You'll see it for yourself soon enough. We'll be all moved in before the month is out."

"No doubt."

"By the way," Cara said, changing the subject, "any more newspaper gigs?"

Leigh smiled. The ordeal at the Fischer/March house had had one positive effect. The story got reported just as she wanted it—because she had written it herself and sold it freelance. It was the first "real" story she'd ever gotten published, and a copy of the check was still taped to the refrigerator in her new apartment. "No more freelancing for a while, no," she answered. "I think I'll be plenty busy."

Cara smiled. "So Jeff Hulsey finally won you over, eh?"

Leigh grinned. She had to admit she'd been enjoying the account rep's ceaseless badgering. Several key members of her old team had decided to start up their own agency, and they wanted her on board. Badly. On the bright side, there would be no more random layoffs. On the down side, they could all starve together. "It's a scary proposition," she answered, "but as soon as Jeff gets the financing together, it's a go. And I'm in."

"And staying in advertising is really what you want?" Cara asked tentatively.

Leigh thought about the negatives—losing accounts for spurious reasons, the occasional late-night marathons. But she couldn't help but think of the positives—rolling with laughter over a facetious ad campaign, collecting checks for dreaming up the same dumb stuff she'd been spinning off effortlessly ever since she was a child. And now she had a chance to be her own boss.

"Yes," she said confidently. "It's really what I want."

"Then you can do it," Cara encouraged. "I know you can."

Leigh turned her head, embarrassed, and spotted a bouquet of pink balloons just behind the recliner. She pointed at them, puzzled. "Is this an effort at neutralizing sexism, or does Mathias have a twin sister I don't know about?"

Cara grinned broadly. "Mathias isn't the only one with a birthday today. Did you think I would forget?"

Leigh looked from the pink Happy Birthday balloons to the smiling face of her cousin, and her eyes grew moist. How could she expect her to remember? Today of all days?

"I won't even make jokes about your age," Cara said slyly. "But we both know it doesn't have a two in it anymore."

Leigh blinked forcefully and gave her cousin another hug. "That's OK. Sometimes change is for the better."